THE COTTAGE AT CLAMSHELL BAY

SARA JANE BAILEY

Storm

PUBLISHING

Ebook ISBN: 978-1-80508-121-0
Paperback ISBN: 978-1-80508-123-4

Cover design: Leah Jacobs-Gordon
Cover images: Shutterstock, Depositphotos

Published by Storm Publishing.
For further information, visit:
www.stormpublishing.co

ALSO BY SARA JANE BAILEY

The Bakery at Clamshell Bay

ONE

"The rituals and rhythms of flour, water and fire allow me to process a changing world."

TARA JENSEN, A BAKER'S YEAR

Libby Brown was kneading like she'd never kneaded before. Banging the dough onto her granite countertop so hard the *thwack* reverberated through the kitchen and she felt the shudder up her arm. Her baking teacher, Cleo Duvall, had told her students that kneading could be therapeutic, a great way to release stress and anger. At the time, she'd felt grateful for her perfect life, one where she didn't have to punish bread dough to make herself feel better.

Strangely, that baking weekend last May had been the turning point for Libby. She'd come home to find her husband looking both guilty and belligerent, telling her he wanted a divorce. His business interests had been taking him to Eastern Europe more frequently and for longer stretches, and it seemed some of that business had been very personal.

Like a leggy model from Prague personal.

Panic still clawed at Libby's chest whenever she thought back to those terrible first few days when she'd learned her safe, perfect life was shattering and she couldn't fix it. Victor had promised he'd take care of her and the kids. She wasn't to worry.

Thwak. She could have used her top-of-the-line mixer for the dough, but Cleo had been correct. Kneading by hand helped channel a bit of the anger and panic. At least temporarily. She shaped the bread dough into a ball and placed it into a greased bowl and covered it with a cloth.

Victor had been in such a hurry to leave that he'd been more than generous, giving her the house, primary custody of the children and healthy alimony and child support. She didn't contest the divorce. What was the point? So, he'd been free of her in just over four months.

Libby put the oven timer on for an hour. On the wall was a calendar with inspirational quotes she'd bought to keep her thoughts positive. It was January. A brand-new year and the featured photo was of skaters on an outdoor rink sparkling in the sunshine and a Helen Keller quote, "Keep your face to the sunshine and you cannot see a shadow."

As if. A letter was propped up on the granite kitchen counter like the shadow of a huge boot about to crush her.

What a fool she'd been with her positive thinking and motivational quotes. "It's always darkest before the dawn," that was another one she used to throw out like sparkles to brighten a sad day. Now she thought that had to be one of the stupidest expressions she'd ever heard. Libby had raged her way through plenty of middle-of-the-night blackness lately, and when the birds started chirping to announce dawn, she never felt lighter or more positive. She merely felt one day closer to the edge.

While the bread rose, she showered in the en suite and dressed in the plush bedroom of her dream home on the outskirts of Clamshell Bay in Washington State. Victor had insisted they could afford it and so she'd bought the kind of furniture she'd only ever seen on TV growing up. Her mahogany dressing table gleamed as did the matching chest of drawers empty of Victor's things. The king-sized bed that was too big for one person.

What was she going to do?

She went back to the kitchen and sat sipping a mug of coffee at her kitchen table while she read over the letter once more.

Victor was two months late on alimony and child support payments, though he'd found the money for extravagant Christmas presents for the kids. He'd told her he was in a cash crunch but would make everything up to her soon. Fool that she was, she'd believed him. Not until she'd received the letter from the First Bank of the Pacific Northwest yesterday had she glimpsed the depth of his betrayal. The word *foreclosure* jumped out at her from the midst of the careful, corporate wording like a skeleton leaping out of a closet. They weren't foreclosing quite yet, but the threat was there. Not only had Victor stopped paying her, he hadn't paid the mortgage, either. Ominously, he seemed to have disappeared.

Was that why he'd been so generous? Because he knew he'd never fulfill his obligations? The thought made the surface of the coffee shiver as her hand shook.

He might leave her, but he'd never abandon his own children.

Would he?

The naïve part of her wanted to believe that something had happened to him. The cynical side wasn't buying it.

Draining her coffee mug, she rose and began baking oatmeal-raisin muffins for breakfast. It was part of her morning routine now, along with baking homemade bread. As though knocking herself out to be the perfect mom could balance Victor's role as the homewrecker.

She liked baking. The activity soothed her and gave her

some measure of control over the mess of her life. Not that she was fooling herself that a few muffins and a loaf of whole wheat could make up for a missing dad, but she had to work with what she had. Apart from learning to bake bread, her baking class had also given her new friends. Women in Clamshell Bay who cared about her. They weren't other moms from school or couples she and Victor had socialized with, so they'd become the people she could rant and vent to safely.

Libby didn't know what she'd do without them. Cleo, who owned the only bakery in town, famous for its cinnamon buns. Brooke Mattson, a gorgeous former model who now lived in Clamshell Bay most of the year with her billionaire husband, and Megan Alexander, a painter and decorator who lived in overalls and work boots and usually had paint in her hair. Four very different women, and somehow they'd bonded over bread dough and secrets.

By the time she woke the kids, the smell of comfort food filled the kitchen and she'd put the letter back onto her kitchen counter.

She had to shake eight-year-old Tyler twice to get him to wake. "Morning, sleepyhead," she said, smiling down at his sleep-pinkened cheeks and the one skinny leg sticking out from under the duvet cover patterned with vivid insects.

He groaned and rolled over. "Hi, Mom."

He wasn't functional until he'd been up for a few minutes, so she ruffled his hair and left him with a reminder to make his bed. "Fresh muffins," she said, glancing back. "Your favorite."

Then she stepped into her three-year-old daughter's room.

Mia, like her, was a morning person. Her daughter was already awake, sitting in bed and chattering to her stuffed dinosaur. She had a mixed herd of stuffed animals and dolls in her bed and she could amuse herself for hours.

"Mama," she cried, holding her arms out.

With a big smacking kiss for her daughter, Libby followed

the morning ritual of greeting the animals and dolls before helping her baby to the bathroom and then to get dressed. Mia was in a pink and purple fashion stage. Even at her tender age, she was fussy about what she wore. Dresses were preferred, in pink and purple, obviously, but there was a final test. The dress had to be a good spinning dress. If it didn't bell out when she twirled, well, what was the point?

Mia was enrolled in tiny tot ballet and had decided she was going to be a dancer or a princess when she grew up.

The two women of the house walked down the stairs hand in hand. Libby took a moment to feel the tiny warm hand tucked into hers and watch the soft bounce of blond curls. The kids were growing so fast sometimes she had to stop and concentrate on a moment so she could hold on to it and hopefully program it into her long-term memory.

Mia was halfway through her second muffin and her apple juice when Tyler stumbled into the room.

"Before you sit down, can you get me a knife from the drawer?" Libby asked him. Cucumber and cream cheese was one of his favorites, though she was running low on cream cheese and felt a niggle of unease about how she was going to keep buying groceries if Victor didn't send her money very soon.

"Sure." He yawned and did as she asked. He yanked at the drawer and even as she exclaimed, "Careful," it was too late. The drawer front plopped into his hand.

"Oh, oh," Mia said.

Oh, oh, was right. How many times had she told them that drawer was loose? She couldn't afford a handyman and her carpentry skills were in the slim-to-none category, edging strongly on the none end.

She quelled the urge to snap at him. It wasn't Tyler's fault. "Sorry, Mom," he said, looking stricken.

"It's okay," she said, taking the drawer front from him and putting it on top of the counter.

His gaze followed the action, his expression serious and worried. "Zach Gillis's mom said I come from a broken home," he said dubiously, looking at the drawer in pieces.

Libby's eyes stung suddenly. She did not want pity and she really didn't want other moms talking about them like they were a defective family. Sure, they'd fallen apart, but she could hold things together. She had to.

"I have a special glue," she said. "Fixes everything. We'll have that drawer back together in no time." In fact, there were two items in her toolbox. A single screwdriver with multiple heads, most of which she had no idea what they were supposed to screw, and a tube of carpenter's glue, which was really amazingly versatile. "We're fine."

Tyler nodded thoughtfully. "I told him it's not our home that's broken, it's our family."

———

Once she'd got Tyler off to school and Mia dressed, Libby drove to the appointment she'd made with a loan officer after she'd received that letter yesterday. She sat in the bank parking lot in her car, while rain drummed down on the windshield, reading that devastating single page one more time. Helpless rage spurted through her. "Victor Brown, how could you do this to me?" She didn't even realize she'd vented aloud until her daughter chirped, "Daddy?"

"No, honey." Libby turned to the child in the back seat, and her heart twisted. So much love and innocent trust shone from the cherubic face with the cascade of blond curls. "He's not here."

Mia opened her mouth and Libby waited for, "I want Daddy," but after quivering a moment, the pink lips closed again. Libby pursed her own lips hard to keep them from quivering as childishly and opened the door.

She hadn't lost everything yet, and she wasn't going to. The children still had a home and a mother. They had friends and a decent school. And she would do anything, anything at all, to make sure they kept the precious stability of remaining in the only home they'd ever known.

By the time she'd waited ten minutes past her appointment time, Libby was bristling with righteous indignation. Her ex-husband was supposed to pay the mortgage. Why was the bank bothering her?

A short, unsatisfactory interview with Mr. Lizst, the lending officer who had written the letter, explained why they were bothering her. If the mortgage wasn't paid, the loan would be called. Then foreclosure would begin. "But," she argued, "I've got all the paperwork showing that my ex-husband signed over the house to me."

He checked the computer records and said, "Since you were on the original mortgage documents, you can pick up the payments without any problem." He glanced at her and then at Mia. "But the house is the collateral for the mortgage, Mrs. Brown. Is there someone who could lend you some money to get yourself back on track?"

She blinked. "What about you? You're a lending officer at my bank?"

He shook his head, giving her a small, sympathetic smile. "Sorry. You wouldn't qualify for a loan with us. No income, house payments in default." He was sorry, but that was it. When she tried to explain her situation, he looked at her as though he'd heard a thousand stories like hers and had no sympathy left. "Maybe you should trade down," was his only suggestion.

Trade down? She'd spent her childhood moving from place to place, always trading down, never up. She felt a shiver of pure childhood fear crawl over her skin at the words, and a vision rose up of her last home with her parents—the awful trailer across the highway from Friendly Hank's Used Cars on Federal Way.

He fished around in a drawer and came up with a couple of pamphlets which he handed her. She read the title of one, Avoiding Foreclosure, and crumpled the wad of papers into her bag.

In shock, she stumbled out of the cubicle, heading numbly for the daylight coming from an outside door.

"Mama, you're squishing me," Mia complained.

Around them, people ebbed and flowed to banking machines, tellers and suited bank reps like Mr. Lizst in cubicles. A sea of people with money to deposit, withdraw, invest. And she, Libby Brown, former wife of successful entrepreneur Victor Brown, had just been informed she was responsible for a debt of more than twenty-six thousand dollars in back mortgage payments, plus extra interest and late fees. She had thirty days to pay it, and resume regular mortgage payments, or the bank would start foreclosure proceedings on the house.

Stubbornly, her Chanel flats, that had seen better days, refused to carry her out of the building.

There had to be another way.

Libby hadn't done anything wrong. She'd followed the rules she'd first learned from those wonderful TV families. She'd married the right man, had the right children. She'd entertained clients graciously. Done everything she could to help Victor prosper.

Her thanks was to get dumped.

Well, she'd had enough of men like Victor and Mr. Lizst taking things away from her.

A guy in a baseball cap and a wet rain jacket jostled her on his way past where she stood trying to figure out what to do. An armed guard lounged in a corner of the marble lobby and looked at her with mild curiosity. Anger at the unfairness of it all began to bubble inside her. No, she wasn't leaving this bank until she had a better solution than selling her house, taking her children out of the neighborhood, with the good schools, and trading down. She stalked to the bank directory and scanned straight to the top of the listed names.

Jeremy O'Toole, President and CEO of the First Bank of the Pacific Northwest. He was her man. Before the anger could dissipate, she hiked Mia higher in her arms and marched to the elevator.

The executive offices on the third level were hushed and unhurried. Her worn shoes tapped against the gleaming oak floors.

"Can I help you?" a cool female voice asked.

"Yes. I'm looking for Mr. O'Toole," she told the perfectly groomed gray-haired woman behind an expensive-looking reception desk.

"Do you have an appointment?"

"No, I—"

"I'm sorry. He's in a meeting. Perhaps someone else can—"

"No. It's very important that I see Mr. O'Toole today."

"He's not available today. The earliest appointment he has is two weeks from Wednesday."

"I need to see him today."

"Well, you can't."

Later, she'd realize that was the moment she snapped. But at the time, it seemed like the best course of action was to find the one man who might help her, and to do it immediately. Libby walked past the reception desk and headed into a hushed labyrinth of offices and meeting rooms.

"Wait! You can't go back there. Stop! I'll call security."

Libby hardly heard the words.

She felt all the exhilaration of breaking the rules for the first time in thirty-four years. If a little rule-breaking would keep a roof over Mia's and Tyler's heads, it was a small price to pay. She stalked forward, knowing instinctively that the farther she got from the reception desk—and the paying public—the closer she'd get to the real power in the bank.

It had been one hell of a morning, and the day wasn't getting any better. Jeremy O'Toole's stomach felt like it was being attacked from inside with burning knives.

Which left him in no mood for the weekly executive meeting.

He eyed the silver carafe in front of him with a combination of longing and dread. Coffee was the worst thing he could stick inside his already suffering body.

He tried to think about something else, but cups rattled against saucers to tease him, while the aroma of fresh coffee tickled his senses.

His doctor had warned him to stay away from the stuff. But then his doctor had never sat through one of these meetings. He poured a long, fragrant, black stream into the empty cup in front of him and drank deeply.

"Well, Jeremy? What do you think?"

Glancing up at the eleven faces around the board table, he took a moment to replay as much of the discussion as he could remember. He took another hit of coffee, stalling for time, then focused on the ad campaign the marketing director had presented.

A series of mock-ups of digital ads beamed at him from the big screen.

One showed a smiling middle-America family; one dad, one mom, one boy and one girl, in front of a brand-new house complete with a two-car garage and green velvet lawn. A second pictured a young woman proudly polishing her new red sports car, while the third displayed a young couple hanging an Open sign in front of a trendy coffee shop. All the ads carried the same headline: *The New Face of Banking.* And the subhead read, *We're banking on YOU!*

Irritation spurted along with the gastric juices that were torturing his gut. "I think they're tired, trite, and unimaginative."

A grunt of exasperation escaped from Melanie Kwan, the bank's marketing director. "Jeremy, these ads went over great with the focus groups. They show ethnic and sexual diversity, they're aspirational, emphasize trust in our brand."

"You asked for my opinion. I'm giving it." He felt churlish, miserable, and sick. He drank more coffee.

Melanie gestured at the ads. "They're realistic."

"You want realism?" He poked his index finger toward the first ad layout. "There's a fifty percent chance that family's going to break up and the biggest argument will be over who pays for the kids' braces."

He pointed at the second ad. "That woman won't be smiling when she finds out she's sick of her car in a year and she's stuck paying for it for five. And as for those kids," he jabbed his finger toward the spiky-haired, black-clad twenty-somethings in front of the café, "Seventy-five percent of new business fail within three years, flushing their dreams down the drain."

"What do you suggest?" Melanie snapped. "Clamshell Bay is an expensive place to live. It's affluent. Crime is low. People here have money to invest. They come here to holiday or to retire. Grandparents have money to help out the younger generation." She pointed at the ads again.

He knew all this. "Do you have anything else we—?" Before he could finish his question, the door to the boardroom flew open, hitting the mahogany-paneled wall with a resounding thump. In charged a red-faced woman clutching a chubby toddler in her arms.

All eyes turned to stare at the woman, whose own eyes

snapped fire. Big hazel eyes, ash-blond hair, and a curvy body. He blinked, wondering if he'd conjured this woman out of his bored imagination. But a second glance told him she was no fantasy; she was a flesh and blood woman—and she was rigid with anger. Her hair was pulled back off her face exposing the taut jawline. Her breathing was short and shallow, her creamy cheeks were flushed and she faced the room square on. You didn't need to be an expert on body language to see this lady was humming with fury.

Jeremy's masculine eye noted the tall, slender length of her body; his banker's eye noted that she wore an expensive coat and accessories that had seen better days. She also wore that attitude, and it crackled. Almost before he realized what he was doing, Jeremy found himself rising out of his seat.

Her gaze snapped to his face. "Mr. O'Toole?"

Yep, the voice was exactly what he would have expected. Soft, a little sweet. She was clearly furious but she didn't raise her voice. He admired that kind of control.

He put a neutral expression on his face as he answered calmly. "Yes, I'm Jeremy O'Toole." Fifteen years in banking had taught him that irate customers were always easier to deal with if he could defuse their anger first.

Linda, the executive receptionist, piled in behind the woman, a uniformed security guard in tow. "Sorry," she gasped, glaring at the woman. "I told her she couldn't come in here, but she barged past me."

"I'm a customer of this bank, and I'd like a moment of your time, please. Now." The words were delivered in the same softly determined voice, but Jeremy heard the quaver underneath, and recognized the naked desperation in her eyes. Every chivalrous instinct surged within him. Maybe he couldn't cure cancer, but he could certainly help a mother who was having a problem with his bank.

He opened his mouth to speak when his VP Jonas

Carrington beat him to it. "As you can see, Mr. O'Toole is busy now. I'm in charge of customer services. If you'd like to make an appointment, I'll try and see you next week."

"That's not good enough."

"Ow, Mama, you're squeezing me."

"It's all right, darling." That voice was definitely quivering now.

Jeremy watched the faces around the table. The expressions ranged from embarrassment to boredom. No wonder those customer ads were all crap.

"Here's the reality," Jeremy said, looking at each of the executives round the table. When he had their attention, he gestured to the woman inside the doorway, "*This* is the new face of banking. Linda, please seat this customer in my office." Then to the woman, he said, "I'll be with you in a moment."

She was still furious. He could see it in the line of her body, the way she held her chin up. For a second he thought she might refuse to budge, but then, after glaring at him for another moment, she nodded stiffly and stalked out behind Linda.

The security guard wiped his forehead as he closed the door.

"Really, Jeremy, I would have thought this meeting was more imp—"

"That's where you're wrong, Jonas. That woman is the reason we're in business. Never forget it."

He glanced coldly at each person in turn. "Excuse me, I have to see a customer."

Then he smiled for the first time that day.

TWO

Libby had expected the bank manager to be old. Fatherly. Someone who might be won over by the thought of homeless children. She didn't want Jeremy O'Toole to be close to her own age and good-looking.

After Victor, she no longer trusted handsome men.

With shaking hands, she settled Mia on the floor, near a rack of glossy brochures advertising the bank's services, and perched at the edge of a gray upholstered visitor's chair.

After icily showing them into the office, Linda had marched off leaving, Libby and Mia alone, and Libby realized she needed a minute or two to calm herself. She'd never felt such anger— and never in her memory had she acted so brazen. She was a pleaser. A giver. She didn't take or demand. All her life, she'd given, taught from an early age that was the best way to avoid getting yelled at.

Recently, being a pleaser hadn't worked out so well for her. Only raw desperation had given her the courage to walk into a meeting without permission.

Now she had the attention of the man at the top, all she had to figure out was how to make the most of it. She took deep calming breaths while she tried to collect her thoughts. How would she get through to the bank president that he had to let her keep her house?

A quick glance around the office revealed little in the way of inspiration. It was an executive office like a million others. Neat, professional, impersonal—except for the bag of crisply laundered shirts hanging from the door handle with the dry cleaner's tag still attached.

The dozen or so shirts themselves had about as much personality as the bag, spanning an entire rainbow from white to pale blue. Dull, corporate, and respectable. She bet all his suits were navy or charcoal and all his ties had burgundy in them. He was probably a guy who always followed the rules. Like she used to. Somehow, she had to make him bend them in her case.

Apart from the bag of shirts, the only signs of the man's personal life were a squash racquet propped against one wall and a single picture on the rosewood desk in front of her. Leaning forward she turned the frame around and peered at two identical faces grinning back at her. The twin girls looked to be about ten years old, identical except that one was missing a front tooth in the photo. They had curly brown hair and sweet faces.

In her earlier career as a pediatric nurse, she'd treated all kinds of children. The twins looked like high-spirited mischief-makers through and through. And vaguely familiar.

"Their names are Olivia and Grace."

With a start, Libby replaced the frame and stood to face Jeremy O'Toole. "Thanks for seeing me. I thought I was going to be thrown out on the street like a bank robber."

He winced like a man in pain. He must take his job pretty seriously. "Sorry about that." He seemed like he wanted to say more, but thought better of it. He squatted down to Mia's level and asked, "Would you like some juice?"

Mia was absorbed in assessing the various merits of a glossy new mortgage, a financial plan that made sense in today's volatile economy, and a retirement package that promised she'd spend her golden years golfing and fishing. She glanced up from the fan of glossy brochures on the floor and, after observing the man for several unsmiling seconds, handed him a brochure with a crumpled corner.

He glanced at it. "You'd rather have an on-demand line of credit? Very sensible, especially if you're taking your mom toy shopping." He smiled at the little girl and, obviously deciding she'd found a friend, she smiled back.

Libby hoped he'd be as nice to her.

Straightening, he turned and extended his hand. "Jeremy O'Toole."

"Libby Brown." She gave her hand, which still trembled faintly, glad he didn't seem worried about Mia mauling bank property. He had a nice warm handshake, no he-man wrestler's grip, just a pleasant squeeze. He looked to be a pleasant, no-nonsense man as well, although the nurse in Libby detected that his skin was unnaturally pale and his eyes had a dull glow she associated with pain. She hoped whatever he had wasn't contagious. The last thing she had time for now was a flu epidemic on top of eviction from their home.

"Would you like some coffee, Mrs. Brown?"

She'd like a reprieve from her mortgage and worries. She'd like to sleep at night. She wanted her old life back.

But a cup of coffee would be a start. "Thanks, cream and sugar. And Mia would love some juice."

The banker didn't push a button to summon an underling. He said, "I'll be right back," and turned back toward the doorway, only to pause when he spotted the dry cleaning.

"Sorry about this stuff," he said as he picked up the hanging bag and moved to open a closet door. Inside hung three jackets:

one navy, one navy pinstripe, and one charcoal. Half a dozen burgundy ties hung on a tie rack.

Libby didn't realize she was smirking until he caught her at it.

"I don't really live here. I keep some things at the office because I don't have a lot of time in the mornings."

"I'm sorry. I wasn't thinking you live here, only that all your clothes look alike." *Oh, great. Start her meeting to ask for money by insulting the bank manager.*

His eyes crinkled when he smiled. For a second, Libby forgot why she was here and basked in the warmth of that smile. "It's the conservative look. They teach it in banking school."

A chuckle was surprised out of her. His sense of humor definitely didn't go with his boring wardrobe.

"Mornings are hectic enough. I don't have time to worry about putting the right shirt with the right tie. Everything I own matches everything else. Simple."

Now she understood. She'd felt the same way when, as a new mother, she'd cut her waist-length hair and tossed out her hot rollers.

"I'll get that coffee."

By the time he returned with a plastic tray containing two steaming mugs and a glass of orange juice, Libby had worked herself back to nervous. She took refuge in fussing around, arranging Mia in a position where she'd be least likely to knock over her juice. Then she sat down and took a sip of coffee.

Glancing up, she saw Jeremy O'Toole, now seated at his desk, doing the same, and couldn't miss the grimace that crossed his face after he swallowed. *Gastric trouble,* she diagnosed him mentally.

"You should try to avoid coffee," she said without thinking. Then gasped at her tactlessness. First, she'd critiqued his wardrobe, now his health habits. She had to get a grip.

"Great, now my doctor's sending out spies." He rolled his eyes in an expression of comical horror.

Libby couldn't help but smile. "I used to be a pediatric nurse. Sorry."

"I didn't know caffeine addiction was on the rampage among children." He was teasing her, and the half smile on his face creased his cheeks into deeply attractive lines.

"You can get gastric troubles at any age," she said in her best nurse voice.

"I've cut way down on coffee but I'm only human."

A typical stubborn man. She was glad he wasn't her patient. "Ulcer?"

He shook his head. "Acid reflux."

"Try herbal tea."

His disgusted expression told her what he thought of that idea. "If Dr. Kim didn't send you to check up on me, what can I do for you?"

Licking her lips nervously, she glanced up into gray-blue eyes fringed with black lashes. If he still felt pain he wasn't showing it. He had a nice face. Not magnetically handsome like Victor's, but nice. A face that grew more appealing each time she looked at it.

"You can let me keep my house," she blurted.

A crease formed between his brows and the look of pain flashed again in his eyes. He reached for the computer keyboard on his desk, then, without so much as touching a key, paused and dropped his hands. His gaze shifted back to Libby. "Why don't you tell me about it?"

It would be easier if he could find out everything he needed to know on his computer. She didn't want to have to tell him, or anyone, what a fool she'd been. But he was waiting, so she pulled in a breath.

"My husband asked for a divorce. He said I could keep the house. But he seems to have disappeared." She stopped to swallow hard. She'd cried enough tears over Victor, she wouldn't embarrass herself in front of a stranger.

"What do you mean he's disappeared?" He passed a box of tissues as casually as though most of his meetings were conducted in tears.

"He's g-gone. He's always traveled a lot on business but he's stopped calling. The kids haven't heard from him in weeks." She yanked out a tissue and blew her nose. "I had no idea he'd stopped paying the mortgage until I got this letter." She pulled the now wrinkled document out of her purse and waved it.

"You have a written agreement?"

She nodded.

"Where does he work?"

"He's self-employed. I tried calling yesterday, when I got the letter, but his phone's not working."

His focus on her sharpened and the crease between his eyes deepened.

"His home phone? Office? Cell?"

She shook her head and sniffed.

"Does he own his home or rent?"

"He didn't bother renting anything when he moved out. He was on the road too much. He told me he'd get things settled in the fall. And I believed him." She swallowed. "He's gone."

He pulled the letter closer, and started typing.

She'd already been through all this with Mr. Lizst but she didn't bother telling him that. Maybe his computer would give better news. Hah. And maybe this was all a bad dream.

Jeremy O'Toole took a longer time to scan the screen in front of him than Mr. Lizst. He also pushed a few more buttons, clearly taking more of an interest in her case. Libby began to feel hopeful.

Then she saw him glance at Mia, who was happily playing on the floor. There was pity in his eyes. "The mortgage hasn't been paid in more than sixty days."

She nodded. "I got the letter yesterday. I didn't know anything about it." She felt her anger returning.

"I'm sorry, it's bank policy to call in a loan after ninety days of non-payment, Ms. Brown." He looked truly sad.

"But I've got young children. I'm sure I can catch up with the payments now I know about the problem. I need time. You can't throw us out on the street."

A glimmer of humor crossed his features. "In spite of the way you've been treated today, we do try to look after our customers. Under the circumstances, I can give you an extra thirty days to put a plan in place."

"Thirty days. I was supposed to get the house. It's in my name." She was speechless with shock and anger but at least the urge to cry had dried up. "This is *not* my problem."

"I'm afraid it is. The house is in your name all right, so whatever equity you've built up is yours, but the bank holds the property as collateral against the outstanding mortgage balance."

"You mean my house belongs to you?"

"We don't want it. The last thing a bank wants is a foreclosure. We'll help you any way we can."

"For thirty days." She pictured the trailer where her father still lived and shuddered.

Still watching her, O'Toole heaved a sigh. "Do you have any idea where your husband is?"

"Ex-husband." Libby glanced down at Mia, glad to see she was busy finger-painting juice on one of the brochures, seemingly too caught up in her activity to listen to the grownups. "He transferred the house to me." She paused and shrugged, knowing she'd been played for a sucker. "He got behind on child support. He said he was going through a cash crunch and promised to pay me everything he owed as soon as things got better. I haven't heard from him since Christmas."

She shook her head. "I trusted him. He's an entrepreneur.

All our married life he had ups and downs financially, but we always ended up fine. I trusted him to take care of his children. I assumed he was a better man than he turned out to be."

"Have you contacted a lawyer?"

She shook her head. "I thought he was going through something." She looked at their beautiful child playing quietly. "I thought he'd come back."

"Any other investments? Pension?"

"It was all tied up in Victor's company. All I wanted was the house and the children." Her voice shook again. "I can't believe he'd abandon us."

"The police might be able to help. Do you think he's still in Washington State?"

"I doubt he's in the country. Victor was excited about the opportunities in Eastern Europe." She glanced at Mia and lowered her voice. "There's a woman in Prague." She glanced up at the banker. "I only know her first name, Irina. Oh, and that she's twenty-two and models."

"A bit of a cliché."

"He said he was sorry, but that Irina was his future. I didn't even contest the divorce. I made it so easy for him. And this is how he treats us?"

"Does he have partners? Employees? Someone must know where he is."

"I've called everyone I could think of. Our mutual friends, former clients of his." She shook her head. "His parents went back to Germany after they retired. His mother's still alive, but she says she hasn't heard from him either." She stared at the bank manager with the pain-dulled eyes. "How could anyone leave the family they were supposed to love?"

There was a strange moment when something flashed between the two of them, some pull of understanding or sympathy so powerful she felt her breath catch.

"Do you have other sources of income?" he asked brusquely, dropping his gaze to his keyboard.

"I do some landscape design, but the business is so young. It's not enough to support the kids and me. It covers groceries."

He nodded. "Have you thought about going back to nursing?"

"Of course, I've thought about it. By the time I retrain and then pay for childcare for two children, we'll hardly get ahead." She rubbed her forehead where a dull headache thrummed. "I've scaled back our expenses to the bone. My car's ten years old and I rarely drive it. We don't buy anything we don't absolutely need."

"You've built up some equity. The way house prices are rising in your area you could sell and move to a less expensive home."

"No!" He glanced at her, obviously startled at her loud cry. She forced herself to calm down. "I have watched my children suffer enough. Do you have any idea what it's like to see their confusion and hurt when they lose a parent?"

She saw his jaw clench once, hard, and then he nodded.

"At least they've got their home and their mother. They can go to the same school and play with the same friends. I'll do anything to keep that much for them. Anything."

"It's not—"

"I've always paid my bills. Always. I don't have so much as an unpaid library fine in my past. I am going to make a good life for my children. I promise you. There must be something you can do."

Her passion must have reached him, and her determination.

"Here is the best I can offer. We can extend your mortgage to thirty years and renew you early at a lower rate than you're now paying. It's going to cut your payments almost in half, but of course you won't be getting very far ahead."

"And the back payments and fees?"

He stared at her for another moment, obviously debating. She held her breath and tried to look like exactly what she was. A woman who stood by her commitments. Who paid her dues.

At last he said, "I'll add the full amount to the mortgage principal. You'll pay it, but over time."

Relief made her feel dizzy. "That's okay. That's wonderful. When do I have to make the first payment?"

He sighed. Seemed to wrestle with himself. "Let's say sixty days from today."

She didn't care if she never paid down the mortgage if she could keep the house. "Thank you. I won't let you down."

"Mrs. Brown, I suggest—" The phone on his desk rang, and he frowned at it. "Excuse me," he mumbled, and lifted the receiver. "Linda, I asked you to hold all my calls. What? Oh, put her through."

There was a pause, during which he glanced at his watch and the frown intensified and then, "Hi, honey, is there a problem at school?"

The look of concern changed to horror. She heard hysterical babbling sounds coming from the receiver.

"What? Where are you? How much blood?"

THREE

Jeremy O'Toole jerked to his feet, glancing at Libby with blatant appeal in his eyes. "You're a nurse. My daughter's throwing up blood. I can be home in ten minutes. Should they call 9-1-1?"

"How much blood?" She repeated his own question.

He looked completely baffled. "Hard to say."

She thought quickly, then shook her head. "The children are already panicked. I think it's better if you take her to the hospital."

He nodded once, then spoke into the receiver with a calmness at odds with the raw fear on his face. "Hang on, honey, I'll be right there." He hung up and turned to Libby. "Would you come, too?" With her, he didn't bother to disguise the fear.

"It could be flu." She stood watching him grab his coat, root for keys.

"Please?"

He'd helped her out of a tough spot and even though it had been more than eight years since she'd nursed, her first aid training was current. "All right."

She glanced down at Mia, who'd picked up the atmosphere

in the room and was staring anxiously at her mother. "We're going to help a little girl who isn't feeling too well."

Hauling Mia up in her arms and ignoring the crumpled mess of brochures littering the rug, Libby scurried to keep up as Jeremy O'Toole's long legs strode at top speed ahead of her. He yelled something to the astonished Linda on his way past. He didn't pause at the elevator but charged straight for the stairs with Libby following, her shoes clattering on the gray cement, one arm firmly around Mia, the other clinging to the handrail.

By the time she emerged from the street exit he was a dark shape sprinting toward the parked cars. Even as she started forward he leaped into a maroon Volvo. In seconds he was peeling out of the parking space and roaring toward her. His impatience was palpable as she carefully buckled her daughter in the pull-down child's seat in the back.

Thank God they were in the safest car known to man, she thought, as they roared out of the parking lot. She buckled her own seat belt and turned a watchful eye on Jeremy O'Toole. His face was set in a grim mask, all the emotions locked down, hands steady on the wheel. Only the speed at which they were traveling gave away his distress. She had a strong feeling he wasn't a habitual speeder.

"You won't help your daughters if you get in an accident," she warned him.

He didn't answer. Nor did he ease off on the accelerator. He removed one hand from the wheel, dug out a cell phone and pushed a button. The phone was shoved her way. "It's Grace and Olivia."

"Where are the girls?"

"My house."

"It's ringing...Alone?" She couldn't help it if she sounded critical. It was obvious the children were too young to be alone.

"They're supposed to be at school."

"Where's their mother?" She couldn't imagine her kids

approaching Victor with a problem, it was always to her that they'd come.

"Their mother's dead."

"Oh. I'm sorry." She shook her head. "Went straight to voicemail," she informed the man next to her. She clamped her teeth together to keep from screaming as they careened around a corner, narrowly missing a delivery truck.

They shot into a tree-lined boulevard not far from her own neighborhood. The homes that flashed by were a blur of well-kept colonials and Tudors.

She was thrown against the passenger door by the g-force as he peeled from one crescent into another.

"Whee!" squealed Mia.

Moments later they jerked to a halt. He was out of the car and running up the path that bisected the only ragged lawn on the crescent. Quickly, she helped Mia out of the back seat.

"Where we going?"

"We're going to visit a little girl who's sick. Can you be very good while Mommy's busy?"

Mia nodded solemnly, and Libby couldn't help hugging her as she pulled the child into her arms once again and ran up the path, already reviewing what she knew of internal bleeding.

The front door was wide open, and as she approached it she could hear the crying. In stereo.

Libby sucked in a deep breath and crossed the threshold.

After locking the front door behind her, she secured Mia in the cluttered living room to the right of the front door. A quick survey told her there wasn't any clear danger to Mia, so she sat her on the floor near a pile of books and Legos with instructions to stay put.

Libby followed the sounds of crying up the stairs and along a hall, where her nose was able to help pinpoint the twins' location. The air was sour with the scent of vomit.

"Daddy, I can't stop throwing—" the tearful voice was cut off by a bout of retching.

Libby poked her head around the open door to find one curly head bending over the toilet, heaving. An identical head was bent over the sink, similarly occupied.

Relief struck her immediately. If they were both vomiting then it was either flu or something they'd eaten. She could put away her sketchy knowledge of ruptured blood vessels and cancer in kids.

"Do everything together do they?" she asked, squeezing into the crowded bathroom.

Jeremy O'Toole stood poised in the middle of the floor in his business suit, arms stretched to their limit so he could rub both heaving backs simultaneously.

He shot her a helpless parent look that took her back to her days on the emergency ward. "Do something. They're bleeding their guts out."

"If they're both sick, it's a good sign," she said soothingly, keeping her voice calm but positive. How easily she slipped back into the nurse role.

Stepping behind him, she managed a good look in the sink. "Which one started vomiting first?"

The one in the sink pointed to the one bent over the toilet.

"Still think it's flu?" Jeremy O'Toole asked her.

"Could be." She did a rapid check for fever by putting her forearm on the back of each bent neck. "They're a little warm, but that could be from exertion."

She gently lifted the wrist of the girl closest to her and found the pulse rapid, but nice and strong. "What did you girls eat last?"

The one over the sink groaned and started heaving. The one at the toilet stopped crying long enough to gasp, "Brownies. We made them ourselves."

Libby glanced at their father, who appeared horrified at the news. "They don't know how to bake."

"Hang on, I'll check the kitchen," she said.

She ran down to the kitchen and sure enough there was a large cake pan, empty but for a couple of remaining lumps of tar-like substance.

Pigging out on a whole pan of brownies was enough to make anyone sick, in Libby's opinion, but not so violently. Puzzled, she studied the perfectly ordinary brownie recipe staring at her from an open book on the counter.

Every ingredient the girls had used seemed to be on display, from baking chocolate to an oozing jar of corn syrup, to sugar and vanilla. There was nothing unusual, except that the flour canister looked undisturbed in the far corner.

In the interests of medical research, Libby pinched off a lump of the brown stuff in the pan. It smelled like chocolate. She bit off a tiny bit and chewed. Careful not to swallow, she rinsed her mouth out at the sink. Along with the strong chocolate taste, she noted a peculiar flavor.

She sorted more carefully through the ingredients strewn all over the counter. The only thing she didn't instantly recognize was an unmarked white plastic container with white powder inside. Beside it was a plastic measuring cup with powder residue almost up to the two-cup mark.

Using the tip of her tongue once again as an instrument of science, Libby tasted the powder and wrinkled her nose: baking soda. The girls had obviously mistaken it for flour. No wonder the little stinkers were heaving their guts out.

And, in the midst of the kitchen counter, was a pitcher of bright red cranberry cocktail and two nearly empty glasses of the red stuff. So much for the "blood."

With a muttered prayer of thankfulness that they'd ingested nothing worse than bicarb of soda, she went back upstairs, sticking her head in the living room on the way to see Mia happily singing to herself as she pretended to read one of the books.

Back in the bathroom, the crying had started up again. "My stomach hurts," wailed one little girl, doubled over. The other one was now sitting on the toilet seat as though she knew she'd never get far.

Jeremy O'Toole had his arms wrapped round the girl with the cramps. "I'm taking them straight to the hospital."

"Seems they made a pan of brownies using bicarb of soda in place of flour, and drank it down with red juice."

"And you think that's funny?" He turned an evil eye on the smirk she couldn't prevent.

"That's what was turning their vomit red. Not blood."

As her words sank in, he slumped against the vanity, panic ebbing out of his face. But the worry was still there. "Thank God. But they're really sick. What should I do?"

"It won't do them any permanent damage. If they were my kids, I'd put them to bed." She shrugged. "But the hospital can give them a shot to stop the vomiting. It's up to you."

He pulled the second girl into his embrace and hugged both children to him fiercely. "Right, come on, girls. We'll have you feeling better in no time."

"Who's she?" asked one.

"This is Mrs. Brown. She's a nurse, and she's here to help you." O'Toole glanced over at Libby as if wondering how to proceed next.

"Why don't I get the girls' coats and maybe a couple of buckets."

"Coats are on the hooks by the back door. There should be some buckets in the garage."

She finally unearthed the jackets on the floor in the living room. There might have been buckets in the garage, but Libby figured she'd end up in hospital herself if she tried to wade through all the junk in there. Back in the house, she emptied a couple of overflowing wastepaper bins to serve instead of the missing buckets.

"Mia and I live near here. Maybe you could drop us off?" she asked once everybody was buckled into the car.

"Aren't you coming with us?"

"I can't. I have to be home when my son gets off school at three o'clock. It's after two now."

He glanced at her and she almost read his mind. He was going to suggest she call a taxi, but she couldn't afford one.

"Please, it's on your way," she said, and quickly gave him directions.

When they reached her house, he barely waited till she had Mia out of the car before roaring off, leaving Libby saying, "I hope you feel better," to the empty road.

———

"Hi, Mom, I'm home." Tyler's voice bounced high with excitement. At eight, he still thought she was the greatest being in the universe and he held a special place in her heart as the only male who'd ever really loved her.

"Hi, darling, how was your day?" Libby gasped as he squeezed her in a bear hug.

"Hi, Tyler." Mia ran up to get her turn at a bear hug, then laughed as her big brother lifted her feet clear off the floor.

"Guess what?" With all the importance due to the only member of the family whose daily activities took him outside the home, Tyler plunked down at the kitchen table for his daily recitation of the day's events.

"What?"

"We're going on a field trip to see a play about space. It's gonna be so cool."

At the words field trip, Libby's heart sank. Field trips cost money.

Tyler glanced around the kitchen hopefully.

Libby prided herself on the wholesome home baking she served her family but today she hadn't had a lot of time for baking. She'd sliced carrot sticks and dug out a dozen chocolate chip cookies from her emergency stash in the freezer. She had a packet of brownies in there too. She shuddered and pulled out the cookies, put them on to bake, then poured the milk.

While they were catching up on his day, there was a knock at the kitchen door and Tyler bolted out of his chair.

"Wait till I see who it is," Libby reminded him.

"It's Josh," he said with the intense frustration of an eight-year-old who wants to play with his buddy *now*. Libby was fairly certain he was right, but she still checked the window above her son's head to be sure. And broke into a smile.

Josh wasn't alone. His mother and little brother, who was only a few months younger than Mia, were also there.

"Hi," she said to them all. "Come in." Then she lifted her eyebrows to Paula Lowenstein, her neighbor and friend. "Want some coffee?"

Her friend looked sheepish. "I'd love to but I've got a doctor's appointment I forgot about. I could drag the kids along, but..." She looked at Libby hopefully.

"They can play here. It's fine."

"I owe you. I'll watch yours anytime."

The kids made short work of the cookies and carrots and then bounded downstairs to the basement playroom. The three-year-olds needed help with the stairs, but once ensconced down there, everybody was safe and Libby could process her day.

She'd called Cleo earlier to let her know what had happened at the bank and asked her to tell the others. She knew the group of baking friends were all sending her positive energy and that helped.

Libby brewed coffee and for a second smiled, thinking of

Jeremy O'Toole's face as he'd drunk coffee that was so bad for him.

The doorbell went again and she wondered if Paula had forgotten something, but to her delight, she saw three of her favorite people in the world standing outside. Cleo Duvall was in her fifties, long and lanky with graying red hair she usually kept tied back. Brooke Mattson was nearing forty but still kept her supermodel looks. At six feet tall she towered over the others, her hair a perfect blond curtain, her eyes the most remarkable blue. She'd married a billionaire and you'd think she'd be the most envied woman in town, but she was too nice for that. Besides, she had her own troubles. She wanted a child desperately and it didn't look like it was going to happen.

Megan Alexander had obviously come from a job based on the green streaks of paint in her curly brown hair. "I stripped off my overalls," she said as she came in, "so I won't mess up your pretty house."

"Might not be mine much longer," Libby said, so relieved to have these women here when she needed them. No need to pretend everything was fine when it was the opposite of fine.

Cleo carried a bag of her famous cinnamon buns. "Good baking makes everything a little better," she said, giving Libby a hug.

Just the aroma made her smile and start to feel lighter. She wasn't alone. She had friends.

"No," Brooke groaned. "Don't tempt me. I'm going to the Caribbean next week."

"You're going to the Caribbean?" Libby turned around to stare. "Oh, how wonderful. White sand beaches, turquoise water—"

"Two-piece bathing suit."

She laughed. "What's the occasion?" Not that rich people needed them.

Brooke paused for a second. "Our tenth anniversary."

Libby would never see her tenth wedding anniversary, but she didn't let that stop her. "Hey, that's great. You know, Kyle almost deserves you. He reminds me that there are good men out there. And you remind me that some women do have good judgment."

"Cleo put an arm around Libby. We all make mistakes, hon. I know I did the first time."

She nodded, taking them into her kitchen. She poured the coffee and they settled around her kitchen table with the plate of cinnamon buns and the rest of the chocolate chip cookies she'd baked. "He certainly fooled me," and she proceeded to tell the three women in detail about her meeting today.

"I can't believe your husband just left and stopped supporting his family," Brooke said, sounding genuinely shocked.

She nodded. "I tried to convince myself that twenty-two-year-old Irina was some crazy phase Victor was going through. He was forty years old and having a mid-life crisis. It was humiliating but it would pass." She swallowed. "And now he's left us as though we never existed."

"What an ass," Megan said. "We knew he was a bad man, but even I didn't think he'd turn out to be a deadbeat dad."

Libby blinked. Her friend was right. She'd fallen for and married a man who turned into a deadbeat dad.

"What are you going to do?" Cleo asked.

"I'm not letting go of this house," she said with a combination of panic and fierceness. "The bank president turned out to be a pretty good guy. He's working out something so I pay a lower monthly mortgage payment. Of course, I'll pay it forever, but if I can hang on until the kids are out of school..."

"If you need a loan to get you through the next few months..." Brooke said, sounding hesitant. "I can write you a check right now. Kyle doesn't have to know anything about it. I have my own money."

She felt warmed by the offer even as she knew she'd never take charity from her friends. "I'm fine. But thank you from the bottom of my heart for offering."

"Hey," Brooke said, leaning forward. "It's what friends do. Anytime, the offer stays open. I still have a nest egg from when I worked. It would be between us."

"No. I have to do this myself. I wanted to build my landscape design business." She shook her head. "Now I've got sixty days to figure out how to pay for everything. I'll have to find a job."

Megan reached for a chocolate chip cookie. She stopped mid-chew and moaned. "Libby. You are the only woman I know who bakes better than my mom. Cleo, these might be better than your cookies."

Libby laughed and Cleo took a cookie to see for herself. "Not bad," she said, nodding.

Megan continued. "And you cook healthy food, you raise gorgeous kids." She swallowed and said, "I know what you should do, you should run a school for moms."

Libby laughed. "Better still, I should be a stand-in mom for kids who don't have one." And she told them about the banker's unsupervised daughters and their little baking experiment.

"They could have killed themselves. Why weren't they at school?" Brooke asked.

"I get the feeling that their dad is having a rough time controlling two high-spirited, motherless girls."

"Of course," Megan said, slapping her forehead. "That's what you should do."

"What?"

"Offer childcare from your home." She leaned forward, her eyes widening as she got excited by her idea. "You're a trained pediatric nurse, you bake everything from scratch and your house is so child friendly it's obsessive. One of my clients has been complaining about trying to find decent childcare. You'd be perfect."

"That's a fantastic idea," Cleo agreed.

"If I ever had kids, I couldn't imagine anyone I'd trust them with more than you," Brooke said, a little sadly.

Libby stared at her friends for a long moment and then nodded slowly. "You're right. That's the perfect solution. And I know a couple of kids who could sure use my help."

Megan glanced at her phone. "I have to get back to my project, and I think our work here is done."

Cleo wanted to get back to the bakery in time to close up, and Brooke left with the others.

When Paula returned to pick up her kids, Libby asked if she'd watch Mia and Tyler for a couple of hours after dinner.

"Sure."

Quickly, she explained her new venture and Paula was immediately excited and said she might know someone who needed before and after school care.

Libby began to hope she could make enough money to scrape by. "I've got to pick up my car and then I've got some marketing and promotions to take care of."

"I'll drive you to your car," her friend offered.

"I owe you."

"Hah. Don't worry. I plan to use the services of your daycare."

"Any time. For you, it's not a business. We're friends."

FOUR

Jeremy glanced in the rearview mirror at the two children's bodies sprawled in sleep, dark curls mingling. They were going to be fine. His heart squeezed with a painful feeling of relief.

And guilt.

He wasn't good enough.

If only Kelly were still here, none of this would have happened. She'd have made them a pan of goddamn brownies if they wanted them. And she'd for damned sure have made certain that his kids weren't sneaking home at lunch hour to an empty house.

Kelly.

He tried not to think of her. It hurt too much. It was going to the hospital that brought it all back. St. Paul's was where she'd given birth to the twins.

And where she'd died.

And where, that last day, he'd promised to be mother and father to the girls.

He was failing miserably, and the torture chamber that used to be his stomach punished him every day.

This time, he'd been lucky. The doctor hadn't even pumped

their stomachs, merely put them both on an IV drip for a few hours with some anti-nausea meds and something to rehydrate them. His daughters were going to be fine. But he felt his reprieve like a warning; his current childcare arrangement wasn't only unsatisfactory, it was downright dangerous.

The car headlights guided him into the driveway. When he cut the engine, everything went black and Jeremy cursed himself for not flipping on some lights earlier.

The house looked dark and unwelcoming. He wished with all his heart that Kelly was here waiting for them. Kelly with her good-natured laugh and generous loving. "Aw, baby, I miss you," he whispered under his breath as he dragged his exhausted body from the car.

And froze.

His heart jerked painfully against his ribs when a female figure rose gracefully from the front steps and glided toward him.

The hair stood up on the back of his neck and he felt his flesh break out in goose bumps as the ghostly apparition moved closer. "Kelly?" his voice croaked.

Even as he whispered the name, he knew the woman moving toward him wasn't his wife. She was too tall and too slim.

"It's Libby Brown," she answered softly, her voice floating smoothly through the night air.

Disappointment crushed him. He wanted his wife, even if only for a brief ghostly visitation. He was tired, lonely, and worried about his children. The last thing he needed was this woman with her mountain of problems.

He could barely shoulder his own burdens, never mind hers.

She hadn't been so all fired up wonderful as a nurse, either, now he thought about it. He sighed. That wasn't fair. She'd been perfectly professional, but the twins needed their mother, not a nurse. He hadn't thought the evening could possibly get worse. Looked like he was wrong.

"This is a surprise," he managed to get out.

"How are the girls?" She was closer now and he could make out the pale blur of her face.

"You were right. They spent a few hours on an IV drip and they've been sent home to sleep it off." He opened the back car door and unbelted Olivia.

"If you hand me your house keys, I'll open the door for you," that calm voice suggested. He hesitated then handed her the keys, and by the time he had Olivia hoisted in his arms the outside lights were lit and the front door wide open.

Trudging into the house and up the stairs with his sleeping burden, he felt suddenly grateful for the woman snapping lights on upstairs and pulling the bedclothes down so he could slip Olivia into bed. She'd guessed wrong, but he didn't think the girls were in any shape to notice they were in each other's beds until morning.

"Would you like me to put her nightclothes on while you get her sister?"

"Thanks. Her nightclothes are...ah..." He glanced around the cluttered piles of clothing all over the floor until he recognized a cotton night shirt with a picture of kittens on it. "Here."

He bolted back downstairs and by the time he returned with Grace, Olivia was tucked in and sleeping peacefully.

Within a couple of minutes, Libby Brown had Grace tucked in efficiently and she'd done something to the beds so they appeared smooth and freshly made.

She nodded and quietly left the room.

He kissed them each on the forehead, promising silently to do better for them in the future. He crept out of the room—or tried to. A stray fashion doll, naked as the day she was molded, tripped him up and sent him crashing against the doorjamb.

One of the girls muttered in her sleep, then sighed.

He cursed softly. The house was a pigsty.

He'd let it go because the current housekeeper was a trained teacher unable to find a job. She'd seemed like a responsible young woman, and Jeremy liked that she wanted to be a teacher, figured she'd be fantastic with kids.

Now that he knew how irresponsible she was, he hoped she never got a teaching job. In his opinion, the education system was in enough trouble.

When he returned downstairs, Mrs. Brown stood at the bottom of the stairs holding a brown paper bag from which wafted a mouth-watering aroma. "I brought some vegetable soup," she said. "I didn't imagine you'd have time to cook dinner. If the girls wake up hungry, this would be good for them. Easily digestible and very nutritious. I brought enough for you, too."

"You didn't have to do that," he said, feeling awkward and embarrassed.

"Well, I wasn't merely being neighborly. I do have an ulterior motive."

He tried to keep his face neutral even though he wanted to kick something. This was not the first casserole he'd received that felt as though it came with very thick strings attached. "I see." He knew her financial situation, possibly a little better than she did herself. If she asked him out, on this very day when she'd discovered she was in a financial jam, he wouldn't know how to turn her down without embarrassing the pair of them.

It was his own fault for panicking when he got that call and thinking he might need her training.

He took the bag she offered and, since he couldn't put it on the floor, he walked through to the kitchen, suggesting she follow.

"What a mess," he said when he saw the baking disaster in the kitchen. He'd forgotten all about it.

"I could help you clean it up."

"No," he said, louder than he'd intended. He blew out a breath. "Sorry. I'm pretty beat. Why don't you tell me what's on your mind?" He motioned to one of the kitchen chairs and she pulled out a chair and sat.

He put the bag on the kitchen counter. "Thanks for your help today." Pushing a stack of newspapers to the floor, he sank into a chair and leaned back, exhausted. He was almost relieved that Mrs. Brown was here. She'd shared part of the crisis with him, and even if she did have a not very well-hidden agenda, at least she cared enough to check on the children and bring them soup.

He felt like he'd aged ten years in one day, rushing the twins to the hospital then soothing them through the examinations, rubbing their backs each time a new spasm of retching shook their slight bodies, and finally watching them sleep as the drugs took effect.

The only time he'd left them was when he phoned that useless nanny and fired her.

"You're welcome." She smiled at him faintly and he thought again what an attractive woman she was. Even prettier, he imagined, when her eyes weren't etched with worry and she put some effort into hair and makeup.

There was silence for a moment. He couldn't summon up small talk, so he left it to her. Finally, she asked, "Who's Kelly?"

"What?"

"You called me Kelly."

"Kelly was my wife." He let his tone resonate with finality.

"What happened to her?" She asked the question as normally as if she were asking what he liked for breakfast. He felt like something was smothering him. His chest labored to draw breath.

"Cancer. She got breast cancer, and they did the old poison, slash and burn treatment. But it spread, first to her spine, until she couldn't walk." He let all the anger and viciousness he felt spill out as though it were all her fault Kelly had died.

He knew it wasn't, but she should at least have the decency to leave the woman dead and buried, not question him for all the gory details. Well, if she wanted details, he could give her enough to make her sick to her stomach. "Then it spread to her brain and some days she didn't know who she was, didn't recognize her own children. Didn't understand why she was in so much pain." He gasped at the pain he was feeling.

"You must have loved her very much," she said softly, and he realized it was hopeless to try and intimidate a former nurse with illness details. She'd probably seen it all.

"Yeah."

"She was lucky."

Something exploded in his brain. "Lucky? What's so lucky about having your flesh and bones, even your brain, eaten away by disease? What's so lucky about dying at thirty-five?" His voice was raw and hoarse.

"I meant she was lucky to be able to leave this world knowing she was loved, and that there was someone to care for her children when she was gone."

"Huh. And a piss-poor job I'm doing at that. The twins are only ten years old. They could have set the house on fire while they were making brownies, or cooked up something even more poisonous."

"You said you had a childcare provider?"

"She was supposed to be there all day. Instead, she sneaked off to her boyfriend's, probably."

"From the state of the house, I'd say she was doing a piss-poor job, too."

Even though she was repeating his own words, the sound of a vulgarity coming from Libby Brown's mouth shocked him.

"Yeah. I fired her."

She nodded. "Good." She glanced at him, then at the brown

paper bag on the counter. "Would you like me to warm that soup for you?"

"I'll shower and change before I eat." He was pretty sure he smelled like vomit.

"Look. I thought of a way we could help each other out."

She appeared mildly embarrassed. He never knew how to handle these awkward situations. Not that he'd been in that many of them, but in three years he'd had some offers, usually from nice women he didn't want to hurt. Like this one.

"I really don't think so," he said as firmly as he could, hoping to cut her off at the pass.

Her brows rose. "You don't even know what I'm going to suggest."

Yeah, he did. But he waited anyway. If she wanted to make this more difficult for both of them, he was too tired to stop her.

She licked her lips. That was a mouth made for kissing, he thought, surprised at himself for thinking it. What if she did ask him out?

What if he went? This was the first time he'd seriously thought he might, but then he remembered it wasn't his killer bod and winning personality she was after. She wanted him to help her keep her house.

So he squelched the tiny spurt of male interest and waited.

"You remember when we were talking in your office today, about my situation?"

"Of course."

"Well, obviously I'm going to have to do something to earn enough money to pay for the mortgage and bills."

"Right. We talked about this."

"I think I've found a way to do that."

"Already?"

"I'm going to offer childcare in my home. I'm an excellent cook, a trained pediatric nurse, as you know, and I renew my first aid certification every year. My home is clean and childproofed, I have a fenced-in yard and I live within walking distance of the school."

"That's a good plan," he said, stifling a yawn. "Do you have any kids lined up?"

"That's why I'm here, Mr. O'Toole. I'm going to suggest you and your daughters might benefit from the arrangement."

He stared at her blankly for a second, then almost laughed. On the good side, she hadn't asked him out, although his ego was oddly stung. On the bad side, he couldn't do it.

"I'm not sure that's a good idea."

She looked taken aback. "Oh."

There was an implied question mark at the end of her, "Oh," so he went on. "I think it might be unethical for me to use one of my bank's customers as a daycare provider." It was a bogus excuse but all he could come up with.

She stared at him with her eyebrows slightly raised and he could see she didn't believe him for a second. Well, who would? His doctor and dentist both banked with the First Bank of the Pacific Northwest as did his grocer and any number of other people whose services he used. He couldn't explain why he felt uncomfortable about her proposition, he simply did.

"Well," she said, rising. "I'll let you get on with your evening then. Sorry I disturbed you."

He got to his feet too. "You didn't disturb me. You were a big help today. I appreciate it." He held out his hand and she shook it. Odd to be so formal with a woman standing in his kitchen at seven thirty at night.

She walked toward the front door and he followed her. In her jeans and sweater, he noticed the shape of her, which wasn't something he wanted to think about right now.

They got to the door and she turned again to say goodbye and he blurted something he'd been thinking about while he sat beside his sleeping girls in the hospital. "Why didn't you go after your husband earlier?" She might have at least been able to keep him current in payments before he vanished to the other side of the world.

As he contemplated her in exasperated silence, her head dropped and color flooded her pale cheeks. How did she do this to him? One minute she was the cool, capable nurse, the next she was this vulnerable woman.

In the long silence he heard a dog barking somewhere outside, but, even though he strained his ears, no sound at all came from the girls' room upstairs.

"I thought he'd come back," she whispered at last.

His spine prickled. Any fool could see it was hopeless. Mr. Brown was a deadbeat dad, a species of men who would leave the country rather than support the family they'd helped bring into the world. The woman standing staring at her shoes was crazy and pathetic to think he'd come back.

As crazy and pathetic as Jeremy himself, who no more than half an hour ago had whispered his dead wife's name out in front of the house.

"If I hear of anyone looking for a decent daycare, I'll tell them to call you," he said.

"I'd appreciate that," she said. "Good night." And she was gone.

FIVE

Up in his bedroom, he shrugged thankfully out of the scratchy puke-smelly suit and dashed into the bathroom for a quick shower before dressing in jeans and a navy polo shirt. He kept his eyes averted from the queen-size bed, still with the same yellow chintz comforter Kelly had chosen the year before she died. His eyes burned. He stabbed his feet viciously into sports socks and grabbed his sneakers.

Back in the kitchen, he warmed the soup the Brown woman had brought. God, the woman was amazing. Not only was there a Tupperware container of soup, but she'd included a loaf of home-baked bread, round and crusty.

Okay, he thought, as he settled down with the first home-cooked meal he'd eaten in a long time by someone, unlike him, who could actually cook, she'd gone the right way about advertising her services. Not only was the flavor fabulous, but the soup tasted wholesome. He somehow knew the herbs in there were from her garden and that no cans, packages or shortcuts of any kind had been used.

Wow.

Maybe if he'd tasted the soup first, he wouldn't have turned her down so hastily. He tore into the bread and discovered it tasted as good as he'd imagined it would.

Would it be so bad to try her out as a childcare provider?

But no. That woman had a mountain of problems to wade through, and if he ended up having to foreclose on her home, he didn't want his kids involved.

Turning her down had been the right thing to do.

But, as he rolled up his sleeves and washed up the brownie disaster, he kept seeing her again, the way she'd efficiently figured out what was wrong with the twins, the natural way she'd tucked them in, as though she did it every night.

Well, maybe her new business wasn't for him, but he bet whoever ended up using Libby Brown's daycare was going to be very happy.

Tomorrow, he'd take a day off, watch the kids, work from home and find some other arrangement. He wouldn't use the same agency who'd found him the useless, unemployed teacher. He rubbed a tired hand over his face, so hard that his wedding ring scratched his cheek. Maybe his sister would have some ideas. Tracy was a grade-school teacher and a resourceful woman.

Dishes done, he wandered into the den and accessed his office email from his computer. With luck, everything was running smoothly. He could leave Linda a voicemail that he wasn't going to be in tomorrow and then head to bed.

That hope died an instant death when he saw the subject of several emails.

Couldn't one single thing go right? With the crisis with the girls, he'd forgotten that tomorrow was the directors' meeting. The reason he'd been reviewing next year's marketing plan when Libby Brown stormed into his life.

If he missed tomorrow's meeting, he might as well kiss his

job goodbye. He had to present the bank's strategic plan for the next twelve months at ten o'clock tomorrow morning. He'd intended to spend the bulk of today preparing his presentation. First Libby Brown, then the twins' baking disaster had knocked the whole thing out of his mind.

The plan was in place, including Melanie's crap ad campaign, but he still had to write his speaking notes and polish up his presentation.

He started typing, then stopped. What was he going to do with the girls tomorrow? He'd been told to keep them home from school for a few days. He certainly wasn't about to un-fire the nanny for one day.

Panic settled in his stomach, and the gastric juices began churning his guts into the pit of hell.

He picked up the phone on his desk and called his big sister. "Hey, Tracy," he said when she answered, feeling better just hearing her voice. As she grew older, she reminded him more and more of their mom. "What's up?"

"I'm considering petitioning congress to outlaw cell phones to any child under twenty-one. I had a girl's cell phone go off in the middle of a math test. I confiscated it and later her father called. Not to apologize, you understand, but to warn me never to touch his daughter's personal property again." She blew out a breath. "How was your day?"

"I win in the crap day department. Mine was worse." He told her about the baking and the hospital visit and Tracy made all the right sounds of outrage and sympathy. Being able to tell her about it made him feel a little better. "So, now I'm stuck with no childcare tomorrow and two sick kids."

"Oh, Jer. I'm so sorry. Look, I can call in a sub and take a day off tomorrow. Believe me, after the cell phone incident, I need a mental health day."

"I love you for offering, but no. I'll find another way."

There was a short pause. "You know Mom would fly home and help out." Their parents had retired to Florida two years earlier. They'd owned the condo in St. Pete's for a few years before that and he knew that they'd held off moving to support him and the twins through Kelly's illness and death and the first terrible year after she'd died.

"I know she would. But then Dad wouldn't want to be left alone, so they'd both come and it's not fair on them. They're enjoying their lives. Besides it would only be another temporary fix. No. I've got to find a better solution." He scratched his head. "If only the twins weren't such..."

"Monsters?" his sister suggested with a wry note.

He made a face she couldn't see. "I've spoiled them, haven't I?"

"Well, you let them get away with murder, but you've also got two great kids who are getting through a tough time as best they can. Anyhow, they come by the monster gene honestly. Remember what we were like?"

And suddenly he laughed. "Mostly, it was you who thought up the stunts and me who got caught."

"They're going to be fine, Jeremy," she said, somehow answering the worry he hadn't voiced. "They'll grow up to be wonderful people. We did."

"I know you're right. Thanks. It's tough having nobody to share the worry and the responsibility."

"I know. I guess Kelly's parents wouldn't—"

"No." he said with finality. He'd met his wife at college, which he'd attended back East. She was from Chicago and her family still lived there. Kelly's parents never really got to know Olivia and Grace all that well, and after Kelly died, the contact dwindled to gifts and a phone call at birthdays and Christmas and a check each year toward their college fund. He couldn't understand how her parents could dismiss all that was left of Kelly, but he suspected they found it too painful to be reminded of their dead daughter in the twins, who looked so much like her. He tried to understand.

Kelly's brothers and sister all had their own families and seemed to take the lead from her parents.

"I do have one option," he said and he told Tracy about Libby Brown.

"She sounds perfect," his sister said after he'd described the way his bank client had helped him through the brownie fiasco and he'd described her qualifications. Seen through his sister's eyes, of course, Libby Brown was perfect. "Why are you so hesitant?"

He didn't mention one reason. That he was attracted to a woman who was as messed up emotionally as he was. "I don't know. Maybe because she was talking about being a landscape designer at ten o'clock this morning and nine hours later, she suddenly opens a daycare. And if we have to foreclose, I'd be in a tough spot."

"I wish I had an easy answer for you. The offer stays on the table. If you want me to take a day off tomorrow, you know I will."

"Thanks, Tracy. You're the best." He rubbed a hand absently over his belly. "But I'll figure this out."

"Sorry, I'm later than I thought I'd be," Libby said when Paula opened the door. "I had to wait for them to get back from the hospital." Briefly, she told Paula about her evening.

Her neighbor glanced at her wrist. "Fifteen minutes late. I'll have to punish you by feeding you coffee. Come on in, I made some decaf."

"Don't you want me to take the children straight home?"

"They're watching the new Disney video. Wild horses won't drag them away until it's over and the princess bags her prince. Besides, Ben's got a partners' dinner tonight, I can use the company."

Libby snorted, following her neighbor into a warm oak kitchen. "I'm thinking about launching a petition against all movies where princes and princesses end up happily ever after. Why poison their little minds with…What are you doing?" While she'd been speaking, Paula had dragged a chair across the kitchen. Now she climbed up on it to reach the cupboard above the fridge.

"I sense we need a little kick in our coffee," Paula said, dragging out a bottle of Irish cream liqueur which she handed down to Libby. With a grunt, Paula clambered down and bustled around collecting mugs and the coffee pot.

Libby watched, bemused, as her friend poured rich, dark streams of coffee into two mugs and then sloshed a healthy dose of liqueur into each mug. "Hell, we might as well go all out," she announced and opened the fridge and pulled out a slim carton. "Real, one-thousand-calories-a-teaspoon whipping cream."

Soon they were sitting at the kitchen table, steaming coffees in front of them. Libby sipped, enjoying the tickle of cream against her upper lip, and the kick as the drink hit her stomach. For a moment life felt like it used to be.

"Well?" Paula asked, reminding her that life was completely different than it used to be.

She shook her head. "He said, no."

"How could anyone say no to you? What's the matter with the guy? Is he too cheap to pay for decent childcare?"

"We never even discussed money. It wasn't that." Her brows drew together in a frown. "I don't have a clue why he turned me down. He said something about ethics, but I don't think it was that."

"Maybe he really wants the kids looked after in their own home," Paula suggested. "And getting the childcare provider's exclusive attention."

"Maybe. And they could definitely use a housekeeper. That place is a mess."

Her friend shrugged. "His loss. We'll put the word out among school moms and have you turning down customers in no time."

Impulsively, Libby reached across and touched the other woman's hand. It was freckled and warm. "You've already helped, taking the kids tonight. Taking in other children is the perfect solution for now."

"I agree."

"Do I need some kind of a license or something?"

Her friend shrugged expansively. "I don't know. You can check it out tomorrow."

Excited chatter erupted from the basement, indicating the movie was over. Feet pounded up the stairs, and four bright faces burst through the doorway into the kitchen.

"Hi, Mom," Tyler shouted, running forward and then sliding to a halt in his stocking feet when he realized his friend Josh was watching.

Mia had no inhibitions about hugging in public. She threw herself into her mother's arms. "Mama."

When she'd finished tucking the kids into bed, Libby poured herself a bath—one of the few indulgences she still allowed herself. She was a little punchy from lack of sleep and a day that had pretty much been all dramatic peaks with not enough valleys in it to catch her breath and regroup.

Knowing Victor had abandoned them still stung cruelly, but there was a sneaking sense of determination that Libby hadn't been sure she possessed. Deep down, she knew she was going to be okay. With a lower mortgage payment, some daycare clients and her landscaping business, she was going to survive.

"You've got this," Cleo Duvall said when she struggled over a difficult bread recipe, and Cleo was always right.

Her first attempt at recruiting daycare clients hadn't gone so well, she reminded herself as she stepped out of her robe and sank into the warm, bubbly water.

Those girls were obviously a handful, but the mother in her responded to their plight. Sure, it was bad to have your father abandon you, but to have your mother die of cancer was so much worse. And Jeremy O'Toole was no doubt a first-rate bank manager, but she got the strong feeling he was out of his depth in his domestic life.

Oh, well, if he didn't want her, he didn't want her. Bubbles tickled her neck and her breasts peeked through the white foam, pink and wet.

And it hit her so hard she sat up, sloshing water.

He did want her. That poor, broken man, calling to his wife's ghost on the front lawn, had wanted her in that elemental way a man sees a woman and responds. There'd been a time when that happened so often, she barely noticed, but in the last couple of years, she'd caught that look, that certain current of energy, so rarely she'd almost forgotten what it was like.

Was that why Jeremy O'Toole had turned down her offer? Because he was attracted to her? She tipped her head back and inhaled the gardenia fragrance. Probably it was a good thing he'd turned her down if that was the case. She didn't have the time or the energy to let a man down lightly. Better they remain strangers.

He'd awakened feelings, though, feelings she'd almost forgotten she owned.

She'd noticed him glancing at her the way a man eyes an attractive woman. She thought about him. Realized she'd found him appealing too.

If anything, his painful love for his dead wife increased his attraction. Fidelity was an attribute she no longer took for granted.

While she was in the tub anyway, she decided to shave her legs. And she really needed to do something about her nails. Just because she was alone was no reason to let herself go.

In the middle of the second leg, the phone rang. It was a habit to bring her cell into the bathroom with her, so she was able to reach one bubble-dripping hand out of the tub to the small wicker table that held candles and some fancy soaps and a basket of polished rocks with inspirational words on them. A drop of water hit a stone with Courage carved into it. She picked up the phone. "Hello?"

"Libby? It's Jeremy O'Toole."

Now, there was a voice she hadn't expected to hear. "Um, yes?"

"I hope I'm not calling at a bad time."

"No. It's fine." What on earth did he want? She flashed back to the way he'd looked at her earlier, and the way she'd felt his admiration of her as a woman. *Oh, no*, she almost moaned. *Please don't ask me out.* She didn't feel up to rejecting the man who'd given her a chance to save her house.

Regardless of the fact that he didn't want her looking after his children, she didn't want to hurt him.

"I have a problem," he said, sounding tired and serious.

"Join the club."

He chuckled in an exhausted way. "I was planning to stay home tomorrow with the girls but I've got a critical meeting in the morning."

Okay, it seemed like he wasn't asking her out. She let out her breath, relaxing so the water sloshed up over her shoulders.

"Uh-huh?"

"Frankly, I'm reconsidering your childcare offer. Pardon me for asking, but are you reliable? I can't keep changing sitters, it's bad for the girls."

She might not be certain she wanted his business, but she was very certain of her skills. "I am completely reliable, my home is spotless and my brownies haven't killed anyone yet."

"Okay. Can you start tomorrow?"

"Well, since it's an emergency, I suppose so."

"What's your address?" he demanded. "I was in such a hurry earlier, I didn't pay much attention."

She gave it to him. "I live even closer to the school than you do." She'd figured out that the twins had seemed vaguely familiar because she'd seen them at the school. Being twins, they stuck out in a crowd. She'd never seen Jeremy O'Toole at the school as far as she knew. With a little shiver, she wondered if she'd ever seen his wife.

"I'll be right over."

"What?" she squeaked, sitting up so bubbles and water streaked over her torso. The half-shaved leg splashed as she dropped it back into the tub. "It's ten o'clock at night."

"I need somebody to look after the girls tomorrow. So far, I've gotten absolutely nowhere. If you want my business, I'll have to check out your home."

"But..." She was about to tell him she was naked and wet, then thought better of that idea.

What on earth had she done? "I'll be charging higher rates than most childcare providers because of my medical training," she said, in a last-ditch effort to head him off.

"Fine. I'll be right over."

She hung up and scrambled out of the tub, threw on some clothes, ran a brush through her damp hair and dabbed on lip gloss.

She ran downstairs to make sure everything was tidy and realized the stupid broken drawer front still sat on her kitchen counter. She ran down to the basement, found her glue, and ran back up.

Following the directions, she squeezed glue onto both the

drawer front and the drawer pieces and stood with her hip against the loose piece.

Was she a handywoman or what?

———————

After begging his good-natured sister to watch the kids for a few minutes, it took Jeremy less than five minutes to drive to the Brown house. An elegant Tudor, it rose a foot or so higher than its neighbors, presumably so it could look down on them.

The outside lights illuminated a lush garden straight out of a glossy magazine. Annoyance sparked through him. The first thing that woman needed to do was fire her fancy gardener. She needed to save her money to pay the mortgage and feed her family. He trod up a whimsical, winding flagstone pathway with dark leafy shapes shadowing either side, leading to two steps. Up he trod and, ignoring the doorbell, so as not to wake her kids, banged the brass lion's head door knocker. In the dim light the brass glowed as though it was polished regularly. He couldn't help but compare the outside of her house with his; she must employ an entire staff to keep the place up.

She must have been waiting for him, for the door opened almost immediately. His eyes widened when he saw her. The woman holding the door open looked like she'd just stepped out of the shower, smelled like it too, he noted as he entered the house. Her blond-brown hair curled damply around her flushed face in steamy tendrils. Her face was equally pretty without makeup, more vulnerable somehow, and she smelled like flowers.

He shut the front door behind him. Check out the house, that's why he was here. Glancing around the front hall he noticed how neat it was. Soft blue walls, gray-blue carpeting that still bore the ridges of a recent vacuum job. All the electric outlets had child-proof covers.

"Would you care to come into the kitchen?" she asked in her soft hostess voice.

Nodding, he followed her lead. Glancing into the unlit living room he got the impression of a room rarely used. It seemed lifeless, somehow, and the formal dining room across the hall looked like it hadn't seen a dinner party in a while.

He followed Libby's back. She wore jeans and a flowered T-shirt and he approved of the way it looked from behind.

The kitchen was obviously the heart of the house. It was done in blues and yellows that looked vaguely French. They sat at a round pine table with not a crumb or a sticky patch in sight. Jeremy wasn't sure how to begin, what he wanted to ask her. She seemed suddenly shy.

"Would you like something to drink?" She smiled slightly. "Herbal tea?"

"I'm fine, thanks." He smiled, trying to ease the atmosphere between them.

Her house was obviously clean and well organized. A quick inspection showed the outlets in here also had childproof covers. His own pair were more devious than any toddler. He wondered how she was planning to keep them out of trouble.

"Well, Libby," he gazed at a wall calendar with pictures of flowers and optimistic inspirational quotes. The squares for each day filled with notes about school events and after-school activities. "What do I get for my money?"

If she was taken aback by his bluntness, she didn't show it. "Apart from emergency medical response on demand, I'll also provide wholesome home-baked snacks after school, I'll supervise the girls' homework, encourage them to play outside in nice weather. You can drop them off in the morning on your way to work, I'll walk them to school with my eight-year-old son."

"What if I'm late picking them up at night, do I get charged overtime?"

It was obvious she hadn't thought of this possibility. He

watched her struggle with herself, clearly wondering how far she could push him. "Of course," she finally answered.

"I tell you what, let's try it for a month and see if it works out. You'll have to keep them home from school tomorrow."

"I can do that."

He paused, then voiced his biggest concern, "The girls are a little lively sometimes. Do you think you can handle it?"

The slightest smile of superiority teased her lips. "In my experience, Jeremy, the best way to keep active children out of mischief is to keep them busy. I'll do my best." She rose. "Would you care to see the fenced yard out back?"

He nodded and stood.

She crossed the kitchen to a pair of French doors and flipped on a light switch. As he came up behind her he could see an immaculate fenced backyard with a swing set and child's playhouse. A round patio table and chairs were made for sitting outside with a book and a coffee.

The backyard looked fine. Too fine. "Who does your garden?" he asked. He'd try and slip in a subtle reminder that she needed to cut non-essentials like professional gardeners out of her budget.

"I did it myself," she said, not without pride. "Gardens are my passion."

What a fool he was. She'd told him this morning she designed gardens. "It's beautiful," he said. So was the line of Libby Brown's jaw since she'd relaxed and stopped clenching it. Her neck was slender and the skin appeared silky soft. If he moved forward an inch his chest could touch her back. He breathed in the scent of gardenia and woman. In that moment, he couldn't remember what Kelly had smelled like. He tried to recall the scent of her perfume, or shampoo, but the flesh and blood woman in front of him overpowered his memory.

Jerking backward, out of the spell of her woman's magic, he

drew in a ragged breath. "I'll drop the girls off at eight tomorrow morning."

She turned and nodded. "That's fine."

He unhooked his jacket off the chair and shrugged into it. The sound of something falling and hitting the ground with a smack had him turning.

"Oh, I thought I fixed that," his hostess said with an irritated tone. On the floor was a wooden drawer front. Everything in her kitchen was so pristine that the broken drawer made him feel more at home somehow.

He walked forward and picked up the wooden drawer front. It was solid maple he noted. No particle board for the Brown home. "How did you fix it?"

"A tube of glue. It's about the only handyman thing I know how to do."

He nodded, pleased somehow that he could do something better than her. "It needs a vise. To hold the pieces together until they're dry."

"A vise. Oh."

He stifled a grin. "Want me to take it home? I can bring the drawer back in the morning."

Her eyes closed for a moment. Then she opened them and he saw she wasn't annoyed, as he'd feared, but grateful. "That would be so wonderful. You know, I try to watch YouTube videos, and I've got a couple of books, but I'm not very handy."

"Well, I can't cook worth a damn."

A silent laugh shook her. "Between the two of us, we make a great single parent."

He was too busy pulling the drawer all the way out and placing the plastic cutlery tray onto the counter to answer her.

"I'll bring this back tomorrow with the girls."

She followed him slowly to the door. "Do I need to worry about the twins sneaking home for any more illicit cooking sessions?"

"Not anymore. I confiscated their house key."

"Good."

"See you tomorrow." He opened the front door and plunged out into the darkness before she had even reached the door. He felt a sudden urge to run.

SIX

Flipping off lights as she went, Libby made her way up to bed then lay awake for a long while wondering.

First, she wondered where Victor was. Did he ever think about them? Was he sorry? Had he really run away rather than support his own children? She preferred to think he'd hit a bad patch in business and was too embarrassed to tell her. A tiny, angry voice inside her whispered that his twenty-two-year-old girlfriend was probably the recipient of the money his family needed. How had she been foolish enough to love such a man?

She was going to have to track him down somehow and make him resume his responsibilities.

From Victor, her mind drifted to another tall handsome man who'd come into her life and pretty much shunted it onto a whole new course, all in one day.

She bet Jeremy O'Toole would have been faithful to his wife forever; she could tell from his painful grief that his love had been the forever kind. It seemed an odd irony that the man who'd loved his wife so faithfully should lose her in such a cruel way, while the man who'd had it all, healthy wife and children, should abandon them.

Jeremy had been furious when she'd called his wife lucky. He couldn't understand the stab of envy that had shot through her for the woman who'd been loved so deeply that her husband was still calling out her name long after she was dead.

What would it be like to be loved by a man like that, Libby wondered as she rolled over and tried to find a more comfortable spot. What would it be like to love a man like that, a man you could trust? To know that when he had to work late, he kept his pants on. To know that when he was out of town on business, he slept alone.

That love extended to his children. She smiled in the dark, recalling the frightened love in his eyes as he tried to comfort both vomiting girls at once. She shuddered to think what would have happened to her kids if she'd been the one to die young and Victor had been left with two children. She doubted somehow that Irina was the motherly type.

Well, her new home business was starting out with a bang. She was completely unprepared to entertain a couple of convalescing ten-year-olds tomorrow, but she needed every dollar she could earn. Plus, some extra goodwill with her bank manager probably wouldn't hurt.

Feeling like she'd tossed and turned all night, Libby finally got out of bed at six thirty, flipping off the alarm that was set for seven.

Tired and dispirited, she put on coffee, then jumped into the shower while it was brewing.

Toweling off, she glimpsed her naked body in the mirror and sighed. Nothing was quite as perky as it used to be, although she was slim enough, too thin, really. Since she'd given up her fitness club membership, her body had lost its tone.

Not that it mattered. She'd been discarded. Victor had

taken everything she had to give, from her virginity to her trust, and treated them like worthless junk-store gifts to be used and then tossed.

She was thirty-four years old, she reminded herself. Not old enough for the scrap heap. Still, she dressed quickly. An image of the taut young nymphet Victor had finally left her for flooded her mind while she automatically dried her hair, wondering how soon it would turn gray.

By eight o'clock her own children were breakfasted and dressed and she'd sent them up to tidy their rooms and make their beds before school. Three-year-old Mia imitated her older brother in everything, and there was often a pout when they dropped Tyler off at school and she had to accompany her mother back home.

By eight-fifteen Libby was beginning to wonder whether the bank manager had had a change of heart, or a better offer for childcare. But, as she was getting ready to walk Tyler to school at eight thirty, the Volvo pulled into the driveway and one very harassed looking father emerged, followed more slowly by two sullen faces that told their own tale.

Even though she knew she was the probable source of the long faces, Libby had to bite back a smile. Jeremy O'Toole was a poster boy for the hopelessly manipulated single dad. His face was red, as though he were bottling up a mighty temper, when he stomped up the path with two identical red knapsacks that looked high tech enough for a Mount Everest climb. He dumped the bags unceremoniously in the front hall. His gray-blue eyes looked like a stormy winter ocean and there was a large nick on his chin where he'd cut himself shaving.

"The girls aren't too happy about this arrangement," he

grumbled. As if that was news. She could see them slouching up her driveway with mutiny written all over their pale faces.

"Are they feeling better?"

"Well enough to make the kitchen this morning a war zone."

Instinct warned her not to leave those two unattended in her house even for the fifteen minutes it would take her to deliver Tyler to school.

While her children made short work of a cheap but nutritious hot oatmeal breakfast, she'd told them she'd be looking after the girls.

Tyler had looked disgusted that more girls would be invading his home until he found out they were twins. That put them firmly in the cool category. He eyed them now with open curiosity, his eyes huge blue pools as he discovered they really were identical.

Jeremy said, "Sorry, I gotta go, I'm late." His face was drawn and tired, his eyes underlined by dark half-circles. He was backing away even as she opened her mouth to ask him questions.

"But, what about—"

"I'll call from the office," he muttered, then turned and strode back to the car. As he passed the twins, still only halfway to the front door, he grabbed each in turn for a quick hug, to be treated to two icy rebuttals. The girls' actions did nothing to raise them in her esteem.

"Oh, here," he said from the car and reached into the back seat, emerging with her kitchen drawer.

She walked down and took it from him, noting how solid it felt, like it might actually stay fixed this time. He must have fixed the drawer last night when he probably should have been preparing for his big meeting today. "Thank you. And good luck with your meeting."

He nodded and got into the car, pulling away before she'd

recovered from the fact that he was dumping two very grumpy looking girls on her for the day.

"Tyler, honey, go knock on Josh's door. You can walk to school with him today."

"But..." his eyes were still glued to the twins.

"Don't worry, the girls will still be here when you get home from school. You'll get to know them then." *If you still want to,* she thought, noting the glances of open disdain the twins were throwing his way.

"Hi!" he chirped, with his eager friendly smile.

"Hey," they both muttered, sounding as though they were speaking around wads of bubblegum.

"I see Josh on his front step, go on, Tyler," she urged, giving him a quick hug and a pat on the backside. With a cheery wave, he took off down the sidewalk and she watched him all the way to his buddy's house.

By now Paula was out in front with her coat on. As Tyler jogged up to join her and her son, Libby watched him chatter eagerly to the pair. Paula's head popped up from where she'd been bent over listening and she peered over to where Libby stood giving a thumbs up sign. Her friend pumped her fist in the air and mouthed *Yes!* before heading off toward the school with the two little boys in tow.

Now that she had Tyler on his way, Libby turned her attention to her daycare's first customers. They didn't look thrilled. Without a word to her, they trooped into the house and with a child's uncanny instinct, headed straight for the kitchen.

"Girls." Libby stopped them in their tracks with her nurse voice, pleased to see it hadn't lost its ring of authority after eight years. "When you arrive in the morning, I'd like you to take off your shoes and put them in the front closet. You can hang your coats there, too."

They dragged themselves back up the hallway and one after the other kicked their shoes off into the closet that Libby had opened for them. Biting her tongue against further rebuke, she handed each of them a hanger and watched them shove their red and navy jackets on the wire. She was impressed at the way they both managed to hang their jackets so that they sagged disreputably. Without a word she put the jackets away, knowing they would fall to the ground long before the day was over.

Leading the way into the kitchen, Libby asked, "How are you feeling today?"

"Sick," replied one.

A glance at their pale faces confirmed it. "Have you been able to eat anything since yesterday?"

A firm shake of the head from one and gagging motions from the other answered in the negative.

Knowing they should at least get some electrolytes in their bodies, she sent them into the TV room with a couple of blankets and pillows and two glasses of watered-down apple juice. "This is an exception to my rule," she warned them. "I don't usually allow television until after school when all your homework is done. I'm letting you watch TV today because you're sick. Understood?"

A couple of lackluster grunts answered her.

One day at a time, she reminded herself. Today she was earning real money, the kind that would help her buy groceries and stay in her home. Her first client wasn't going to solve all her problems, but she'd made a start.

When she heard music that didn't sound like it came from a children's show, she popped into the den where the girls were curled up watching a music video. Mia sat on the couch beside them, enthralled by a female K-pop group, and that was as close as Libby could get to identifying the young women singing about girls and power. Mia had a thumb in her mouth and her favorite stuffed bear in her lap as she watched the screen with wide-eyed fascination.

She remembered her own time on the couch watching The

Spice Girls and the Backstreet Boys. When the twins were back at school she'd get Mia back on track, watching educational TV if she watched TV at all. For now, she let them be.

Back at the kitchen table, Libby found an old envelope and a pen and started a to-do list. She hated writing on the backs of envelopes, hated the way the ridges spoiled her handwriting, but nice fresh pads of paper were one more luxury she could no longer afford. She'd discovered it wasn't losing the big things that bothered her. It was the little ones. She could forego new clothes, hair appointments and even, after a struggle, really good chocolate.

It was the dumb little things like giving up boxed tissues and pads of writing paper that irked her the most.

Better for the environment, she reminded herself, as she propped her head on her hand. And wrote:

1. Find Victor
2. Increase income
3. Grow landscape business

What a great to-do list. They looked so tidy, those bullet-point instructions to herself telling her how to fix her life. She chewed her lip for a while, thinking.

The most important item was to track down her ex-husband. She couldn't believe he'd gone off and abandoned his children, gone back on his promise to keep paying for the house.

Maybe something had happened to him?

What if he was dead?

But a moment's reflection told her that was unlikely. If he'd had some kind of accident, she'd have heard something.

No. As much as she preferred to think of him in a hospital somewhere with both legs in traction and a cell phone with no power, she knew that wasn't why she hadn't heard from her ex-husband. He'd run away from his responsibilities.

Well, she wasn't going to run away from hers. She was going to figure this out. She got out her computer and did some searching.

By lunchtime, she was feeling a little more hopeful. She'd discovered a legal aid clinic that specialized in helping women that was open in the evenings. She'd made an appointment.

Her mind revolved around where Victor might have gone and what had happened to his successful business while she warmed up soup, arranged rice crackers on a plate, sliced an apple and poured three glasses of watery juice. She contemplated letting them eat in the TV room but felt she needed to establish some ground rules early, such as no eating in front of the TV. She knew she was a bit obsessive, and she accepted it.

The girls were singing along to a Korean girl band. The young musicians had all dyed their hair a different color and wore miniskirts. Heartbreakingly cute, Mia was doing her best to keep up.

Maybe this was going to work out after all.

"Come on in the kitchen," she said when the song ended. "Lunch is ready."

SEVEN

"I hate soup."

"You haven't tried it yet," Libby reminded the girl, scowling at her. The four of them were sitting at her kitchen table for lunch, though it felt more like they were two battalions preparing for war.

"I hate all soup."

"Can I have milk instead of juice?" the other twin asked.

Spoiled brats. Libby's fists clenched, and she counted silently to ten. "The soup and crackers, and the juice, are easy on your stomach."

"Dad never makes us eat stuff we hate."

"He doesn't let our babysitters make us, either."

Deciding non-confrontation was her best course of action, Libby put her spoon into her soup and started eating.

She refused to react when the twins walked away from the table, leaving their lunches barely touched. She needed to talk to their father about how she planned to handle the girls, and, for this first day, she was curious to see how they behaved. Although curious was turning to appalled.

After lunch, Mia went down reluctantly for her nap. "I want to play with the two twins," she argued.

"They'll still be here when you wake up, besides, they'll be resting too," Libby promised her.

And rest and quiet was exactly what the twins needed. Knowing they would want to watch more TV, Libby was determined, so long as their dad was paying her good money to look after them, that she wouldn't park them in front of the TV all day.

It was time she took charge. She went to her room and dug out *Anne of Green Gables* and *Little House on the Prairie* from among her other favorite books from childhood.

As she returned downstairs, she heard the hum of the TV, as she'd expected. Entering the room, she stopped dead. She'd expected music videos. She certainly hadn't expected to find the twins curled on the couch, surrounded by potato chips and candy bars.

"What on earth?" she cried wrathfully.

"Dad said we could take some snacks," the one she saw as the bolder of the two replied, her chin jutting forward. The smell of grease and chocolate hung in the air, and Libby stared at the bold twin, Olivia, she thought, until the girl's defiant gaze faltered. She was beginning to see subtle differences between the twins, but it would be awhile yet before she could distinguish them unerringly.

Cellophane crackled beneath her fingers as she scooped up the load of junk food from the couch and ordered the girls to wash their hands once more.

"But I didn't finish my Doritos."

"In my house, you follow my rules. No snacks between meals if you don't eat your lunch."

She snapped off the TV even as they cried, "But that's Pretty Girl."

They glared at her like she was an ogre out of a fairy tale before stomping off, muttering to each other.

If they thought she was evil to take away their junk food, she dropped even lower in their estimation when she produced the books.

"We don't have to do homework, we're sick."

"This isn't homework. It's called reading for pleasure."

Glumly, Olivia took the proffered book and then balked again when she read the cover. "Don't you have anything from this century?"

"Sorry, I only have the books I used to read when I was a little girl."

The two identical looks of horror caused her lips to tremble with barely suppressed amusement. "That was shortly after the printing press was invented."

"You read this stuff?"

"Well, only because K-pop didn't exist yet."

"My dad—"

"Would you like to phone your dad and check if it's okay to read a book at my house?"

From the panicked glance the twins shared, Libby confirmed what she'd begun to suspect. They were on their worst behavior for her benefit. Without another word they both opened their books and at least made a pretense of reading. She'd have to ask around and find out what books ten-year-old girls read these days.

"I'm going to start dinner now. If you have trouble understanding any words you can bring the book into the kitchen."

"But we're too sick to read," Grace whined.

"Then you can nap in Tyler's bed."

They had their heads down, eyes to the page in seconds.

Challenge is good. What doesn't kill you makes you stronger. She was reciting her entire calendar of optimistic quotes. She continued her silent pep talk while she returned to the kitchen and started preparing dinner. While she was peeling onions, the phone rang.

"Hello?" she answered, sniffing.

"Libby?"

She sniffed again, and wiped her streaming eyes with her sleeve. Oh, for a tissue. "Hello, Jeremy."

"What is it? Have the twins made you cry?" Jeremy's voice sounded full of dread.

She chuckled wetly. "I'm peeling onions. The twins are fine."

She heard scuffling noises in the hall and suddenly the bold twin bounded in the room gesturing frantically. It took Libby a minute to figure out that the flapping, pointing, and silent begging were a plea for her not to tell Jeremy about the junk food stash in the backpacks. Interesting. Maybe he wasn't the complete pushover she'd begun to suspect.

The sigh that rumbled out of the receiver said more than any words could. "How was your meeting?" she asked.

"Annual directors' meeting. It went all right, but I had trouble concentrating." He paused. "I was worried about the twins."

Was he worried she was being mean to his sweet darlings? His sympathy would have been better placed with their caregiver. She kept these feelings to herself, however, and asked what time he'd be picking them up.

A groan of frustration answered her. "There are a couple of urgent items I've got to clean up. I was hoping you could keep the girls till seven tonight...at your overtime rate of course."

She hesitated. Frankly, she was counting the minutes till she could get rid of the twins, but she heard real anxiety in Jeremy's voice. And he *was* paying her overtime. "All right," she finally agreed.

"I tell you what." She heard the relief in his tone and was

glad she'd agreed to help. "Put the onions away, I'll have pizza delivered to your place for dinner."

"We'll take a rain check on pizza. The last thing those girls need is more junk in their stomachs. I'll make them something wholesome."

He chuckled. "If it's wholesome they probably won't eat it, but you're the boss."

She was thinking that if he used that laughing sexy voice all the time the bank would be swamped with female customers. Even though he and his daughters seemed to have taken over her life, she felt her lips turning up in response. "See you later."

Surprisingly, he turned out to be wrong. Maybe it was because they hadn't eaten anything but a few filched potato chips since the lunch they'd picked at, but the twins wolfed down the chicken and vegetable stew she'd made and got through most of a loaf of whole wheat bread. They looked suspiciously at the rice pudding, but once they'd tasted it, they made short work of that, too.

And they surprised Libby by displaying excellent table manners.

Tyler was so much in awe of them that he spent the entire mealtime staring at first one, then the other twin. Maybe they were used to that kind of attention, for they didn't even seem to notice. Mia didn't stare. She merely copied everything they did.

"How did you get on with *Anne of Green Gables*, Olivia?" Libby asked. They hadn't come to her all afternoon for help so she was suspicious about how much reading they'd done. She'd peeked in on them once and found Olivia reading and Grace sound asleep on the couch.

"It was okay." The girl shrugged and fell silent.

"Did you have any trouble with big words?" Libby persisted.

"Not really."

Had the girl read any of it? Or had she heard Libby's

approach and stuck the book in front of her face before she got caught doing something else? "What did you like about the book."

Olivia stared hard into her rice pudding. Beneath the rioting auburn curls, Libby made out a different shade of red staining her cheeks.

Nobody said anything for several seconds.

Just as Libby was about to ask her what she'd really been doing all afternoon she burst out with, "That Anne was an orphan. If our dad dies we'll be orphans too and nobody will want us." She raised a face wet with tears, her eyes huge.

"Olivia, that's not true." Libby's heart turned over at the real fear she saw in those big wet eyes before the child turned and dashed out of the room. "Olivia, come back," but the running footsteps kept pounding down the hall and up the stairs.

Before Libby could rise out of her chair, Grace let out a sob, and knocking her chair over in her haste, jogged after her sister, beginning her own noisy bout of wailing.

Libby stood up. "Excuse me, children," she mumbled. What had she done?

She followed the twins, but, glancing at Mia, saw her daughter's face start to pucker. She wouldn't understand what the crying was about, but she'd responded to the emotion she'd witnessed.

Tyler looked anxious. He was pulling on the cowlick in the center of his hairline, a habit he had when he was upset. "We don't have a dad. Are we orphans?"

Sudden tears pricked Libby's own eyes. "You have a dad. And he loves you. And you have me." She felt as though a vise was squeezing her ribs. "I won't let anything happen to you...I promise." By this time tears were streaming helplessly down her own cheeks and Tyler's eyes had flooded.

Mia howled, "I want my daddeee!"

At that moment, Jeremy O'Toole walked into the kitchen. "Nobody answered the door. I...what the—?"

———

Jeremy blinked his eyes as though he could reopen them and find the world was back to the familiar place he knew.

It wasn't.

Libby was melting into a puddle right in front of him, and strangely, he felt a powerful urge to take her in his arms and comfort her. Except that she was already moving to offer her own dripping comfort to her sobbing children.

Ominously, he glanced around for his own children. What had they done now? Fear clenched his gut. "The twins?"

Libby pointed upward, her body shaking badly. "I'm so s-sorry," she could barely speak. "The b-book. It's all my fault."

He bounded out of the kitchen and up the stairs without bothering to ask permission. "Girls?" he shouted as he ran, terrified of what he might find. He'd never thought of a book as being a deadly weapon, but with the twins, you never knew. His terror eased a little when he heard noisy sobs coming from down the hall.

They were lying curled up together on a single bed in a room so dominated by pink and purple it must be Mia's. A glance showed him they weren't obviously hurt. There was no visible bleeding or broken body parts. Some of his panic dissipated, and he crossed quietly to perch on the bed beside them.

"Hey, kiddos, what's up?" he asked softly.

"Dad-ee!" they cried in unison and somehow both ended up on his lap, clutching at him. "Don't d-die," Olivia begged him, turning a tear-swollen face up to him.

Even as he opened his mouth in an automatic soothing promise, pain pierced his chest. How could he promise something he had no control over? Who'd have thought Kelly would die? Kelly, who embraced life and who would have done anything to spare her children pain. "I'm right here," he said with a catch in his own voice. It was the best he could promise.

"I don't want to be an orphan," Olivia sobbed. "They make you work like a c-cleaning lady and send you on trains to people who don't even w-want you."

"Who does?" Jeremy was floundering way out of his depth. Cleaning ladies? Trains? Death? What kind of a babysitter was Libby Brown? "Nobody's going to make you a cleaning lady," he soothed.

"That's what happens to Anne. And she finally finds a place she likes but they d-don't like her because she's a girl. Why couldn't we be b-boys?"

"Well I'm glad you're girls." Jeremy latched on to the one part of her complaint he understood. "Your mom and I always wanted a girl, and we were so lucky when we got two of you." He squeezed their slim shoulders to him in a hug.

Grace's body shuddered on a hiccup.

"Who's Anne?" He never remembered hearing about anyone at school called Anne. He thought he knew most of their friends outside of school, no Annes there, either.

"Anne Shirley."

"Anne Shirley?" Now where had he heard that name before. Then he remembered, Libby had mentioned a book. "*Anne of Green Gables*? That Anne Shirley?"

Olivia nodded and sniffed.

"Anne Shirley is a fictional character. And that book was written a long time ago. What happened in the olden days is never going to happen to you."

"Then who's going to look after us when you die?" Olivia demanded.

"First of all, I'm not planning to die for a long time. And if something did happen, Auntie Tracy would look after you. You know that."

"But she has her own kids," Grace objected.

"She'd let us live with her to be cleaning ladies and do all the cooking and the wash," Olivia warned.

"Well, she wouldn't be getting much of a bargain," Jeremy said dryly. "You two would soon have her whole house looking like your bedroom." He squeezed his arms around them in another big hug. "And after yesterday, I don't think she'll be asking you to do any cooking."

A reluctant chuckle answered him.

"How was the rest of your day?"

He caught the guilty glance they exchanged. "Fine."

Dropping kisses on their fiery curls, he said, "Wash your faces and come back downstairs."

Considerably calmer now, he made the return journey to the kitchen. Libby had calmed her kids as well as drying her own tears. She glanced up guiltily when he entered. "How are they?"

"Drying off."

"Children, I want you to go into the den for a few minutes while I talk to Mr. O'Toole. You can watch TV." She gave them each a loving pat as they trotted out of the kitchen. The family tear storm had apparently passed.

She waited until they were out of the room before speaking again, her face creased with worry. "I'm so sorry, Jeremy. I—"

"*Anne of Green Gables*. I heard."

"I loved that book so much as a child. And since it's about a spirited girl, I thought Olivia might enjoy it. I didn't think about how it begins, with Anne as a rejected orphan. I'll put it away and find Olivia something else to read."

"No, wait. I know I read the book in school, but I'm a little fuzzy. Doesn't she run around after some boy named Gilbert?"

Libby's tragic eyes filled with sudden disdain. "No. She doesn't. Gilbert runs around after her, and she won't have anything to do with him. He has to win her slowly, with a lot of hard work." She sighed blissfully. "I loved that book."

Sounded like a bunch of BS to him. "Why do you women always love to make men suffer?"

She rolled her eyes. "We're entering dangerous territory. The point is, Anne overcomes all the obstacles in her life and finds love and happiness."

Jeremy was nodding his head as though she'd helped him win an argument. "Then let's let her finish reading the book. Life is tough. Olivia's already learned that." He sighed and leaned his hips back against the kitchen counter. "She's the older twin, you know, definitely the dominant personality."

Libby nodded vigorously and he smiled a little. She'd figured them out pretty fast.

"She's having more trouble than Grace getting over her mother's death. I've been trying to smooth her path, prevent her from being upset. And she pulls pranks like the brownie disaster." He shrugged. "Maybe reading a book about a young girl who overcomes tragedy will help her."

His stomach churned recalling her plea to him not to die. "At least it brought out a fear she hasn't talked about before."

"That she'll be orphaned?"

"Yeah." He swallowed a sudden lump in his throat. "I told them my sister Tracy would look after them." He shrugged his helplessness. "It's the best I can promise."

She nodded, a crease between her brows. "I suddenly realized that if anything happens to me, my children will have nobody." Her voice trailed away and she turned quickly, moving with jerky steps toward the kitchen sink.

She paused there, leaning against the edge of the counter-top. She appeared to be staring out the window, but Jeremy didn't think she saw anything. Even though her shoulders didn't move, he knew she was crying.

Before he knew what he was doing, he was gripping her

shoulders and turning her to face him. He wanted to offer comfort, but what could he say? She was right. He'd seen this situation before. Unless she was very lucky, or her ex suffered a sudden attack of conscience, Victor Brown was as good as dead to Libby and the children.

"Don't you have any family?" he asked.

She shook her head. "I'm an only child. My mother's dead and my father..." She gulped. "No. There's no one."

The raw pain and fear in her face connected with his own pain and fear. He couldn't offer her any real comfort, but he could hold her while she cried, offering her the temporary comfort of a shoulder to cry on. Gently but firmly he pulled her into the circle of his arms.

She tried to pull away, making little sounds of distress, but suddenly she gave in and clung to him.

Libby fit into his arms perfectly, the top of her head nudging his chin. The bones of her back were slender and prominent beneath his hands. Her frame seemed too delicate for the strength of the sobs that shook her. Her hands gripped his shoulders and her tears soaked through his shirt.

But even through her terrible grief he felt the woman's body shuddering against him.

She smelled like flowers. He'd forgotten how exciting all those fragrances were. The hair products that always smelled like flowers. The powders and lotions so numerous that Kelly's side of the medicine cabinet overflowed into his half. Razor, shaving cream, toothbrush, toothpaste, deodorant. That's all he needed. He used to tease Kelly about renting a storage locker to keep all her junk in. Now he had lots of empty shelves. And he missed the little spills of makeup goo on the counter. But most of all he missed the delicate flowery scents of all that stuff.

"It's going to be okay," he murmured over and over, stroking her hair as well as her back.

He wouldn't have even made it to this morning's meeting if it hadn't been for Libby.

Not only had she been there all day with his daughters and fed them healthy food, she'd convinced Olivia to read a work of literature instead of watching TV. No other babysitter had ever bothered.

A wet sniffle coming from the direction of his right shoulder called his attention back to the matter at hand. The sobs seemed to have ended as quickly as they began. She didn't raise her head though. Instead her hand reached out behind her, fingers splayed, bouncing along the counter top searching.

Puzzled, he let his gaze scan the counter, but he didn't think it was the pot scrubber or the dish detergent she was after.

The hand suddenly clenched and pulled back. "I'm out of tissues," she mumbled into his chest.

Jeremy smiled into her hair, dug into his pocket and pulled out a handkerchief which he placed into her hand.

With a muffled "thanks" she kept her head lowered while she wiped her eyes and nose. Only then did she raise her head and glance at him. "I'm sorry. I shouldn't have done that," she whispered.

"Feel better?"

Her face flushed. "A little. Mostly I feel stupid."

Stepping back, he shot her a smile he hoped was brotherly. "Crying is supposed to be therapeutic."

"I've never found it good for much except sore eyes. I try to be a doer not a crier," she said on a hiccup.

"And how are you doing?"

A frown appeared between her brows. "I found out I'm not the only person whose spouse ever left the country and forgot to send support payments. I have an appointment with a legal aid clinic for women. If I could find Victor..." She glanced up quickly. "I made an evening appointment so I'll be here for the girls, of course."

Jeremy tried to look positive, but it was tough. He'd seen a few of these cases at the bank. Everybody hated them. He didn't think Victor Brown planned to keep paying child support for children he no longer saw, and mortgage payments on a home he no longer lived in.

If Libby's hunch was correct and he was in Eastern Europe, things didn't look good.

The sooner Libby realized she was on her own, the better. But he was too tired and too smart to tell her that, not while her eyes were still wet and her voice husky. She'd find out soon enough.

She blew her nose once more, then handed the soggy hand-kerchief back, only to stop with an embarrassed, "Oh! Why don't I wash this and return it."

He would have taken it, but he could see she was uncomfortable and, with a shrug, said, "Sure, thanks. No starch."

She grinned at his lame humor and tucked the hanky in her own pocket. "Would you like some chicken stew?"

Homemade stew. He'd been smelling it in the air since he walked in. It reminded him of his own mother's kitchen. Libby's food smelled like comfort and a warm hug at the end of a tough day. If it was anything like the soup she'd brought over last night, he'd be sorely tempted. But he paid Libby to look after his kids, not him. "No thanks, I had a big lunch," he lied.

"Same time tomorrow?" she asked while they both tried to pretend they hadn't heard his stomach growl in frustration.

"Yes, I'll get the girls. Oh, and here." He dug into his pocket and pulled out the check he'd written. "A week's pay plus time and a half for the overtime tonight. I don't think I'll be late again this week, but if I am, I'll add that to next week's check. Is that acceptable?"

She flushed slightly as she took the folded paper in her hand. She didn't open it, but stared at it with her head bowed. "You know, I used to babysit for people all the time. Working moms, neighbors with dentist appointments. I've never taken money. If we'd met under different circumstances, I would have been happy to look after your girls. I wouldn't have charged you."

"Working for money is nothing to be ashamed of, Libby. Welcome back to the real world."

Her head jerked up, and he saw her eyes widen. But it wasn't anger, but amazement on her face. "You're right. I've been living in a dream world. I was like one of those TV women from the sixties, Mrs. Cleaver, maybe. I wanted to stay home with my kids, that's all."

"Hey, kiddos!" he bellowed up the stairs. "Time to go."

The bustle of sticking the girls in their coats, collecting up their belongings and saying the goodbyes got him out of the door without having any more intimate chats.

EIGHT

Jeremy banged the proudly shining Lion's head, wondering how often Libby polished him, and when she found the time. She was one remarkable woman. He couldn't believe his luck.

They were into their third month of the new babysitting arrangement and so far, things were going so well that his stomach had almost stopped eating away at itself.

The twins were happier than they'd been since their mother died. They were doing better at school, acting more like little girls than hellions—most of the time.

Even their room was marginally tidier. He'd caught them making their beds without being reminded on one memorable occasion.

Libby was making her mortgage payments. She had another child, around Mia's age, who was usually gone when he came to pick up the twins, and she seemed fairly busy with the landscaping. Thank God. He would not have wanted to foreclose on this woman's house. Of course, she was treading perilously close to the financial edge, but she knew it and she was doing everything she could to make things work. He admired her.

It wasn't Libby who opened the door, as he'd expected, but

Grace, looking both important and mysterious. Always a bad combination in his experience.

"Hi, Dad." She opened the door wider and he stepped into the hall. It was the first time anyone but Libby had opened the door to him. His stomach clenched.

"Hi, kiddo. Where's Mrs. Brown?"

"She's on the phone. She's been on for ages."

His stomach sank. How long had the twins been unsupervised? "Oh. And what have you been doing?"

Grace swept her gaze in all directions like a cartoon spy before whispering, "We're having a secret meeting."

"What about?" Kids' secrets in his experience usually turned out to be unpleasant surprises for parents.

His daughter put her finger to her lips and motioned him upstairs.

He relaxed a bit knowing she wouldn't invite him to join the secret unless it was something she thought he would approve of. Which limited the possibilities from life-threatening to merely dangerous. Until he remembered the time the girls had invited him to watch them play Mary Poppins, with his golf umbrella as the featured prop. Olivia was practically out of their bedroom window preparing to jump when he'd lunged across the room and grabbed her ankles. Libby's second floor windows were even higher than his. He increased his pace to a run, heading toward the sound of children's voices hissing in exaggerated whispers.

With a sigh of relief he saw nobody was on the roof or doing anything more death defying than hanging their heads over the bed. They looked a little red in the face, the row of three all regarding him from upside down.

"Hi," he said.

"Shhhh!" they all hissed fiercely.

"This is a secret meeting, Dad, you gotta promise not to tell Libby," Olivia ordered him.

"Why are you all upside down?"

"It's our secret signal."

"Well, I'm happy to join the meeting but I can't do it upside down."

"Well, since you are kind of old...if you promise not to tell, I guess it would be okay," Olivia decided.

"I can't promise not to tell unless you give me a hint what this is about."

"Dad, you're so lame," his oldest informed him. "It's Libby's birthday on Friday and we're planning her surprise party."

A wave of relief rolled over him, as well as pride that they were planning something nice for Libby. "I guess I can keep that secret. What do you have planned so far?"

"Spray streamers that come in a can." Olivia held up a hand and stuck one finger in the air. Without the extra hand to give her balance her head tilted alarmingly, but she didn't seem to notice any discomfort.

"They spray out like a bunch of different colored worms all over the place," Tyler added.

Jeremy imagined how thrilled Libby would be when she found her pristine house covered in canned confetti and shuddered.

"We're all pitching in some allowance and buying chips and pop and stuff," Olivia stuck another finger in the air. "Can you drive us to the store on Thursday night?"

"Sure."

"And me and Grace are going to bake a cake." When she jutted her upside-down chin at him in her usual defiant mode she nearly toppled over and had to stick her other hand on the ground to rebalance.

Visions of bicarb brownies and a barfing birthday girl danced through Jeremy's head. The twins had come so far since the brownie disaster, but he sure as hell didn't trust their baking skills yet. "How 'bout I buy the cake?" he tried.

In unison Olivia and Grace, who'd managed to get herself turned on her head alongside the others, shook their heads. His stomach started to burn.

A cake.

They wanted to bake a cake and they had no mother to help them. And yet he could read in their sparkling upturned eyes how important this was. "Tell you what," he heard himself say, "we'll make it together."

Yips of joy greeted his announcement. "No mixes, Dad. She never uses them. It has to be from scratch."

Hell, how hard could a cake be anyway? He had a shelf full of cookbooks. And he could always call Tracy if things got too scary.

"And you have to get Libby out of the house so we can decorate and stuff," Olivia said.

If they really thought a three-year-old could keep a secret he wasn't going to spoil the fun. "How am I going to get her out of the house with you guys all here?" he wanted to know. "And who's going to look after you?"

"Auntie Tracy could watch us. And, um, you could tell Libby you want her to go with you to the parent-teacher interview." Was it his imagination or had his daughter's face just gone an even deeper red?

He rubbed his stomach. "What parent-teacher interview?"

"There's a note in my backpack," Olivia mumbled.

"What have you been doing, now?" He felt his good mood crash like the stock market on Black Monday.

"Nothing. Mrs. Lawrence is so mean. She picks on me all the time. It's because we don't have a mom," she said in a wheedling tone he didn't believe for a second. "Please take Libby with you on the interview, she can tell Mrs. Lawrence that we're always good here."

"Are you going to tell me what you did or do I have to ask Mrs. Lawrence?"

"She says it's my attitude, but I didn't mean to talk back. Honest. Anyhow, she wants to see you on Friday after school. If you take Libby with you, we can decorate the house while you're gone."

"You'd better give me the full story, Olivia, before I agree to any party. And you can do it right side up."

With an angry grunt, Olivia hauled herself up on the bed and glared at him. "It's about a guy. You wouldn't understand."

His daughters were ten. Ten. At ten he'd been building models and playing video games, not thinking about the opposite sex. This whole boy thing was starting way too young.

He glanced over at their identical little girl faces.

"And for this your teacher wants an interview?"

Silence.

"Olivia?"

Silence.

"Grace?"

More silence.

"Your teacher will only give me her version. You'd better tell me yourself what happened."

"Evelyn told everybody I like Deakon Beamish. But I don't. I might have called her stupid." Olivia's breath started getting agitated. She met his gaze with a look of furious pain.

He kept his mouth shut and waited, knowing from the way her lips were working that there was more to come.

"Then she told me she's not allowed to play with us anymore cause her mom said that ever since our mom died we've turned into little m-monsters." She choked on the last word and her eyes filled with tears.

"Oh, kiddo—"

"So, I told Evelyn I'd rather have no mother than a stupid bitch like hers." With a sob, she tore out of the room and a moment later, he heard the bathroom door slam.

Grace's head hung down and he could see she was fighting tears.

"Grace?"

"Everybody has a mom but us," she mumbled to the floor. "Even the kids whose parents got divorced still get to see them both."

He knew he should be outraged that his daughter had called a classmate's mother names. But the thing was, he agreed with Olivia's assessment of Evelyn Whatever-her-name's mother. And he could think of a few other adjectives to add to "stupid".

With a sigh, he got up and wandered to the closed door of the bathroom. "Olivia?"

"Go away."

"Kiddo, I'm not mad at you. I'm glad your teacher wants to see me. I've got some things to say to her, as well."

He heard some shuffling and a loud sniff on the other side of the door. "You're not mad that I swore?"

Parenthood was a constant minefield, and he'd just stepped on a good one. "Of course, I'm mad that you swore. But I understand. Sometimes I swear too when I'm really, uh, mad."

"Yeah. You say sh—"

"Okay, Okay," he interrupted. "I shouldn't do it either. Open the door now?"

He heard water running, then it stopped and a moment later, the door opened. Olivia stared up at him with a mixture of belligerence and pleading.

Maybe he should give her a lecture, a detention, force her to apologize. *The hell with it.* He opened his arms, and she tumbled into them, squeezing him so hard he thought both their hearts would break.

"Jeremy? Are you up there?" Libby's voice floated from downstairs.

He whispered into the tangled red mass of Olivia's hair, "We'll sort this out later, huh?"

She nodded and pulled away to scamper back to the others.

"Hi, Libby." He pulled himself upright and ran lightly down the stairs to where she waited at the bottom, a look of suppressed excitement on her face.

He realized with a shock that she was beautiful, with that hopeful glow highlighting her features. Every time he saw her there seemed to be a line of worry marring her forehead. "I got here a few minutes ago, but you were on the phone."

"Oh, sorry. My head's in a whirl."

He smiled at her. She looked years younger. It was easy to see what a knockout she'd been before her life turned sour.

"Looks like you got some good news."

She twirled like a princess at a ball. "I got the job of landscaping the display home in that new upscale subdivision down on Essex Street."

"That's great." In the three months that she'd been looking after the girls, he and Libby had become friends. She'd sent the baking to Grace and Olivia's class for the Christmas party, and she and Jeremy had sat together at the annual Winter Concert where all their kids but Mia had a part.

He'd come to look forward to this part of his day, he realized, when he picked up the girls and he and Libby would share a little of their day.

"Well, it is great. Because, if the people who buy into the subdivision like what I do, they'll hire me too, right? This could lead to a lot of work for me. I've even been toying with the idea of expanding my services to include doing the actual landscaping."

"That's a pretty big job."

"I know. And I'd need employees and things."

"Capital."

She grinned at him. "Good thing I am on such excellent terms with my local banker."

"Have you thought about—"

"Oh, don't worry. I won't do anything until Mia is in school full time. Right now, the design work is keeping me busy. It's amazing how many people know people. Word gets around."

"Well, it's not that I'm not supportive of the idea, because I am, but I don't want you getting any more strung out financially than you can help." He frowned, hating that he had to bring their business connection into her kitchen. "The thing is, you don't have much of a cushion if anything goes wrong."

She slumped into one of her kitchen chairs and he reluctantly sat opposite. Her fingers tapped the tabletop. "I know. Believe me, I know. It keeps me awake at night."

"This is a pretty big house for three people, Libby," he said gently.

She rubbed at her forehead. He'd noticed she always did that when she was stressed. "Do you think I grew up with this? Scale down is the story of my life." She glanced around the kitchen as though for the first time. "I grew up in a crummy old run-down house that seemed like a palace once we got thrown out. I was seven, and that was the first time we scaled down."

"Libby, I..." What? What could he say to make any of this easier?

"It was always somebody else's fault when my dad lost a job. His drinking had nothing to do with it."

He suddenly pictured Libby as a little girl, a little girl who looked a lot like Mia, only living in squalor, and his belly squirmed.

"We played the same scene over and over. He'd get fired, then hang around home drinking. Mom worked as a cashier and waitress to keep food on the table. She always made excuses for him. It was because of his war injuries, she used to tell me."

"What war?" He calculated swiftly. "Vietnam?"

She shook her head and the overhead light reflected gold in her hair. "He did a short stint in the military but got thrown out after a drunken brawl. His real war was against anyone who told him what to do."

"Like a boss, for instance?" Jeremy was getting a strong mental picture of Libby's father, and he didn't like what he saw.

"Yep. After a while we didn't move for jobs anymore, we just moved to cheaper places. I don't think I ever did more than a single year at the same school."

Her index finger traced patterns idly on the tabletop, following the grain of the wood. Jeremy fought the urge to take her restless hands in his.

"By the time I was a high school sophomore, my mom came into a little money from an aunt who died and she bought the trailer we were living in. My dad's still in it. It's an awful place, in a derelict trailer park across the highway from Friendly Hank's Used Cars. But, by some quirk of fate, the high school I got bussed to was pretty good."

Her past explained so much about this mania she had about keeping her house. He admired her tenacity, but he was still worried about her future. Keeping the house was crazy in his opinion. "How did you get to be a nurse?"

"I won a scholarship. Lived in a dorm and swore I'd never go back to that trailer park. I met Victor the year I graduated. Mom was so happy the day I got married, but when we moved into this house, I thought she'd burst with pride. I'm glad she passed away before Victor left me."

Jeremy put a tentative hand out and touched her shoulder. Such slender shoulders for such a heavy burden. "I'm sorry, Libby."

"Well, I inherited a lot of things from my mom. The work ethic, the love of cooking, and bad taste in men."

"Victor took out a million-dollar life insurance policy right after Tyler was born. He said if anything happened to him, he wanted to know his family was looked after. How could anyone change so much? How could he do this to us?"

There was no answer. How could any man desert a woman as special as Libby? He sure as hell wouldn't.

"All men aren't bad, you know."

"I know." She sighed and leaned back. "My friend Paula up the street? She's never lost the extra pounds from her last child. Her husband tells her not to diet. He likes her exactly the way she is. Imagine." She rose and went to the oven to check on something that smelled amazing. As he watched her in the kitchen, he noted one of the cupboard doors hanging askew. She liked things so neat and organized that must drive her nuts.

He got up and followed her, moving the door back and forth. "Looks like you need a new hinge."

She sighed. "Among other things. I wish I was handy."

"What other things?"

She was bent over an oval baking dish, turning chicken pieces that were in some kind of wonderful-smelling Italian tomato sauce.

"I've got cracks in some of the walls from when the house settled. The upstairs bathroom faucet leaks. One of the boards on the back verandah seems soft." She shrugged. "Little things I need to figure out how to fix. Dumb things."

"Was Victor handy?"

She gave a snort of laughter. "Not remotely. But when he was around, we could afford to hire people." She paused. "At least, I thought we could."

He took another look at the hinge, feeling pretty pleased that the despicable Victor couldn't even fix a cupboard door. "I could fix that."

She glanced at him over her shoulder. "Thus proving that you are a better man than Victor?"

Had she read his thoughts? "You already know I'm a better man than Victor," he said evenly. He wasn't a violent person, but he felt a strong impulse to pound the missing and unlamented Victor Brown.

"Yes," she said, turning away quickly. "I do. You're one of the good guys."

He stared at her back, so straight and elegant. He was aware of an urge to kiss the junction of her shoulder and neck where the skin looked so soft he almost knew how it would feel under his lips, warm and silky.

"Have you dated anyone since he left?"

Her hands stilled. "No." She bent to replace the casserole and when her head was practically inside the oven she asked, "You?"

"I tried online dating and met some nice women but nothing clicked. Plus, there was an awkward dinner party where I was paired with a single woman I've known socially for a while. I think our hosts were disappointed we didn't fall madly in love over their prime rib."

"Oh." Did she sound relieved that he wasn't dating?

Was he relieved that she wasn't?

Something was definitely floating between them, some spark of attraction that they both ignored. Maybe it was time to see if it wanted to go anywhere.

Or not. There were more reasons to steer clear of Libby than good reasons to pursue this budding attraction.

NINE

"Be careful not to scratch it," Libby cried out as two burly guys in blue overalls man-handled the gleaming walnut dining table out the front door.

Not that she should care. It didn't belong to her anymore. A beam of sunlight hit the surface and reflected the deep colors of the wood: gold and amber and a swirl of butterscotch. The rich patina was due not only to the quality of the walnut and the age of the piece. She had to take some credit for the hours she'd spent polishing that table in the years it had been hers.

"What are you doing?" Jeremy O'Toole's unmistakable voice carried through the open door a moment before she glimpsed him hurrying up the front path.

"Redecorating," she called out breezily. Darn it, she'd especially booked the pickup for midday when she hoped everyone from curious neighbors to nosy bank managers would be otherwise occupied.

"Hold it right there," Jeremy ordered the guy closest to him, who paused and turned a sweaty look of inquiry on Libby.

"Nonsense, keep going," she replied, making forward

motions with her hands, and glaring at Jeremy, who fumed on the other side of the walnut barrier.

"This is crazy. You can't sell your furniture." Jeremy stood in the middle of the steps directly in front of the table.

"Would you keep your voice down?" She glanced up and down the street, but all remained quiet. She breathed again. "I've already sold it," she said. And given herself an emergency financial cushion that she'd appreciate a lot more than a dining table she rarely used.

Jeremy's face flushed. "You can't—"

"This thing weighs a ton. How about you kiss and make up after we go, huh?"

After glaring at the delivery guy, then at Libby for another moment, Jeremy stepped aside and watched in silence as the men eased the table the rest of the way out the door and headed for the truck waiting at the curb.

As soon as the table was clear of the door, he strode over the threshold. "What are you doing?"

"I needed a change. I'm tired of the traditional look, I decided on a more minimalist style."

Jeremy glanced into the dining room, where a lone table lamp rested on the floor. China was stacked neatly along one wall. He could see indentations in the blue carpet where the furniture had been. "Minimalist, huh?"

"I decided on a Bedouin dining room. My guests will eat cross-legged on the floor." She glared right back at him, daring him to say one more word.

A reluctant grin tugged at the grim line of his lips. "Maybe you'll set a new trend."

"I got five thousand bucks for that dining suite, so if you're here to evict me, you've wasted the trip."

He smiled, one of those rare smiles of his that made her go weak at the knees. "I came to see if I could take you and whatever kids are in residence to lunch."

"Oh." She took a step backward. The hall seemed to have shrunk since he'd started looking at her with that warm expression in his eyes. "Lunch."

"It's a common custom to eat something in the middle of the day." The expression turned teasing. "Even the Bedouins take lunch, I believe."

She stalled for time. "I've only got Mia home today, but she isn't very good in restaurants."

"That's why I had the deli pack us a picnic. It's such a nice day, weirdly warm for February. We could go to the beach if you like, or I thought we'd eat in the park by the river. There's a nice play area for Mia." Clamshell Bay had some nice public beaches, but it would be cooler by the ocean. The park would be easier with Mia.

He'd arranged a picnic lunch and thought through the logistics. That was so thoughtful of him, but also ambiguous. What did it mean? Was this like a date? How did she feel about going on a date with Jeremy? While she stood there not knowing how to respond, he said, "I want to talk to you about the girls."

"Oh. Well in that case." She stopped herself and then caught him grinning at her.

"I'll get Mia."

Libby licked a dab of mayonnaise from her lip and sighed, lifting her face to the weak sunshine. With their jackets on it wasn't cold at all. The river burbled its way past the park where they were sitting at a picnic table watching Mia tackle the jungle gym in the adjacent playground.

After weeks of rain, it was beyond nice to feel sunshine on her face.

Odd to feel so content when she'd lost one of her prized possessions, but Libby was a lot less bothered by the loss of her precious dining suite than she'd expected to be. She'd spent months searching for the right furniture and that suite had fit perfectly into the dining room. It was old and grand and if she tried hard enough, she could pretend it had been in her family for years.

Victor had told their dinner guests that once. He always insinuated that Libby came from a privileged background. She used to believe it was to save her embarrassment. Now she knew better. He'd wanted to impress their friends and his business associates that he'd won a prize in Libby. Libby herself apparently wasn't enough of a prize.

There was a lightening somewhere in her chest. Maybe getting rid of that table with its twelve matching chairs, buffet and china cabinet, was like setting a lie straight. Cleansing.

And she'd save hours in polishing time. She breathed deeply of the soft air. "Thanks for bringing us here."

"I'm enjoying it myself."

This impromptu picnic was like a mini-holiday, as pleasant as it was unexpected. She glanced over to her companion and provider of the feast. With his white shirt rolled up at the sleeves and his tie loosened, he looked exactly like what he was, a businessman father stealing away from the office for lunch in a playground.

Only Mia wasn't his child, and she wasn't his wife.

She gazed at him, at his black hair lightly threaded with silver, the straight nose and firm jaw, the deep smile lines in his cheeks. A nice face, an attractive face. She wondered what it would be like if appearance was reality and he was hers.

He sat facing the playground, as she did, his back leaning against the tabletop. He took a bite of his sandwich and she watched his square hands with their blunt-tipped fingers. Strong hands for a desk-jockey. Her gaze traveled to his forearms, muscular with black hairs catching the sun. "How do you stay in shape?" she found herself asking.

He finished chewing and swallowed. "Squash. Four lunchtimes a week." He turned to her. "I canceled today."

Feeling absurdly flattered that he'd canceled another

commitment to be with her, she took refuge in scolding. "I hope you still eat something in the middle of the day. With your stomach trouble, you should eat regularly."

"Yes, Nurse," he replied with false meekness.

What was she doing? She had no right talking to Jeremy O'Toole that way. He was her bank manager and employer, not her child or her lover.

"Mia, why don't you try the other slide?" she heard him say, and jerked her attention back to where Mia wobbled uncertainly on the bottom rung of the biggest slide in the playground. Libby half rose and then sank again as her daughter moved to the small slide without complaint.

He's a good father, a mushy voice crooned within her chest.

With a jerk she pulled herself up from foolish fantasy. What was she thinking?

"You wanted to talk about your daughters?" she asked tartly.

He turned his head to look down at her, a frown drawing his brows together. "I'm sorry, I didn't mean to interfere with Mia."

"Oh, no. It's not that...I mean...Jeremy, why did you bring us here?"

Consternation turned to puzzlement. "I don't know," he said slowly. "I thought about our conversation yesterday. We're obviously both pretty gun-shy, but..." He gazed off at the river for a long moment. "I wanted to spend some time with you," he said at last, and she could tell from his tone that he was as amazed to say it as she was to hear it.

Something funny happened to her chest. Like her heart tried to cram about a year's worth of heartbeats into a nanosecond. "Oh," she said. Could he possibly be interested in her? Not as a loser bank customer, or as an efficient daycare provider, but as a woman? Even as the possibility fluttered across her imagination, he doused it.

"Oh, hell, forget I said that."

She was only too happy to forget it. More complications in her life, she really didn't need. "Consider it done. Um. What about the girls?"

Another age went by before he answered, and Libby felt a struggle going on inside him. It must be as tough for him to face an attraction to another woman as it was for her to think about another man. She watched Mia taking turns on the slide with a giggling boy, listening to their shrieks of laughter. A smile tugged at her lips as the kids shared the instant intimacy of children.

She and Jeremy were at the opposite end of the intimacy spectrum, forced into closeness by circumstances and doing their best to remain strangers.

She felt rather than saw the movement beside her as he wiped his hands on a napkin and then picked up his soft drink. "Olivia's in trouble at school."

"What?" Libby was genuinely surprised. She'd seen enormous progress in the child's schoolwork and attitude in the months she'd known her. In fact, once she'd realized she wasn't going to get away with her old lazy habits at Libby's house, she'd exhibited a natural curiosity and intelligence that made Libby as proud as if she was her own child. Grace, who followed Olivia in everything, had improved enormously, too.

"She got into a fight at school and the teacher overheard her call some girl's mother names."

He recited the facts tersely, and by the end Libby was furious. "How could any mother be so cruel? Olivia's been doing so well, I hope this won't set her back."

"Her teacher wants to see me Friday after school. I think it would help if she saw there was an important woman in Olivia's and Grace's life. I want the teacher to meet you."

An important woman? He thought she was important to the twins? Well, he was right. But she was surprised he'd noticed. And she'd love to tell that teacher a thing or two. Even more, she'd like to have a few words with one very insensitive mother. "I'd love to come."

"I was hoping you'd say that."

"But what about the kids? Who'll look after them while we're gone?"

"If it's all right with you, I've asked my sister Tracy to watch them at my house until we get back."

"Oh. Tracy...Your house?"

"Tracy is great with kids, and her own are teenagers, so they can fend for themselves. I picked my house because I thought Tracy would be more comfortable there."

"Well, I guess that would be all right then. If you're sure your sister won't mind."

"She'll love it."

Friday was her birthday, but obviously he didn't know that. Oh, well. It's not like she had anything better to do than attend a parent-teacher interview. Victor used to take her out for a nice dinner and he and the kids would put on a party for her. One more thing she had to get over. She'd at least give herself a night off from cooking and order in pizza. That would be fun.

Jeremy stretched his arms over his head and Libby's mouth went dry as she watched the pull of muscles beneath the white shirt. Catching her gaze, he held it a moment, then said, "How would you like to take a walk along the river?"

"I'd love to." She raised her voice. "Mia, let's go for a walk."

"I'll get her," Jeremy said. As he walked to take Mia's hand, the three-year-old cried, "Daddy," and put her little hand into his.

For a stricken moment, Jeremy and Libby stared at each other. "She copies the twins in everything," she said, trying to make light of the comment.

They avoided looking at each other by packing up the picnic remainders. They went for their walk, but the brightness of the day had dimmed.

Jeremy wedged himself into the child's chair feeling like Gulliver in Lilliput. It didn't help that Mrs. Lawrence had chosen to sit facing him and Libby in her adult-sized teacher's chair.

He didn't like her. Not only did her ridiculous chair power game annoy him, but her face looked like some giant hand had accidentally squeezed it too hard. All her features were shoved together in the middle of her face in a frown.

There were lots of fabulous teachers, men and women, who took pride in their work and inspired kids. He knew that. He couldn't imagine a better or more dedicated teacher than his sister. So far, the girls had been lucky enough to experience some first-rate educators. But not, unfortunately, this year.

It was like going back in time. The room smelled like chalk, old apple cores, and the bodies of ten-year-olds. He glanced over at Libby, squeezed into the desk next to him and had to squelch an urge to reach over and pull her hair. Or slip her a note.

As though aware of his gaze, she glanced back, and he knew, from the twinkle of mischief in her eyes, that she'd read his thoughts.

Suppressing a grin, he turned to the unsmiling face above him. Mrs. Lawrence had a file folder open on her lap and was regarding it sternly. She made them wait for a minute while she completed reading.

"Have Olivia and Grace told you why I requested this meeting?" she asked at last, letting her eyes bore into both of them, as though daring them to come up with the wrong answer.

"Yes." He bit back the "ma'am".

She nodded. "Good. I've called you in today because this is by no means the first such incident. Olivia used foul language about another student's mother. I feel it is only fair to inform you that the mother in question has also been to see me, she is naturally extremely upset."

"But she—"

The teacher raised a finger. "Please, Mr. O'Toole, allow me to finish. You will have your turn."

Damn, he'd forgotten to take an antacid pill before the meeting. He tried to ignore the pain as anger prodded his gut.

"We have a zero-tolerance policy for bullying in this school."

"I understand, but—"

"I believe it would be appropriate for Olivia to be taken to Mrs. Morgan's house and forced to apologize for her behavior."

Jeremy tried to rise but he was jammed tight in the desk. He wanted to be standing above Mrs. Lawrence when he told her what he thought of that idea. But Libby beat him to it.

"And will that woman apologize to Olivia for *her* rude comments?" Her voice was strong and clear, and angry. "Olivia's a ten-year-old, a child who's lost her mother. Mrs. Morgan's comments were cruel and insensitive, and maybe her daughter would have done better not to repeat them to the twins."

There was utter silence for a moment. If possible, Mrs. Lawrence's mouth pursed even more. "You, I believe, are the babysitter."

But Libby wasn't to be intimidated so easily. He watched in admiration as she said, with her quiet dignity, "I'm also their friend."

Turning her attention to Jeremy, the teacher said, "I have here a written record of the times one or both of the twins have been reprimanded."

"You keep a rap sheet on ten-year-olds?" Jeremy spluttered.

She shot him an acidic glance as though to say, "now I see where the girls get their rudeness from". "Olivia is the worst offender, but Grace follows her lead. I believe the girls are a bad influence on each other. Now, the school cannot force you to make Olivia apologize, that is up to you and your conscience. However, I've spoken to the principal about splitting them up into different classes."

"You'd separate then?"

"For their own good."

"But they've always been together. Since their mother died, at least they've had each other." The school bell rang, idly he wondered what for when all the students had left for the day. He hated the idea of splitting the girls up. And he determined not to let it happen. He'd go to the principal, the school trustees, as high as he had to. Once again, he tried to wrestle himself out of the chair.

Once again, Libby's voice stopped him. "Mrs. Lawrence, I've noticed a real improvement in the girls' behavior over the last weeks, would you agree?"

"I would have said that, before this last incident, yes."

"And I've seen the good marks they've been getting on their work. Olivia is really enjoying the project about famous women. It's so good for girls to find role models."

He could see the odious woman beginning to soften. "I want the girls in my class to aspire to great achievement."

"Perhaps you would consider giving the girls a trial period to see if the improvement continues?"

"Does Mr. O'Toole plan to make Olivia apologize to Mrs. Morgan?"

"No." Jeremy said.

"Then—"

"But Mrs. Brown is a trained pediatric nurse. She's an expert on treating children who've dealt with trauma. Since she's been working with the girls, we've all seen an improvement. You've admitted it yourself. If she believes a trial period would be beneficial, I think it's worth a try."

He could see the old biddy's wheels turning. Did she dare defy an expert? He was still holding back his trump card, hoping he wouldn't have to use it.

"I'd be happy to work with you on this, Mrs. Lawrence." Libby smiled. "I believe at this stage in their recovery, separating them could have disastrous consequences."

The teacher's eyes narrowed even more. She was obviously out of her depth. "You have professional credentials and references, I assume?"

Libby's brows rose. "Of course."

"They may stay together for the time being, but I'll be watching them carefully," she said to Libby.

Jeremy finally ejected himself from the desk and he and Libby got out of the school as quickly as possible. Their steps echoed down the hallway that smelled of cleaning solution, past the rows of pint-sized lockers. Once out of sight and hearing of Mrs. Lawrence, Jeremy grabbed Libby's hand and bringing it to his mouth kissed her knuckles. "Thank you."

She squeezed his hand briefly, then pulled away and he noticed the delicate color creep up her cheeks. "And thank you for making me into some bogus expert."

"Not bogus." He pushed the metal bar on the outside door and held it open for Libby. As they passed out into late afternoon sunshine, he said, "Even Mrs. Lawrence had to give you credit for what you've done for the girls, especially Olivia. Maybe I haven't said anything, but I've noticed it too."

She blushed even deeper, and he knew his words had pleased her.

"And, thanks to you, I didn't have to play my trump card on the Wicked Witch of the West."

"Trump card?"

"The school principal is one of my squash buddies."

She laughed, a sweet sexy laugh. "I'm beginning to see where Olivia gets her bad habits."

"I'm wondering if we should get both girls moved to the other class. What do you think?"

He watched her face as she considered his words. "I think for the time being they should stay where they are. They have friends in the class and learning to deal with difficult people in authority is a skill they'll have to pick up. I think the teacher is trying to do the right thing, she's just old school."

He thought about it and nodded. "Okay, you're the expert. Let's go get the kids." They made their way to his car. He'd been careful not to do anything stupid like wish her a happy birthday, but now that it was time for her birthday surprise, he felt as jumpy and excited as the kids had been for the last couple of days. Libby didn't say anything, but he had to wonder if she suspected.

"Don't forget to drop me at my place so I can pick up my car," she reminded him.

He wanted to drive her to his house. Wanted to prolong their conversation and their time alone together, but he'd make her suspicious if he didn't drop her off, so he said goodbye in her driveway and roared off to warn the birthday party surprise crew.

TEN

Libby slumped for a moment behind the wheel, giving her cheerful act a break. Thirty-five years old today, and what had she achieved in her life? She'd become a cliché: the divorced single mom, dumped for a younger woman. And on top of that, she was fighting to hang on to her home.

She was as bad a loser as her mother.

No, she was worse. Even her mother had managed to hang on to her husband.

Libby gave herself a mental shake. She had two beautiful children, more work than she needed, between the garden design and the daycare. She didn't love living on the financial edge, but she felt herself moving slowly toward safer ground.

As a birthday present to herself, she decided to take a night off from worrying. Putting the car in gear, she headed for Jeremy's place. After she picked them up, she'd take the kids out for pizza. When was the last time they'd had a treat like that? And instead of spending the lonely hours after they were in bed on work, she'd choose a good book and pour herself a bubble bath and a glass of wine.

Libby pasted the smile back on her face as soon as she

reached Jeremy's house. It took a while before anyone answered the door. As she was about to ring a second time, it opened and there was Jeremy smiling down at her.

"Hi," he said. "Kids are waiting in the living room. Come on in."

The living room? A stifled giggle and furious whispering came from somewhere behind his left shoulder. Surely, they hadn't remembered. Another quick glance at Jeremy's face and she could see they had remembered. He was as keyed up as a little kid.

"Oh, Jeremy."

"Don't spoil it," he whispered and, grabbing her arm, dragged her into the living room.

"SURPRISE!" Young bodies bounced out from behind the furniture, and they all threw themselves her way. Foggily she noted balloons, clumsily twisted crepe paper, and long, looping strings of colored goop all over everything. Then she was being hugged and Happy Birthday'd by four kids at once. Blindly, she hugged them back.

Above their heads, her gaze met Jeremy's, and she thanked him silently. Something crazy happened when he gazed right back at her, something soft and sweet and very, very new. Libby experienced a sudden surge of elation. She felt her heart pick up the pace, her mouth felt dry, and her breathing ragged.

He took a step toward her, his eyes dark and serious, and then, as though he'd suddenly noticed they weren't alone, he stopped.

Everything that had receded in that moment came crashing back.

Especially the noise.

All four kids were talking at once, shouting as they tried to claim her attention. They were telling her how many times they'd almost blown the surprise, whose idea it was to get the potato chips, how many cans of spray streamer they'd emptied.

"How about we let the birthday girl take off her coat?" Jeremy suggested. He stepped forward to help her out of it and managed to turn the simple courtesy into a caress that left a wake of gooseflesh down her arms.

A woman with a big smile who looked to be in her early forties emerged from the kitchen. "Hi," she said. "I'm Tracy. Happy Birthday."

"Thank you. I think." She shook Jeremy's sister's hand and decided she could see a faint resemblance.

"This is your chair, Mom." Tyler pointed to one of the Queen Anne chairs decorated with balloons, bows, and ribbons.

"I feel like a queen," she assured him after he arranged a footstool under her feet and thrust a bowl of potato chips at her.

"Do you want some swamp water?" Grace asked. "We bought four kinds of soda then decided to mix them all together."

Libby swallowed and hoped her smile didn't waver. "Why thank-you, Grace."

"Tell you what, Grace, you get the kids' drinks, I have some-thing special for the adults." He turned to Libby. "I got cham-pagne, but if you prefer something else, name it. I have wine and a fully stocked bar. Also soft drinks."

"I love champagne. I haven't had it in ages."

"Three glasses, coming right up."

"Not for me, bro," Tracy said. She turned to Libby. "Tommy, my oldest, is playing basketball tonight. I have to go watch." She glanced from Libby to Jeremy and back again. "Have a great evening, you two. Happy Birthday again," and then she was gone.

He looked as though he was going to say something, then gave up. He disappeared in the kitchen just as Mia walked in proudly holding a lumpy red-wrapped package.

"It's a present." She confided in a whisper and placed the package at Libby's feet.

"Come here, you," Libby growled and hauled her giggling daughter onto her lap for a giant hug.

Soon she had a stack of presents at her feet and a foaming glass in her hand.

"Open mine first," Mia begged.

"I'll open them from the youngest to the oldest. Is that all right with everyone?"

Everyone agreed so she picked up the lumpy red parcel carefully and slowly unwrapped it. Inside was a terracotta plant pot painted with bright craft paints. "Oh, Mia, It's beautiful. Why look at that big happy yellow sun, and an apple tree, and so many different colored flowers, and there's even a rainbow."

"And that's you." Mia jumped up and ran over to point at the stick figure with a huge smile. "You're in your garden."

"This is the most wonderful present, Mia. Thank you."

"Grace helped me," Mia told her, pointing at the blushing girl.

"I knew you liked plants and stuff," Grace mumbled.

"Thanks. It's perfect."

With a big smacking kiss, she set Mia aside as Tyler stepped forward to present his gift, a grocery-sized box wrapped in newspaper. He unwrapped it for Libby, pulling out a mobile on a bent coat hanger.

"This is me in outer space. See, here are all the planets. And that's my spaceship. Jeremy lent me a book about space so I could get the planets in the right order." Somehow, Mr. O'Toole had become Jeremy to the kids. She wasn't entirely sure when it had happened or whether she approved.

But the twins called her by her first name, so what could she do about it? Jeremy looked as embarrassed as his daughter had when she thanked him for helping her son.

"We can hang this in the kitchen so I can enjoy it every day."

"And when I go into space, you can look at it and remember where I am."

The laughter helped ease the lump in Libby's throat.

"You next, kid sister, you're five minutes younger than me," Olivia said.

After rolling her eyes, Grace said, "Mine's the yellow one."

"I love tulips and daffodils," Libby said as she opened the package of spring bulbs.

"I bought them with my allowance," the young girl said proudly.

Olivia presented her with a pastel drawing of a girl holding a hank of red hair and frowning. "Carrots" was scribbled underneath.

"Why, that's Anne of Green Gables. Olivia, you are a very talented artist."

"I know you like that book."

"I love it. It's something we have in common. Thank you." She rose and crossed the room to hug first Grace, then Olivia.

When she returned to her seat there were two neatly-wrapped packages still at her feet. "But what are these?"

"The green one's from Auntie Tracy," Olivia piped up. "The huge one's from Dad."

"Tracy? She shouldn't have bought me a present. And what a pretty vase. I'll be able to put the flowers that grow from your bulbs in here, Grace."

The last package was the biggest of all. When she tore off the paper she found a hardware store box. Inside was wall plaster and a metal applicator, tile grout, some assorted tools and a hinge exactly like the one on her kitchen cupboards.

She glanced up. "Thank you, I think."

"It comes with a handyman," he explained. "I'll come over and fix the cracks in the plaster, and the other things you mentioned. I noticed your upstairs tub needs grouting. Make a list. You've got yourself a weekend handyman."

"A handyman," she breathed in rapture. Maybe it was sexist, but she didn't care. She'd tried to figure out the basics of home repair, but she couldn't hammer in a nail straight.

"Everybody else got a hug, doesn't my dad?" Olivia asked loudly.

Libby laughed shakily. "Yes, I guess he does." She rose, and slowly crossed the room.

He stood to meet her, the expression in his eyes intense, hungry. He put out his arms and pulled her flush against his solid body, where she clung for a moment, letting her head rest against his shoulder. She heard the beat of his heart—a little fast perhaps for a man who played squash four times a week, but still slower than her own frantic pulse.

"I can't thank you—"

He interrupted her words with a quick, hard kiss on the lips. "Happy Birthday, Libby."

ELEVEN

It was just a little birthday kiss. A peck, really, yet she felt she would have fallen on the floor if she hadn't been clinging to Jeremy. Her lips still tingled with the remnants of heat from his mouth. She wanted...

"I'm starving. Can we have pizza now, Jeremy?"

"Ty-yler! Come in the kitchen," Olivia ordered, then she gestured frantically at the other kids who scrambled to obey.

"Oh, dear. Is she feeling upset?" Libby pulled away and straightened her perfectly straight blouse.

"No-o. I'm not the child expert, you are, but I think she likes to see us kissing." Jeremy picked up his glass and drained it.

In the awkward silence that ensued, Libby busied herself picking up wrapping paper and folding it neatly.

"The girls chose music they thought you'd like," he said, as Taylor Swift's voice filled the room. "Shall we see if dinner's ready?"

She nodded her agreement, and they headed into the kitchen where pizza steamed on a round oak table laid with what was obviously the best china.

It felt so right, sitting there with Jeremy and his children.

Grace was helping Mia to a second slice of pizza. Olivia scolded Tyler in a low voice about the way he picked every vegetable off his pizza.

And there was Jeremy, caressing her with his gaze every time their eyes met. She almost choked when she caught him staring at her mouth. She licked her lips, wondering if she had a blob of pizza sauce on them. Jeremy seemed transfixed by the movement of her tongue on her lips.

She felt hot and excited and nervous. Like a woman being pursued by a man. And she realized that's exactly what she was. The pleasure she felt was totally out of proportion to the casual interest she was certain he felt, but it was still nice. It had been such a long time.

After they'd all stuffed themselves with pizza, Libby made a move to start clearing the table.

"Sit," Jeremy ordered. He and the twins cleared the table and then everyone but Libby disappeared. Within minutes they were all singing, Happy Birthday to you...And around the corner came the cake, carried by Grace.

"We made it ourselves," Olivia proudly exclaimed.

Libby shot an alarmed glance at Jeremy, remembering the disastrous brownies the girls had once baked, but it was Grace who calmed her fears. "Dad and Aunt Tracy and me and Olivia all made it together."

"And me and Mia helped decorate it," Tyler said.

"It's the most beautiful cake I've ever seen." And it was. From the candy heart decorations to the crooked lettering. "Come on, everybody, help me blow out the candles." She pulled the kids around her.

"Wait."

She paused on a big indrawn breath and glanced up at Jeremy's command as he snapped a few photos.

As soon as they'd consumed the chocolate cake and ice cream, the kids begged to watch a movie.

"I don't know. It's getting kind of late." Libby checked her watch.

"You should probably have some coffee before you drive home. We have lots of room if the kids want to doze off here."

"Can we have a sleepover?" Tyler begged.

"Sleepover, sleepover." Mia jumped up and down.

"I don't know. I hate to impose."

"There's plenty of room, you're all welcome to stay," Jeremy said in a too-casual voice that sent shivers of excitement up her spine. He was inviting her for a sleepover as well.

"Please, Mom. Please."

"I'd like you to stay a while," a much deeper male voice chimed in.

"Well, maybe for a little while."

"Come on." Tyler wasn't waiting any longer. And with the maximum possible amount of noise, four kids bounded off.

In the relative quiet after the stair-pounding died down, Libby fussed about clearing the dessert things off the table, keeping her hands busy while her brain reeled. Jeremy wanted her. Unless the champagne was giving her delusions.

Bent over the table picking up scattered birthday candles, she peeked up at him through her lashes. He seemed engrossed in measuring coffee into a filter, but she sensed he was as keenly aware of her as she was of him. It was like an invisible current hummed between them. She tried to imagine what it would be like to make love with Jeremy.

"How do you like it?" he interrupted her thoughts.

Her eyes widened and her jaw dropped. She liked it pitch black and under the covers where sagging boobs and stretch marks didn't show. And she did not like discussing sexual pref- erences in a well-lit kitchen with a man she hadn't yet decided she would sleep with. She dragged her jaw back up and glared at his back.

"Black? Cream and sugar?"

Coffee. Oh, God, he was asking her how she liked her coffee. "Libby? It's decaf, if that's what you're worried about."

"Oh, good. Yes, cream and sugar, please."

Gathering up the dessert plates, she cursed herself for a fool. But as she eased behind Jeremy to load the plates in the dishwasher, she felt it again. No way all that heat was being generated from her. Working together in the shaped kitchen brought them into close contact.

Even as she ran water over the dishes and stacked each one carefully into the dishwasher, she felt his movements where he worked scant feet away. The aroma of coffee filled the air. Good thing it was decaf. Any more stimulant and she might go spinning off into space.

"Here," he said, handing her a cup.

"Thanks." She added cream and sugar and followed him into the living room. For a few minutes conversation was stilted. He told her a dull story about the bank. She told him a cute story about Mia and Grace, then had an awful feeling she'd told him the same story the day before.

Suddenly, he laughed. "This feels strange, doesn't it?"

"Yes," she agreed. "It does."

"We're friends, at least I think we are?" He glanced at her and she nodded confirmation. "But this feels like a date."

"I know." She didn't mention the strange undercurrent between them that was making her so jittery.

"What do you think would have happened if we'd met socially? Instead of the way we did?"

"What do you mean?"

"If I'd met you somewhere, a party through mutual friends, say, would you have said yes if I asked you out?"

"I don't know." She put her empty coffee cup down. "Would you have asked me?"

"I think so. I hope so."

She put her head on one side and studied him, trying to

imagine meeting him for the first time without the fear of losing her house topmost on her mind. "I probably would have said yes."

"Okay." His eyes crinkled at the edges when he smiled. "So I'm asking."

"You're asking me out? On a date?"

"Yes."

"When? Where?"

"I don't know. Dinner. Next week some time."

"Who'd look after the kids?" she asked, stalling.

"A sitter, I guess."

She blew out a breath. "I thought I'd finished dating in my twenties. I'm thirty-five today."

"I'm thirty-nine. And we'll still be thirty-five and thirty-nine whatever we do."

He was asking her to take this unspoken attraction out into the open. Was she willing to? She glanced at him. "Okay."

"Excellent. How about next Friday?"

"Sure, so long as we can find sitters." She rose and carried their cups to the kitchen.

"More coffee?" he asked.

"I'd better not. I should get the kids home."

She put their cups in the dishwasher and noted the machine was full.

"Where do you keep dishwasher detergent?"

"Under the sink. Here let me." But she was already moving and even as his words registered, she was too late to stop. He'd moved forward at the same time. She felt the soft, warm impact behind her as he toppled over her. His hands grabbed the counter on either side of the sink.

For a stunned second, neither of them moved, then she made a noise in her throat, not a moan or a sigh but a combination of both with a hint of nervous giggle thrown in.

His hands came down off the counter and wrapped around

her, straightening them both in the process. He held her like that, his front warm and solid against her back, his arms wrapped around her torso, below her breasts. She let herself lean into him and absorb his warmth, his scent. In a slow caress, he brought his hands to her shoulders and slowly turned her to face him.

She gazed into the blazing hunger of his eyes, and then his face blurred as he claimed her mouth in a kiss. She splayed her hands in the springy hair at the back of his neck, letting her fingers learn the shape of his head. She wanted to learn all of him. The curves and ridges of his entire body. And she wanted it now.

Her own urgency embarrassed her.

Pulling away, she dragged in a lungful of air. "This is crazy," she gasped. "I'm not sure it's a good idea." She'd gone as far as agreeing to a date. That was a big step for her.

"Don't analyze it, Libby, please. Let it happen." The urgency and dark promise of his words sent passion skittering along her nerve ends.

He was right. They were out of their minds to be doing this. If she stopped to think about it long enough, she'd call a halt. And she couldn't bear to stop, not now.

She ran her tongue over her swollen lips. "Let me check on the kids."

"Okay. But hurry."

She crept downstairs to the family room and smiled. There was a pull-out bed and all four of them were sprawled on it, sound asleep. A woolen throw had fallen to the floor, so she picked it up and lay it over the kids. The TV blared. She flicked it off so that only one child's soft snores could be heard and left a lamp burning, then crept back upstairs.

Jeremy was waiting for her. The dishwasher hummed, so obviously he'd turned it on. She knew how the thing felt.

"Everything all right?"

"They're all sound asleep."

"Good." He reached out and dragged Libby toward him. He kissed her softly, then ran his fingers down her cheek. "I feel like a teenager sneaking around while his parents are asleep. You never imagine you'll have to sneak around behind your children's backs."

She laughed softly. And then he kissed her again, long and slow. His hands traveled over her back, cupped her butt and then moved up the front of her blouse. When he reached her breasts, she moaned. His lips moved steadily downward, stopping to kiss whatever they passed. Her cheeks, jaw, chin, neck. When his lips reached the vee of her blouse, he started undoing her buttons.

Nerves fluttered in her stomach. There was far too much light in the kitchen. "We should go upstairs," she whispered. "In case the kids wake up."

He hesitated, then with a quick kiss on her lips, grabbed her hand and led her down the hall and slowly up the stairs.

She was buzzing with a combination of desire and nerves. She'd only ever been with Victor. She was so wrapped up in her own feelings that when they reached the top of the stairs she didn't notice the tension radiating from his body until they paused before a closed door. Turning her toward him, he kissed her again, hard and hungry but with an edge of desperation. Then, taking her hand, he led her forward once again.

They entered a bedroom and to her profound relief he didn't turn on a light, merely kept kissing her all the while he backed her toward the bed. The curtains weren't drawn so moonlight gave the room a dim glow. It was a tidy room, almost sterile. Lamps on the bedside tables and nothing else. A wooden bureau with an empty vase.

A vague uneasiness settled in her chest, then he was laying her back on the bed and, as his bulk blocked her vision, she gave in to the sensations invading her body. The knowledge that he truly desired her was as intoxicating as the feel of his kiss on her lips. Warmth unfolded within her, traveling stealthily along her limbs until her whole body was pulsing with heat. His hands trailed over her, slow, taking his time molding her shape through her clothes, stoking the fire. He kneaded her breasts, pinching the pebbled nipples lightly so she gasped, wanting more. His hands moved lower, over her abdomen, her hips and down to her knees, then they tracked up her pantyhose and under her skirt, moving slowly and relentlessly up her thighs. He trailed his fingers over the center of her sensible cotton panties and she bit back a gasp of pleasure.

She'd never felt like this, never. She was close to exploding right there and then, from nothing more than a little fully clothed foreplay. But she felt, with Jeremy, something she'd long ago lost. Trust. He would never deliberately hurt her. She knew it as surely as she knew his eye color. Within the warmth of that trust she felt herself blossoming, her sexual urges flowing like sap after the spring thaw. Beneath those demure cotton panties she was wet and throbbing with the need to be filled. Even as she thrust her hips up toward him suggestively, her hands reached for his belt buckle.

With equal urgency, he grabbed at the waistband of her pantyhose and started to pull, peeling the fabric from her skin with hands that were not quite steady.

Perhaps a breeze picked up outside, blowing clouds away from the moon, but just then a shaft of moonlight illuminated the bed, and her, as bright as day.

She shivered theatrically, pretending cold all the while her body burned with lust. "Let's get under the covers, I'm freezing."

He lunged up and dragged down the bedspread. Libby moved to help him, but her questing fingers found only a blanket, and the dimpled surface of a mattress, no sheets. Where were the sheets? A slight musty smell rose from the disturbed bedding. Her earlier dread returned as all the pieces fell into place. The impersonal feel, the lack of any signs that Jeremy inhabited the space. "This isn't your room, is it?"

A glance at his face showed him looking both guilty and confused. "It's the guest room," he admitted. "I thought...ah...it was safer, in case the kids came looking for us."

"Don't you have a lock on your bedroom door?" she asked softly, dread building in her stomach.

"Yes. But—"

"Then I want to go there." Had she been wrong about him after all? Maybe she couldn't trust him.

"We're here now. Can't we stay?"

"I want to make love with you in your bed, where you sleep, like I'm part of your life, not some temporary guest." Didn't she deserve at least that? Or was this some casual thing, a one-nighter with a sex-starved divorcee. A pity—No. Even as her mind shied away from the term, she knew Jeremy wouldn't treat her so shabbily. Anguish was coming off him in waves.

"All right," he said almost angrily. "Come on."

They padded back down the hall, not holding hands this time, to the doorway where he'd paused earlier. He had intended to take her to his bed then changed his mind. She was getting a really bad feeling about this. Coward that she was, she wished she'd shut up and let nature take its course in the guest room. But it was too late to turn back now. With a deep breath, Libby entered his bedroom. It was dark, but she had to see the room, she knew that. So she snapped on the overhead light.

"Oh, Jeremy," she said with all the pity in her heart.

TWELVE

The room was a shrine to a dead woman. He was living in his own personal Taj Mahal. Pictures of a young woman with mischievous eyes, and a short, sassy crop of curly brown hair smiled at Libby from half a dozen picture frames.

She moved softly to a wedding photo. A much younger Jeremy with a smile that held no shadows hugged his bride. Beside that photo was Kelly with the newborn twins, and pictures of family vacations, Christmas, happy family mementos.

It wasn't only the pictures; it was the bright yellow flower printed chintz draperies and bedspread that spoke of a woman's touch. The lacy pillows monogrammed with J and K. The brushes and perfume bottles on a spindle-legged dressing table. Libby could have sworn there was even the faint scent of another woman in the air.

Her mind was obviously playing tricks on her. And yet... She glanced at Jeremy, standing in the doorway, looking so lost and confused she wanted to take him back to the guest room and simply offer him what comfort she could.

But she'd learned a lot about grieving in her nursing career.

That light floral scent hovered in the air like a ghostly presence. Which was ridiculous. Unless...

Libby grasped a drawer handle on the dresser and pulled.

"No! Don't do that."

But it was too late, she'd already spotted the neatly folded nighties and lingerie, and she knew without looking that the rest of Kelly's clothes would be neatly stacked in the drawers and probably still hanging in one of the double closets.

"Oh, Jeremy," she whispered again, her heart breaking for him. The scent was stronger with the drawer open and in a rush of embarrassment that she had barged into his private shrine, she swiftly closed the drawer. When she straightened and turned around, Libby was alone in the room.

She heard Jeremy's tread thumping down the stairs and decided to give him a few minutes to recover. She needed some time, herself.

The lump in her throat threatened to choke her. She picked up the nearest photo. Kelly in a flowered summer dress laughing at the camera as though she'd been caught unawares. "You were one lucky woman," Libby whispered. "Please understand, I don't want to take your place, I want to help him. How do I do that?"

But the pretty young woman kept smiling. If she was sending any message, it was that Libby was on her own.

Carefully, she replaced the picture exactly where she'd found it and quietly left the room.

She found him sitting in the darkened living room sipping coffee. He didn't offer her a cup, didn't even acknowledge her presence, but Libby knew he needed her as strongly as if he'd sobbed on her shoulder.

Walking to the kitchen she poured herself a coffee, adding cream and sugar from the set he'd prepared earlier, then returned to sit across from Jeremy.

They sipped silently for a while.

"The girls look a lot like their mother," she said at last.

"I'm sorry." His voice was gruff and full of pain.

"I'm sorry, too."

He was staring at the floor, his elbows resting on his spread knees, the cup held in his hands. "I thought I could handle it. You're the first woman I've wanted...since...I mean...Oh hell, you know what I mean."

"Yes. I misunderstood. When you took me to the guest room, I thought it was an insult."

His eyes burned when he glanced up. "I wasn't only trying to get laid, I wanted you."

"I'm glad."

He'd wanted her, but not enough to brave his own demons. Libby sighed. She had to put away her own hurt feelings. Later she could think about how she'd been rejected in favor of a dead woman. But now, Jeremy needed help and she had specific training in grief counseling. As much as the woman in her wanted to run, the professional in her had to stay and help him.

"Do you know about the stages of grief, Jeremy?"

"Yes. Anger, denial, bargaining, depression, and something."

"Acceptance." She let a hint of humor creep into her voice. "You've obviously mastered the first four stages. It seems to be the final one that's giving you trouble."

"I have accepted it. She's been gone for three years for God's sake."

"Three years and how many weeks, days, minutes, seconds."

He let out a startled exclamation.

"Leaving everything exactly as Kelly left it is denying that she's not coming back."

"I'm not a freaking psycho. I know she's not coming back. I never got around to getting rid of all that stuff."

"I know of an excellent women's shelter that would put her things to good use. Don't you think she'd want that?"

"Damn it, I know she would. She'd want us to be up there humping our brains out on her old bed too."

"I'm not trying—"

He glanced up at her and his honesty seared her. "Really. She would. She made me promise I'd get on with my life and find someone else, for me and the girls."

Libby swallowed. "She was a good woman."

"Yeah, she was. The last couple of weeks, the way I've been feeling every time I'm around you. I thought I was ready."

"But, you're not." She sighed, knowing there was something she could do to help him.

He shoved a hand through his hair. "I made a nice mess of your birthday. I'm sorry."

"Don't be. I understand." What she planned to do would hurt him and make him angry with her. She knew that. Sometimes healing really hurt. "Jeremy, I want you to do something for me."

He glanced up warily, his face gray. "What?"

"Tomorrow, I want you to take the girls out for the day. And, I want you to give me the key to your house."

His eyelids jerked as he understood the unspoken message. That she would be cleaning out his wife's things while he was gone. "I don't think I can."

"It's time, Jeremy."

"I thought maybe the girls would want some of their mother's things."

He wasn't going to make this easy. "I tell you what. I'll label everything and put it away in storage boxes. Nothing will be gone, but Kelly's things won't be in your room anymore." She felt the way his body jerked physically when she said Kelly's name.

She bet everyone else he knew never mentioned his wife.

They'd think they were saving him from bad memories. As a grief counselor had once said to her, "As though it might have slipped the person's mind that their loved one is gone." So, he'd bottled all that stuff inside.

She doubted he'd ever had counseling. "Kelly will always be a part of your life, and the twins. You lived a beautiful life together, and part of her lives on in Olivia and Grace." She put her coffee cup down and moved toward him, kneeling so she could look up at him. "But Kelly's not here anymore. And you are. It's time for you to get back to living."

He dropped his head down and nodded once. Then he raised his hips and dug in his pocket, pulling out a bunch of keys. They clattered jarringly in the quiet room as he separated one. Leaning forward he snapped the lone silver house key onto the coffee table in the middle of the room, still without looking at her. "Call Tracy. She'll help. I'll text you her number."

She was forcing him to take the last step in accepting that his wife was gone forever. For now, she was the enemy, and she understood that. She only hoped he would recognize how difficult it was for her to play that part, when she so wanted to be close to him.

But there was no future for them together so long as his wife's clothes lay neatly folded in drawers and her scent permeated his bedroom. Of course, the step she was about to take might kill any hope they'd have as a couple anyway. But, at least, she might help him find peace and eventually he'd be ready to start again with another woman. It was a depressing thought, imagining him with somebody else. It seemed like a lose/lose situation for Libby.

She picked up the key, still warm from being so close to his body and rose. "I'm going to wake my kids up now. It's time we were heading home."

He made an effort to rouse himself, forcing a sorry attempt

at a smile to his face as he stood. "Yeah. I'll text you Tracy's number and then I'll help you get them in the car."

Tyler muttered in his sleep as Jeremy hoisted him in his arms. Mia didn't stir as Libby untangled her from where she'd snuggled in Olivia's arms. The two adults carried their sleeping burdens to the car, but the biggest burden was the unspoken one they both carried. The memory of what had happened upstairs, and of what Libby was going to do tomorrow.

Once the kids were buckled in the car, the engine purring softly as the inside began to heat up, Libby tipped up her face to say goodnight. Her trite "thank you for a lovely birthday" never made it out of her mouth. One quick glance at Jeremy's painfully bleak expression and she was out of the car and reaching for him, her heart yearning to give him comfort.

Wordlessly he held her, so tightly she feared for her ribs. She closed her eyes and leaned in, offering him all the strength and understanding she had. Her head nestled against his neck. "I won't do it if you don't want me to," she whispered, not sure if either of them could bear the pain.

"You have to," he muttered.

She nodded, her cheek scraping against his neck. "Yes, I think I do." Knowing what the cost could be to their budding romance. Would he be strong enough to accept that she must hurt him in order to help him? Or would he forever hold it against her that she caused him this pain?

At last she pulled away and slid back into the driver's seat. "Good night."

"We'll go out early tomorrow." He said in a voice that pleaded with her to get it over with as quickly as possible. She nodded and then put the car in gear and backed away.

The last image she had was of him standing outside in his shirtsleeves, oblivious to the cold, staring straight ahead.

When Jeremy walked up the stairs, he felt like an old man. The girls were sound asleep on the pull-out downstairs and he decided to leave them there for the night. He'd contemplated pulling out a bottle of Scotch and spending the rest of the night slumped in his favorite chair in the den, but he knew that desire for what it was—cowardice. Getting good and drunk wouldn't help anything.

His daycare provider and almost-lover was a master of the gotta-be-cruel-to-be-kind school of do-gooders. But he knew she was right. He'd made an ass of himself and denied both Libby and himself some self-indulgent pleasure they could both use. She'd been so tentative at first, but once she got warmed up she'd been all passion and fire. He ached all over again thinking of what they'd missed.

But Libby had understood what he hadn't. There was a woman standing between the two of them.

Kelly.

He touched the wedding ring on his finger. He and Kelly hadn't had a perfect marriage—who did? They used to have the odd fight, and during the first year after the twins were born, they'd both been frazzled, but Kelly had been exhausted. What with breastfeeding both kids, which she'd insisted on doing, and if one wasn't crying in the night, or teething, or getting a cold, or colicky then the other was, it seemed that they'd barely ever had a full night's sleep. But they'd managed.

And she'd loved those tiny babies with her whole heart. He found he was smiling as he walked into their bedroom, his and Kelly's, as he remembered a night when he'd walked in to find his three favorite females all sound asleep, one baby still attached to each breast, sucking reflexively.

The old anger rolled through him. It wasn't fair that someone like Kelly should be taken so young. And so cruelly. Her daughters needed her. Who would teach them to be women? Who would help them through all that incomprehensible teen girl stuff that was right around the corner? He, being a banker, and a sensible man, had planned for the girls' education the minute they were born, as he had begun saving for his and Kelly's retirement from the day they were married.

She used to tease him about living for tomorrow instead of for today, but he liked to plan ahead. It made him feel safer.

Nowhere in the plan or in his worst dreams had he imagined losing a woman so full of life. He picked up one of the photos on his dresser. It was the only one he had of her after her diagnosis. She was still smiling, and she'd promised him she'd fight that cancer with everything she had.

She did, too. A tear rolled down his cheek. She'd lost that brave battle, but Libby was right. Kelly had left a part of herself in the twins. The fact that Kelly had lived and that he and she had loved each other was evident every day in those two girls who looked so much like their mother.

He wasn't keeping his end of the bargain. He'd promised Kelly that he would make a good life for the girls. She'd told him, near the end, on one of her good days, that he would find someone else. She gave him her blessing. They'd both cried. And at the time he'd believed it would never happen. He would never find someone to replace Kelly.

And, he realized, looking at that bright, laughing face, he hadn't. He'd found Libby. She wasn't Kelly. She wasn't much like her at all. She was quiet where Kelly had been outgoing, meticulous where Kelly had been happy-go-lucky. They didn't look a bit alike, or have any similarities but one. They were both terrific mothers.

Was that what he was doing? Falling for a woman because she was a good mother and his girls were in desperate need of one?

Even as the notion crossed his mind, he dismissed it. He placed the photograph back on his dresser. No. What he felt for Libby was what a man feels for a woman. He wasn't certain how strong it was or where it would lead—probably nowhere now that he'd made a total fool of himself—but it wasn't because she was a good mother that he ached for Libby.

He'd never fallen out of love with Kelly, and he never would. He thought that Libby, of all people, understood that. He opened the closet and fingered a random dress that was no doubt totally out of style and would have long since been donated to charity if Kelly were still alive.

In that moment he realized that packing away her things, like burying her body, didn't mean she was gone forever. Her memory would live as long as he and the girls did. And part of her would go on.

He stood there with his head bowed, knowing this was the last night he'd spend in this room that was still Kelly's. He was still alive. Maybe it was time he started acting like it.

———

The next day, Jeremy put off returning home as long as he could. After breakfast in a pancake house, a shopping trip where the girls picked out new clothes that were totally over-priced and so flimsy they looked like they'd last about a week, lunch in another restaurant, and two hours watching a teen romance movie where he munched antacids at the same speed the girls downed popcorn, they headed home.

He'd told Grace and Olivia over breakfast what Libby and Aunt Tracy were going to do today. They'd gone quiet for a second, glanced at each other, then Olivia said, "Okay."

And they didn't mention it again. Somehow, he knew it was okay. Maybe because they were younger and more resilient, maybe because he'd sent them to the grief counseling he couldn't face himself, maybe because they were optimistic, like their mother. "You know, your mom would be so proud of you two if she could see you now."

"She does see us, Dad," Olivia said, looking at him in surprise. "She watches us from heaven. She told us she would, don't you remember?"

He couldn't speak. He could only nod.

When he couldn't think of anything else to do, they headed home.

He drove so slowly seniors were overtaking him. But, as slowly as the car crawled along with the chattering girls in the back, it arrived in his driveway too early for him to be ready.

"Hurry up, Dad, these bags are heavy," Olivia complained as he stood outside his own front door terrified to put the spare key in the lock.

He pushed the door open. Somebody had left some lights on, for which he was grateful. The main floor of the house looked exactly as he'd last seen it that morning. A few stray strings of spray confetti that he'd missed in last night's cleanup clung to the walls.

He swallowed while the girls clattered past him. "Let's try on our stuff," Grace said as they hauled their loot up the stairs.

When the hall was quiet again, Jeremy took a deep breath and started up the stairs himself. *Just get it over with.* He refused to pause outside the closed bedroom door, but pushed the door open and hit the light switch.

He'd half known what to expect. Even so he felt the air grunt out of his body as though a medicine ball had slammed into his belly.

Nothing was the same.

Oh, they'd been busy, all right. He stepped forward and eyed the green plaid quilt on the bed, which was on the other side of the room from where it used to be. He gulped as he realized they hadn't only taken Kelly's clothing away; they'd removed the dresser she'd kept her stuff in. Those two women hadn't moved the heavy dresser alone. Tracy's husband or the boys must have helped, too. Humiliation burned within him along with rising fury. The whole room was different.

He stalked to the double closet and yanked it open, shocked to find her side stripped bare, even though he'd known it would be. A fireball of rage clogged his throat. Even the yellow curtains were gone. Green ones that probably went with the bedspread now hung on the rods.

They'd even taken her goddam curtains.

They'd left him nothing, those interfering do-gooders. Nothing but the pictures. Kelly still gazed at him from half a dozen frames, but she seemed more distant. They weren't her anymore. They were only pictures.

He sat down abruptly on the edge of the bed. It didn't even smell the same. Those thieving women had taken everything. They would have sucked his very memories up in a vacuum cleaner if they could.

THIRTEEN

An hour and two Scotches later, the doorbell rang. The girls were downstairs in their new clothes, dancing to yet another K-pop group, having declared themselves too full of popcorn for dinner. He'd told them to warm up leftover pizza when they got hungry. That was fine with Jeremy. His stomach rejected the idea of food. The Scotch tasted like drain cleaner, but he figured he needed it.

As the clanging bell interrupted his reverie, he felt his eyes narrow in fury. He stomped to the door, ready to tell that damn Libby she'd done enough for one day.

It wasn't Libby standing on his doorstep, tears of sympathy in her eyes, a steaming lasagna in her hands. It was Tracy.

He wasn't too pleased to see her, either, but for some reason he wasn't as angry with his sister as he was with the babysitter cum psychiatrist who'd suddenly taken over his life.

"Can I come in?" Tracy asked.

"I guess." He sounded as sulky as a schoolboy.

"I thought you might be hungry." She bustled into the kitchen, where he heard the oven door creak open and bang shut. He didn't move from the wide open front door. Hoping that was a strong enough hint that he wasn't interested in a social visit with his sister.

Her heavy tread sounded coming down the hallway toward him. He refused to turn around.

"I'm sorry, Jeremy. It wasn't easy for me, either." Her voice was raspy with tears. "I kept remembering..." She sniffed, and he heard the stifled sob.

Turning, he grabbed her to him, her hefty body shaking with grief. "It's okay, Tracy. It's okay."

"I knew it had to be done. In three years, I haven't had the courage even to bring up the subject. Libby did most of it. I stood around crying all day. I kept remembering things we'd done when she was wearing some of the clothes we packed away. I even shopped with her a few times." She sniffed louder. "Libby warned me you might be angry, but I can't stand it if you are. Please don't be mad at us. Please."

"Libby warned you?" His voice was sharp. How could she have known? Then he remembered. She had training. He was probably as predictable as a textbook. "Why did she do it if she knew I'd get mad?"

"She cares about you, big brother. She warned me that you wouldn't like either of us for a while. She said I should let you alone, give you time. But I couldn't." She shook again in his arms, and the lump in his throat eased.

"I'm glad you came, Trace." He squeezed and let her go.

She dried her eyes and gave him a big smile. "I'm glad too." She touched his shoulder lightly. "This is probably the worst time for me to tell you this, but you know me, I've never been the tactful type."

"Tell me what?"

She sent him a sweet, sassy grin. "I like this one. You can't spend an entire day crying in front of someone and not get pretty close to them, you know?"

He nodded. He'd been so obsessed with his own pain he

hadn't thought about Tracy's. "That must have been hard on you."

"Well, it was. But I love you. I don't want to see you hurting."

"I know."

"Libby's a very determined woman, so organized she scares me, and she's got this quiet way about her, but when she gets going she's pretty damned bossy. I like her a lot." She glanced up at him. "It wasn't that easy for her, either." His sister took a shaky breath. "Don't scare her away."

"Did she tell you about last night?" He didn't think he could feel more humiliated about taking Libby to the guest room, but the thought of Libby and Tracy chatting about him choking made him squirm.

They walked into the kitchen together. "She didn't have to tell me anything. I've got eyes. I haven't seen you look at a woman that way since..."

"Kelly. I know. Tracy, I screwed up royally last night."

"What are you talking about?"

"I...uh, things got pretty hot..." This was so hard to talk about with his sister.

"Yeah, okay, I get it."

"And I took her into the guest room. I couldn't take her into my bedroom."

His sister was staring at him, obviously torn between pity and horror. "You mean you couldn't take her into Kelly's room."

He nodded.

"Big bro."

"Do you think she'll ever give me another chance?"

"I don't know. She seemed fairly professional about what she had to do today." She looked doubtful as she opened drawers and started setting the table.

"Listen, can you stick around for a while? Feed the girls? I'd...uh...well, I need to see her."

"Are you sure that's a good idea?"

"I'm not sure of anything anymore."

Tracy sent him one of the wide smiles she'd inherited from their mother. "Stay as long as you like."

Rejecting the car in favor of a brisk walk, Jeremy let the rhythm of his footsteps soothe him. But it was tough. All the awkwardness of the way he'd made a fool of himself the night before rose in his mind. She'd acted like a dentist's drill, breaking through his protective barrier to get at the soft, hurting part. He didn't like being without his protection. He felt vulnerable, and, if he was honest with himself, frightened.

She'd uncovered his secret pain. Gone through his wife's things. How could he make love to her when she knew him for the coward he was?

How could he still want her?

The lights of her home welcomed him, even though he dreaded seeing her. He picked up the pace a little and was breathless by the time he banged the lion's head.

She opened the door and her eyes widened. "Jeremy." Her surprise was evident in the lilting way she said his name. Then a crease appeared between her brows. "Are you all right? I-I didn't expect to see you." She looked so concerned and so vulnerable standing there with eyes wide, and uncertain that the last of his anger died.

"No. I'm not all right. Not really." He shoved his hands in his pockets as though searching for a tip. "I guess it's going to take a while. But that was a brave thing you did. I wanted to thank you."

A smile both sad and sweet crossed her face. "Would you like to come in?"

"Yes. I would."

She pushed her hair behind her ears in a nervous gesture. "I was putting the kids to bed."

"Can I help?"

"Well, you could read Tyler a story." She sounded kind of doubtful.

"Yeah. That'd be great. I need something to do, something away from my own house." So, he was running from his ghosts. He knew they'd find him again, but a temporary reprieve would be good. Maybe by the time he'd read Tyler a story, he'd have a clue about what to say.

He knew how he felt. But what was he going to do about it?

Tyler was both shy and eager when Libby explained Jeremy would be reading him his story. His hair was damp from a bath and he sported flannel pajamas with baseball players all over them. Jeremy experienced a flash of longing. He loved his girls, but, before Kelly had found out she was sick, they'd planned to have another child. Secretly, he'd hoped for a son.

"Which story do you want?" Jeremy asked.

"Dunno. You pick."

Jeremy scanned the shelves in Tyler's bedroom. Science, nature, space, everything educational. He felt a little intimidated. A Hardy Boys would have been nice.

He eyed the slugger jammies. "Don't you have any books about baseball?"

"No. I don't know how to play baseball."

"You don't know how to play baseball?" Knowing how to play baseball ranked right up there with knowing how to fly a kite or soap windows on Halloween. Quintessential boy stuff. The poor kid had as good as not had a father.

Wide, assessing blue eyes, so much like his mother's, gazed longingly at him. Too scared to ask, but so hopeful Jeremy didn't have the heart to refuse the unspoken request. "Tell ya what, if it's nice out tomorrow, how about we play some baseball? Just us guys?"

Tyler nodded, a smile of pure bliss on his face.

"We have to check first with your mom."

"Check what with me?" The way her voice smiled was as

sexy as a caress, it did things to Jeremy he didn't want to think about.

Jeremy opened his mouth, but Tyler was before him. "Jeremy said he'd teach me how to play baseball tomorrow. Please, can I?"

"Baseball? I thought you didn't like team sports. You never let me sign you up for the teams at school." The smile was gone from her voice and she sounded puzzled, troubled even. It couldn't be any easier for her being a single mom of a boy than it was for him to fathom the whole girl thing.

Tyler was getting an anxious expression on his face, which the little boy Jeremy remembered being could totally relate to. He didn't want to make a fool of himself trying to play a game he didn't understand. Quickly, before his well-meaning mom could ruin everything, Jeremy spoke up. "We're only going to horse around for fun."

The anxious expression relaxed as the boy nodded, the damp cowlick bobbing. Besides, teaching a kid to play baseball might take his mind off his own troubles for a few hours.

Maybe she read his mind. Libby glanced from one to the other and nodded. "That'd be great. Why don't you drop the twins here and we girls will have our own fun?"

He rolled his eyes in Tyler's direction, got a goggle-eyed gagging look in return, and the male bonding had begun.

"Boys," Libby muttered as she headed back down the hallway, her hips swaying in a way that made him very glad there were differences between the sexes.

He dragged a book about telescopes from the bookshelf, but they ended up talking about baseball, anyway. "We'll have to catch a Mariner's game one day," he said, thinking how much fun it would be to take this boy to Seattle and watch him enjoying his first pro baseball game. Then a pang of guilt struck him. What was he doing? His actions encouraged blended family thinking. The last thing the eager little boy beside him needed was another adult male letting him down.

He sat there, his legs looking long atop the bug quilt, reading doggedly about telescopes until the boy dropped to sleep. Then he sat there some more, the soft, regular breathing soothing him as he stared at the open book. What was he doing here tonight? He had no business leading them on, Libby and her kids.

He was a broken man, as he'd so spectacularly proved last night. He wanted Libby in the way a man who hasn't had sex in over three years might be expected to want a woman. But how far beyond that he wanted to go, he did not know.

The lights were dim all through the orderly, polished house as he searched out Libby. He found her sitting at the kitchen table, drawing, a heap of what looked like textbooks surrounding her, some stacked in wobbling piles, some open; it was the most disorderly thing he'd ever seen her do.

He approached softly, admiring her profile. Her expression was rapt as she stared at the page in front of her, frowned, erased something and reached for one of the books.

"Working one of your garden designs?" he asked.

She glanced up with a quick smile. "I'm supposed to call it landscape design. Sounds more important, I guess." She found the book she was looking for and scribbled something on her page before addressing him again.

"This one's for a friend of mine, Brooke. She's got a beautiful oceanfront home, but she still asked me to redesign the garden leading to the front of the house."

"That's great."

"It is. She knows a lot of rich people and she's promised to talk up my work." She nibbled her lower lip, looking nervous. "So long as she likes what I do."

"She'll love it."

"I hope so. I met these three women in a bread-baking class at Clamshell Bay Bakery and Café and we got friendly."

"You mean the place with the great cinnamon buns?"

She laughed. "Everything Cleo makes is amazing, but the cinnamon buns made her famous."

"Kelly and I used to..." He could have bitten off his tongue, but Libby only looked at him, waiting for him to finish the sentence. He tried again. "We used to go there Saturday mornings before the kids were born. We'd get coffee and share a cinnamon bun."

"That's nice. You know, I have the recipe."

"People would kill for the secret to Cleo's cinnamon buns."

She laughed. "One day I'll make them for you." She tapped her pencil on the paper. "One of the other women in the class works on interiors. She remodels and decorates homes, especially old ones. She's going to pitch my services too."

"That's fantastic."

"I'm building a portfolio. If you like, I'll do your garden next. It's good practice for me. Besides, I owe you for all you've done for us."

"You've done a lot for me, too."

She angled her head toward a far book so the hair curtained her face.

He slumped against the doorframe and addressed the huge thing that was sharing air space with him and Libby. "Letting go of Kelly's clothes and things had to be done. I couldn't bring myself to get rid of her clothes and stuff. I knew she was gone and that she was never coming back. But..." He blew out an awkward breath. "I didn't want anyone else touching her things, either. Tracy offered a couple of times, then gave up. It was tough, knowing what you were doing today, and I hated like hell coming home to find everything gone. But...well...thanks."

She seemed mesmerized by the pencil she was rolling between her fingers. "I wasn't sure how you'd react."

"You want the honest truth?"

She looked up and met his gaze. "Always."

"I was so mad I wanted to howl. Now, I don't. Tracy dropped by."

Obvious surprise had Libby raising her brows. "She did?"

"Yeah. She said you told her not to, but she couldn't stay away. In a weird way, seeing her all broken up about today's activities made it easier for me."

"I'm glad." She looked at him as though checking for fever symptoms. "How do you feel now?"

"Like somebody worked me over with a baseball bat."

She nodded. Not even surprised.

What he had to say next had his stomach on fire. "I also want to apologize for last night." He sighed heavily. "For my...it was nothing to do with you...I felt..." How the hell could he explain what he'd felt when he didn't understand it himself? He wanted Libby so badly his teeth ached. And he felt guilty. And scared. God, there it was. He was scared. Scared of feeling again, loving again and getting hurt.

"It was too soon," she said to the pencil.

"No. Damn it, Libby, it's not too soon. It's been three years."

"Chronological time doesn't mean so much. You're not ready."

"Yes, I am." And he knew he was. He was eager, in fact, to take Libby in his arms and prove to her exactly how ready. He crossed to her in two strides and dropped to his knees in front of her, so he could look up into her down-turned face. He raised just his index finger and traced the shape of her cheekbone.

Her lips opened slightly on an intake of breath, and just like that, lust slammed into him like a speeding locomotive. "I am ready," he said, pulling her shoulders until, with a startled exclamation, she tumbled into his lap.

She started to gasp his name, but he stopped her mouth with his lips, kissing her for all he was worth. She sat there in his lap, letting him kiss her, but barely responding. Dimly, he realized he'd hurt her last night. Made her feel he didn't really want her. Words wouldn't express what he wanted her to know. He took her hand and placed it firmly on the one part of his body that would tell her, in no uncertain terms, exactly how much he wanted her.

He felt the little huffing gasp against his lips when her hand closed over him. Then her arms came round him and she kissed him back. Oh, the sweetness of that trim body alive with passion. Kissing him back, her tongue slipping boldly into his mouth.

Need mounting, he cupped her cheek, let his hand follow the line of her jaw and neck, the way his eyes had followed it earlier, and dipping into the jean shirt she wore to cup her breast.

"Mmm," she sighed as he rubbed and kneaded the firm round texture. Wanting to see what he was touching, wanting to put his mouth there, he slipped his hand back out and started undoing the shirt buttons.

As soon as she realized what he was doing, she pulled away, glancing at the kitchen light overhead. "Not here."

He didn't care. The kitchen floor was fine. The front lawn was fine with him. "Let's go upstairs." He tried to kiss her again, but once more she pulled away, and grasping the kitchen table, pulled herself to standing.

She pressed her hands to her cheeks. "No, I can't. What if one of the children needs me?"

"Doesn't your door have a lock?" He gave her back the same line she'd used on him last night.

"No. After Victor left, I took it off. Mia went through a stage where she liked playing with the locks. I didn't want her to get locked in by accident. None of the bathroom doors lock either. I'm sorry."

Even as frustration raged through his blood, a glimmer of

humor peeped through. "We're as bad as a couple of horny teenagers worrying about their parents coming home. I'd invite you to make out in my car, but I walked."

She made a production of rebuttoning her shirt and patting her hair back into place. "It's probably for the best, anyway." She was doing that nurse voice that ticked him off every time she used it on him.

"I'm telling you, I'm ready. I'm so ready, I'll have to have a cold shower and read all the stock market listings before I can sleep."

"Your body's ready, which, if you don't mind me saying so, isn't a real breakthrough in a man. But I don't think the rest of you is ready yet." She glanced up at him, her hazel eyes so clear and yet troubled. "You've been pretty honest with me, and I appreciate it. Jeremy, you need to know," she dropped her gaze to her hands. He noticed they were clasped tight. "I've never been with anyone but Victor. You're not the only one who's got some demons here." She looked up again and he felt she'd forced herself to meet his gaze. "Let's be careful, okay?"

He was shocked at her admission. Then flattered at the implication. But she was right. He had no business messing with this woman until he knew exactly what he was after.

"Whatever is going on here, I don't think it's casual."

She chuckled softly. The sound surprising him. "No," she said. "Sometimes I wish it was." She picked up his left hand and tapped the gold wedding ring he still wore. "Goodnight, Jeremy."

FOURTEEN

The maroon Volvo pulled into her drive on Sunday morning around eleven. She hadn't been sure, after last night, whether Jeremy would come, and if it was only the two of them involved, she doubted he would have made the trip. But he'd promised Tyler they'd practice baseball and, for that reason alone, she'd expected him to show.

He looked tired, with tiny crinkle lines fanning from his eyes. She'd expected that, too.

"Hi," she said to the trio coming up her drive.

"Can we do makeovers?" the girls wanted to know.

"Is all your homework done for school tomorrow?"

Twin eye rolls greeted her. "Yes."

Suddenly she remembered the first day they'd arrived at her house, bristling with bad attitudes. How had they become so dear to her in such a short time? She smiled at the pair of them. "Okay, then. Makeovers it is."

She gave her attention to their father, but he was having trouble maintaining eye contact with her. She wondered if he'd slept at all in his redecorated room. "Are you okay?"

"Yeah."

Jeremy had the box of home handyman stuff he'd bought her for her birthday, which he set on the front porch. She was so used to seeing him in business clothes that she took a moment to enjoy the sight of him in jeans and a gray T-shirt with a navy hoodie over top. He wore a ball cap and perched on top of the box of household fix-it stuff were two leather baseball gloves and a grubby-looking ball.

Tyler came bounding to the door, his excitement beaming out of him. "Hey, buddy," Jeremy said.

He took in the gloves and ball at a glance. "Where's the bat?"

"We're going to start with throwing and catching. The bat's next time."

"Okay."

"Would you like some coffee?" Libby asked. The poor man looked as though he could use some.

She wished she hadn't offered when she saw Tyler's face fall. She realized with a pang of sadness how much this meant to him to have an adult male take an interest in him.

Fortunately, Jeremy saw it too. Or maybe he didn't want to chat with her over coffee. He said, "Maybe later. You ready, Tyler?"

Silly question. He'd been ready when he woke her at seven, asking if Jeremy was here yet. He wore his oldest jeans and a sweatshirt with the name of his school on the front. "I forgot something," he said and pounded back upstairs, emerging in less than a minute with his own ball cap on his head.

"Have fun," she called, as they sauntered down the drive.

They looked good together. Almost as though they fit.

"Will you be back for lunch?" she yelled.

"Naah. We'll probably grab something out."

"Okay."

Please let it go well, she pleaded silently as she went to gather the three girls.

She let them have free rein with her nail polish drawer and each of them had a manicure. Mia, who'd never had polish on her tiny nails before was beside herself with excitement.

"Dad said you and Auntie Tracy decorated his room," Olivia said while she was having bright red polish painted on her nails.

"That's right," Libby answered, doing her best to keep the brush strokes straight on the small nail. Olivia and Grace had tiny, delicate hands. She wondered whether they'd inherited those from their mother. "Are you okay with that?"

"I guess."

"Dad said a swear word when he went in there last night. I heard him," Grace said. "But this morning, when he showed us the room, he said he likes it."

"Do you like it?" How did they feel about having all their mother's things moved?

"It's okay."

"You know, we saved all of your mother's things. They're stored at your Auntie Tracy's house. Any time you want to see them, they're there."

"Okay," Grace said.

Libby didn't sense hostility at her actions. She believed the girls had accepted their mother's death. The loss would always be there and probably would always hurt, but they were healing —a lot more easily than their dad.

After manicures, they moved to lipstick and hair. It was fun taking the time to play with all the girlie stuff. After that they washed up and ate lunch. "I wonder how the boys are doing," she said.

"Dad loves baseball. He made us go on a team last year but we hated it so we quit. He made us practice all the time. Tyler's going to be like totally bored."

But, when the men rolled in around three, it was clear that Tyler was anything but bored. His eyes were vivid with excitement. "Guess what, Mom," he said, bounding into the kitchen. "I'm a natural. Jeremy said so."

"That's grea—"

"And we had jumbo hot dogs and I had two refills of Coke and next time Jeremy says we're going to practice hitting. With the bat. Can we do that tomorrow?"

"I have to work tomorrow. But we'll do it again soon."

"Sweet."

She and the girls were making sugar cookies. The table was littered with scraps of dough and they were decorating cookies in weird and wonderful ways she'd never thought of.

"If you wash up, you can help decorate cookies, Tyler," she told him.

Jeremy said, "Or you can help me. I'm doing some home handyman chores."

She glanced up in surprise. "Today?"

"Sure. Why not?"

"I can help with chores," Tyler said, ultra cool. As though he handled a chain saw every day of his life. She wanted to hug him but was smart enough not to.

Jeremy fetched the box from the front porch and soon he and his helper were replacing the hinge on her kitchen cabinet. "You know," she said, "this seems like a very sexist division of labor."

Jeremy sent her a glance from his tired, blue-gray eyes and halted in the middle of screwing in the new hinge. "Girls, do you want to help with some handyman stuff or decorate cookies."

The twins rolled their eyes in identical motions. "Cookies."

"Cookie," Mia parroted.

"Tyler? Do you want to do handyman stuff or decorate cookies?"

"Handyman stuff," there was an unspoken but implied "like, duh!"

Jeremy managed to stow most of his smirk. "If you ask me, some things are hardwired."

"Well, every man should learn how to cook," she stated.

"And every woman should learn some basic home repair and auto maintenance."

She nodded. "Absolutely. But not today."

Later, when he was upstairs redoing the grout in the kids' bathroom and Tyler was sanding one of the cracks they'd patched, she had a chance to get Jeremy alone.

She liked the way he looked, leaned over the bathtub, his body stretched out, his arm muscles defined.

"Thank you," she said.

He glanced up at her. "For what?"

"For today. With Tyler."

"Don't thank me. He's a great kid. I had fun."

She perched on the closed lid of the toilet. "How are you? After yesterday."

He turned back to his work. He smelled like healthy working man, a little warm and sweaty. "Okay."

"How did you sleep?"

"Like shit."

What could she say? He kept working. She felt dismissed.

"Well, I'll let you get back to it."

She'd walked all the way out of the bathroom when he stopped her. "Libby?"

"Yes?"

He held her gaze, looking sad and tired. "I'm working on it."

"Good," she said softly.

"Hey."

She turned to see him scramble up off the bathtub and wipe his hands on his jeans. He'd been doing that a lot so they were getting pretty disgusting.

"Come back in here a minute."

She did, feeling her stomach flip. Once she was inside, he

shut the bathroom door on them, making the space seem too small all of a sudden.

He appeared frustrated and confused as he cupped her face in gritty hands. He kissed her as though he couldn't help himself. She responded for the same reason.

"If it was only sex, this would be a lot easier," he said.

"I know."

"I feel something for you. I don't know what it is, but there's too much at risk to do anything stupid." His hands tangled in her hair and he kissed her again, taking his sweet time.

Oh, she thought, maybe it could be just sex. If they were careful and discreet, why not?

Except that it was already too late. She had no idea either what she felt for Jeremy, but it was more than lust, though that was a huge ingredient in the confusing mix. It was more than friendship, though he was her friend. It couldn't be love. Not yet, so that left her as confused and frustrated as the man currently nibbling at her earlobe and running his hands over her body.

How much longer did he think he could wait?

That was the question that was taking up a lot of Jeremy's mental bandwidth. Libby was sweet and sexy. A terrific mother. And she was good for him. The first few days after Libby and Tracy had redone his bedroom were tough. He couldn't sleep.

It was like a mini-version of the way he'd felt after Kelly died. But he'd come through it. And he was honest enough to admit that he felt as though a heavy burden had been lifted.

He'd pushed the bed back to its accustomed place because he hated the way those busy women had placed his furniture, but other than that, he'd left everything as they'd arranged it.

He was even thinking about painting the walls, something they hadn't had time to do.

Already his things were creeping over into Kelly's side of the closet and he had to admit that it was easier to find stuff.

He glanced at the clock, grateful it was a squash day and he could exercise away some of his sexual frustration. He grabbed his squash racquet and bag.

They hadn't had their date, he and Libby. After all that had happened, he couldn't imagine a dinner somewhere and then dropping her off at her home. They'd gone too far for a regular first date.

The question of Libby bothered him all morning, along with a question Grace had asked him over breakfast.

The tiny rubber ball bounced and ricocheted round the enclosed squash court like the idea that had taken root in his mind.

He spiked the ball hard, heard the rubber squeak, protesting against the wall and scud off into that sweet, unreachable corner. Raoul, his opponent, lunged and grunted as the ball eluded him.

"Good shot, buddy."

He continued punishing the ball, driving relentlessly until both he and Raoul were sweat-soaked and gasping.

"Feel better?" Raoul asked him after they'd showered and were walking out of the club together.

"You know, I do," he said, limping away to his car.

"Why are you limping?" Libby asked as he hobbled into her hallway later that afternoon, inhaling the scent of warm spices. "Are you hurt?"

"Nah. I pulled a muscle playing squash."

"A hamstring?" she was all eager concern. "I could rub it for you."

"A groin."

"Oh." Her face bloomed with delicate color, and the uninjured part of his groin perked up at her suggestion. She glanced at him, caught the grin he didn't even try to hide and rolled her eyes at him. "Try ice."

He followed her into the kitchen and helped himself to a speckled brown cookie right off the cooling rack and sighed with pleasure as he bit into the crunchy spice cookie. That woman could cook. And always from scratch. He, who'd only recently mastered the secrets of cake in the box, could appreciate the fine art of real baking.

Yep. There were a lot of things he could appreciate about Libby.

And lots of things he could only appreciate if she were naked. It had been two weeks since the disastrous weekend of her birthday, and he hadn't stopped thinking about her in very non-daycare provider terms.

Their little chats when he dropped off and picked up the girls were charged with unspoken messages. Their glances passionate. He must be crazy to try and ignore the obvious.

He wanted that woman in the worst way, and unless he was way more out of touch than he believed, she wanted him, too.

She'd put the kitchen island between them, and was trying very hard to appear unflustered by their conversational exchange about his groin.

"Why don't you call the girls?" she asked. "They're downstairs."

"Not yet. I want to talk to you."

Her forehead creased with anxiety. "They're not in trouble again at school, are they?"

"It's not about the girls. It's about us."

"Oh." She scrubbed at cookie pans that already gleamed.

How to start? How to get out what he wanted to say? "This arrangement. It's not working."

The pans clattered into the sink and her head sprang up. "But the girls are happy here. Aren't they?"

"They love you."

Her face lit up then, as pink and iridescent as a perfect rose. "I love them, too." Pleasure and relief coursed through her voice. She was so pretty, with her lips parted and eager, that he longed to kiss her.

"You know what Grace asked me this morning?"

"What?"

"She asked me if I was going to marry you."

The color faded from her cheeks. "Well, kids think everything's easier than it is."

She slammed the shiny cookie pans into the dish drainer, then sprinkled baking soda in the sinks and started scrubbing.

He grabbed her wrist in the sink to still the frantic scrubbing. "I've been thinking about it all day. It makes sense. We're friends, we love each other's kids, they get on great. And there's obviously a powerful physical attraction here. Why don't you? Marry me."

Even as he felt a jolt of shock vibrate through his bones at his own words, she jerked away, leaning against the island and glaring at him.

"That's not funny."

"It's not supposed to be." His lungs felt like collapsed balloons. He'd gone straight for the blended family, after trying to avoid even thinking about blending their families, doing everything he could to prevent Libby and her kids from getting ideas about him, he'd pulled a childhood TV happily-forever-after scenario out of his pocket and handed it to Libby. And, surprisingly, it didn't seem so terrible now it was out in the open. In fact, them getting married made a lot of sense. Libby could keep her lifestyle, her kids could stay in the same school. And Olivia and Grace would have Libby around permanently.

And, he'd finally get Libby in bed.

There were a lot of positives here.

Libby didn't seem to be seeing it quite his way. In fact, she looked like somebody died. "Why are you doing this to me?" she whispered, her eyes over bright.

"It could work, Libby. You're a terrific person." He scoffed another gingersnap. "You make excellent cookies, and the twins love you."

"What about you, Jeremy. Do you love me?"

She had him there. He wasn't sure what he felt about Libby, where lust left off and love began. But she was a woman receiving a marriage proposal, and she deserved certain things. "I think I'm falling in love with you." It caught a little in the back of his throat, like a stray speck of cinnamon, but he got the words out.

For a long moment she stood there staring at him, a slow flush mounting her cheeks.

"No. You're not. You're still in love with Kelly. I can't ever compete with that."

FIFTEEN

Libby worked in the garden feverishly, but she couldn't find the peace she sought. All she saw was Jeremy's stricken face when she'd turned him down.

Marriage? Was he out of his mind? She'd only been divorced a few months.

Daffodils were starting to bloom, the earth becoming workable enough to get a head start on the weeding and think about the new growing season.

He'd said he was falling in love with her. Convenient. What if he stopped falling before he got there?

She wasn't any clearer about her feelings than Jeremy was. There was so much baggage between them they could open a luggage store. Victor was still AWOL. She and the kids hadn't received so much as a postcard. More than the money, she wanted some kind of closure. And as for Jeremy, he was trying so hard to make everything right, for the twins, for her and Tyler and Mia.

And yet, there was undeniably something good happening. It hovered in the air like an early hint of spring when they said good morning. It teased them with longing when they said good night and their eyes met over the noisy confusion of the four kids all talking at once in the entrance hall.

Was that something love?

Or was it loneliness? Need. Sexual desire rising up like the new shoots in her garden.

She plopped down on the damp earth, the smell of rich dirt and growing things all around her. Idly, she watched a disturbed worm upend itself and burrow back down.

Her anger had finally dissipated and she realized his proposal hadn't been the clumsy act of charity she'd first thought. It wasn't a sincere proposal from the bottom of his heart, either. His eyes had registered shock when he'd spouted out the words. No. He hadn't planned to ask her to marry him. It had come from somewhere deeper inside himself.

Maybe he did love her. She didn't know, and neither did Jeremy. She was no surer of her own feelings. The only thing she knew for certain was that she wouldn't make another mistake.

The trouble was that she definitely had feelings for him. A lot of them purely carnal. The whole sex thing shimmered and teased, promising her a lush paradise in the middle of her desert of a love life. What if it turned out to be a mirage?

If only they loved each other, marriage would be the perfect answer. Still, even if Jeremy didn't love her, he'd become her closest friend. And she'd hurt him.

She was going to have to apologize.

***

"Is something wrong with your phone, Mom?" asked Tyler, hunched on the floor sorting his new collection of comic books, something else he and Jeremy had discovered they both liked.

"No."

"Then why do you keep picking up your phone and putting it down?"

A glib answer came to mind, but she suppressed it. She tried to be truthful with her kids, believing she was modeling good behavior. "I have to apologize to Jeremy. I said something that hurt his feelings. But I'm having a hard time working up the nerve."

Her son nodded wisely. "That's like when my teacher made me tell Josh I was sorry for making his lip bleed. He was real mad. I thought he might hit me. But after I said sorry, it was okay. And I felt better."

"You made Josh's lip bleed?" her voice started to rise.

"Only by accident. Not on purpose."

"Oh my gosh. I should call his mother. Why didn't you tell me?"

Her son put on an expression she'd seen on Jeremy's face a hundred times. "It's a guy thing, Mom. Forget it."

Since Jeremy had taken an interest in Tyler's baseball career, there was a whole new attitude coming from her son. One she didn't always approve of. "And how did this 'guy thing' exactly happen?"

"I was showing Josh how to steal a base by sliding in on your stomach—'cept he hit a rock."

"A rock? Your school field is grass."

"The big kids were using it. So we made our own diamond."

"And the rock?"

"Was third base."

"I see."

"That's why the teacher made me say sorry. Then I didn't feel so bad. You should phone Jeremy, Mom. You'll feel better."

She hugged him to her. "Sometimes you're pretty smart." She turned back to the phone and hit Jeremy's number, restraining herself from ending the call before it went through. The inspirational quote for March showed a field of daffodils and the words: *We must let go of the life we have planned, so as to accept the one that is waiting for us.*

Pretty smart, Joseph Campbell.

After an eternity of ringing, while she cleared her throat and swallowed about six times, voicemail told her Jeremy wasn't available and to leave a message.

How do you apologize to voicemail? she wondered helplessly as the silence stretched. "Jeremy, it's Libby," she spat out at last. "I wanted to, um, apologize for earlier. I think I was abrupt. You surprised me." Another pause. She imagined him playing her message, listening to her make a total fool of herself. "Maybe we can talk tomorrow. Maybe you'd like to stay for dinner?"

She pictured him, a dark angry presence, too angry and hurt to take her call. Why wouldn't he at least let her tell him in person how sorry she was? "I'm not sure what we're having. I was thinking maybe pot roast..." now she was babbling, making things even worse. "With mashed potatoes. Maybe green beans." Another pause. "I'm sorry, Jeremy. And thank you."

Her hands trembled slightly as she ended the call.

"Well, Mom, do you feel better?" Tyler's imitation-adult voice brought a smile to her lips.

"Yep. I feel better. Thanks for the good advice."

He swelled with pride before her eyes, picking up his comics and putting them away before she got around to reminding him to get ready for bed.

The man who dropped the twins off the next morning was the same man she'd imagined standing by the phone refusing to speak to her the night before. He wouldn't meet her gaze. Spoke curtly and didn't even set foot in her house.

"Did you get my message?" she finally asked him, knowing damn well he had.

"Yes." He said to the doorframe.

"Can you come for dinner?"

"I'm not sure, I'll let you know." Then he was gone.

"What's the matter with Daddy?" Grace asked.

Modeling honesty was hard work. "He's mad at me."

"Wow. He never gets that mad at us." Well, that was comforting.

All day she waited for his call.

She received a curt message from him at three o'clock. He'd known she would be picking the kids up from school then and wouldn't be home. Her heart sank. He wouldn't even talk to her. Surprise widened her eyes when she finished listening to the message and she had to rewind and listen to it again, to be sure she'd heard right.

He'd accepted her invitation. And a lovely evening they were going to have with him glowering, refusing even to glance her way. She'd be the one getting gastric trouble next.

Even though she felt gloomy and a little nervous, or maybe because of it, she got Tyler and the twins to help her drag the kitchen table into the dining room and laid the table with linen.

The girls picked daffodils and irises from the garden and made a centerpiece for the table. Tyler sliced the bread, Mia globbed butter on it. And Libby put her heart and soul into a pot roast and salad that said, "I'm sorry."

He arrived punctually at five thirty. After dithering all afternoon about what to wear, Libby opted for something casual. Black jeans and a green cashmere sweater. She didn't want him to re-pitch his proposal. She wanted to get back to the warm and promising friendship they'd had.

Now, as she walked to the door, she wished she'd at least put on a skirt. Not that it mattered. He wouldn't be looking at her anyway.

She opened the door and her eyes widened. He was looking straight at her, big and formidable, the light of war in his eyes. He crossed the threshold. "Where are the kids?"

"In the kitchen."

Before she could move, he grabbed her face between his hands and kissed her. Not tenderly at all, like she was used to, but roughly. If frustration had a flavor, she tasted it on his lips and tongue.

The door was still open. Anyone could walk by. As Jeremy showed no signs of letting go of her, she relaxed into his kiss, letting herself enjoy the moment and the strange excitement of his anger rechanneled into passion.

"We can't go on like this," he said, when he finally lifted his head.

Her heart was pounding and she was having trouble drawing breath. To diffuse the potent emotions swirling around them, she tried for a little light humor. "No, we can't." She reached past him and shut the door. "The neighbors will get ideas."

But he refused to be sidetracked. "I can't stop thinking about you."

"Really?" The thought of the CEO of her bank mooning over her was the sweetest balm to her ego.

He cracked a small smile. "Today, in our executive meeting, I called Melanie Kwan, our marketing director, Libby. I've known the woman for six years."

"You did? Cool."

"Melanie didn't think so."

Jeremy flattering her was infinitely better than Jeremy mad at her. Maybe they could get their friendship back, after all. "Anything else?" She let her fingers trail through his dark hair, intimately aware of the weight and warmth of his hands resting lightly on her hip bones.

"Well, since you're fishing for compliments, let's see...Oh, yeah...I dreamed about you last night."

"You did?"

"Uh-huh." He whispered the words against her lips. "It was a very erotic dream."

Her eyes drifted shut and her lips parted as she waited for him to kiss her again, deep and hard. Instead, she felt his lips trail up her cheek to nibble on her earlobe, then run his tongue round the circumference of her ear before whispering, "I have an idea."

She could hardly concentrate on the words for the delicious shivers running through her body as his warm breath teased the wet flesh. "What?"

"Let's make my dream a reality."

"But where." She stopped and started again. "I mean..."

"I was an idiot. I tried to rush you. I'm sorry."

"No. I'm sorry. It was lovely of you to propose and I was rude and ungracious."

"I don't think either of us can think straight until we get some time alone. I've booked us a cottage for next weekend. For a very dirty weekend."

"You have?" Excitement and nerves warred within her. "What about the children?"

He grinned at her. "They're not coming."

"That's not what I meant."

"You are so predictable. We're not going far. It's a cottage at the edge of Clamshell Bay. A twenty-minute drive from here at the most."

"Oh. A cottage."

"Look. I'd love to take you to New York or Paris and one day maybe I will. But I know you won't go far from your kids. This way, you can relax. If we're needed, we can be back in no time."

"But I don't ever leave my children." Her brain was reeling thinking of how much she wanted to go, and how nervous she was to have anyone else looking after her babies.

"I've booked a babysitting agency that was recommended by a good friend. They'll send someone over for you to interview. And Tracy said she'd check in on the kids."

"Tracy? You told Tracy?"

"Sure. You know what she said?"

"I can't imagine."

"She said it's about time. She thinks it's a great idea."

"But, but..." She wished he'd get back a few feet so she could think. "I'm not marrying you."

"So, you said. Maybe a weekend with me will change your mind."

"Egotist." She was half laughing and totally tempted.

He looked amused and also happier than she'd seen him in a while. "What this relationship needs is some good, healthy sex. No strings attached." He'd come up with the perfect way for them to explore the attraction between them without any obligations. On either side, she realized grimly. It had been a long time since she'd had sex. And much longer since she'd thought of it as "good" or "healthy".

"What if it...ah...doesn't work out?"

His mouth opened, and she waited for a smart answer, but instead said, "Then we'll know. And we can go back to being friends."

Friends. The word had a hollow ring. But then, Jeremy, as a long-term romantic prospect, didn't look so good, either. This could be a big step in the healing process for both of them. It would put another man between her and her bitter memories of Victor. And it would show Jeremy that he was ready to start dating again. Swallowing the quiver of apprehension, she nodded. "I agree. Provided I approve of the sitter, you've got yourself a deal. One weekend away. No strings attached."

"I'll be counting the hours till next Friday."

"Come on in the kitchen. The kids will wonder what we're doing out here."

"They're smarter than you think. Tyler asked if I'm your boyfriend."

Her mouth fell open. "Tyler? He talked to you instead of me? What did you say?"

"I said I'm working on it."

"Oh...Was he upset?"

"Seemed happy about it."

"Huh."

They entered the kitchen, Libby with her cheeks feeling undeniably warm.

"Hi, kids," Jeremy said. Hugging all three girls who'd come running at once, and making a point of leaning over to Tyler, who stood a pace or two back, to ruffle his hair.

What a nice family they made, Libby thought as she dished up dinner. Olivia proudly carried the salad she'd helped make into the dining room, followed by Grace with the fruit punch, Tyler with the bread steaming in its basket, and Mia, who refused to be left out, wobbling behind, her eyes glued to a tottering jug of salad dressing with fierce concentration.

It wasn't the first dinner they'd eaten together at her place, her family and the O'Tooles. But it was without doubt one she would always remember.

It was the way Jeremy looked at her. Every glance held a secret, taunting message. Even though the conversation at the table was general, and mainly child-centered, there was a second conversation going on. It was unspoken. As subtle as the accidental-on-purpose brushing of his fingers against hers when he asked Libby to pass him the salad. As subtle as an innuendo.

"Delicious," he pronounced, and the way he rolled his tongue over the word had Libby suspecting he wasn't talking about her food at all. When she peeped up at him, he winked, and she swallowed so hard she choked.

"You okay, Mom?"

"Just choked on a crumb," she gasped, gulping fruit punch. But an ocean of fruit punch wouldn't be enough to quench the desire the man across from her had kindled.

He didn't try to play footsie with her, or any other obvious action that she could have shut down with a sharp kick. He was so subtle, she wondered if she was imagining things, but when she glanced at him, she was convinced he was deliberately teasing her.

Resolutely, she kept her gaze on the children or her plate. That worked for about five minutes until Jeremy's voice asked her, oh, so politely, if she'd pass the bread.

"Grace, pass your father the bread. You're closer," she retaliated, and got nothing but a sly grin for her pains. He knew exactly what he was doing to her, and he was enjoying every minute.

Come to think of it, so was she.

She didn't even get a kiss when he left. Not that it would have been appropriate in front of the children. All she got was a slow, teasing look as he headed out the door. "Thanks for a terrific dinner. We'll have to do it again sometime, when we have more time." *Like an entire weekend*, his eyes telegraphed.

When her children were in bed, she toyed with her garden design for a while, but it was hopeless. She could hardly hold a pencil straight she was so keyed up. She'd agreed to a weekend of sex with a man she'd already decided she wouldn't marry.

A weekend spent with a man not her husband or even officially her boyfriend might not shock many people, but it shocked Libby. It was a nice change to think of herself as a woman a man desired enough to spirit her away for an entire weekend. It was better than dumped ex-wife, struggling single mom, and the other epithets she could come up with.

She abandoned her design work and ran lightly up the stairs to her bedroom. In the back of her closet was a cream and gold box. In it nestled a nightgown she'd bought last year, after reading an article online titled *How to Rekindle the Fire in Your Marriage*, or something along those lines.

She'd discovered that Victor had been kindling a lot of fires outside his marriage before she ever put the nightgown to the test. It had sat in the back of her closet, all but forgotten—kind of like her sex drive. Quickly she stripped and slipped the gown over her head. Just the feel of the silk shimmering against her flesh made her feel voluptuous and sexy. It wasn't all that revealing, being full length with a silk and lace bodice that hinted at cleavage rather than displaying it.

Feeling younger than she had in years, Libby padded across the carpet into the bathroom where she could see herself in the full-length mirror and flipped on the light.

Her first flush of excitement died when she studied her reflection more critically. It seemed like her breasts had slipped down about half an inch since she bought the gown. And that was definitely a hint of tummy bulge glaring at her where the light hit the silk.

With a sinking heart she turned around and craned her head over her shoulder for a back view. To her critical eye it looked like more than her breasts had sagged.

Maybe she should call the whole thing off.

And then she thought about the way Jeremy gazed at her, the way he made her feel. Anyway, he couldn't reject her. She'd already rejected him. So she could just relax and have a good time.

Just relax.

Ten days. She had ten days to prepare. How fit, toned and perked could one woman get in ten measly days, without major surgery?

She didn't have a moment to lose.

Carefully replacing the silk nightgown in the rustling tissue, she dug out an old pair of sweatpants and a T-shirt, crept back downstairs and found a YouTube HIIT workout that promised a full-body workout in thirty minutes.

At the end of fifteen minutes she wanted to kill the perky hard-body singing the praises of the burpee while every muscle in her body trembled and sweat trickled into her eyes.

She tasted carpet fibers when she collapsed, gasping, on her twelfth push-up. Only the vision of Jeremy seeing her in that gown ('cause no way in hell he'd ever see her naked) kept her going.

"Don't forget to stretch, and make sure you sign up to my channel," the woman reminded her, looking ready to run a marathon or do another hundred burpees for fun.

She rolled off the floor at last and struggled to the kitchen to drink a gallon or so of water.

Before dragging herself up to bed she put a tick mark on the wall calendar. She planned to have a tick mark on every square of the calendar by the time next weekend rolled around.

Jeremy couldn't stop thinking about next weekend. It was kind of embarrassing at his age. But he no sooner had to glimpse Libby, think about her, or even dream about her than he was off in erotic fantasy.

He'd dreamed about her again last night. If his dreams had ratings, he wouldn't be old enough to watch this one. He savored the wispy fragments of the dream as he shaved, wondered if the real Libby would ever do that with her mouth.

"Daddy, we're out of Dino-puffs." Olivia's imperative tones coming from downstairs swept away the last of his dream.

"Eat the granola. It's healthy."

"I only like Dino-puffs."

"All right. I'll be down in a minute." He wiped his face, stepped into the bedroom and put a note on his phone adding "Dino-puffs" to his shopping list.

So much for dreams.

Soon to be dreams no more, he reminded himself. He was still amazed Libby had agreed so easily to spending the weekend with him. It was Monday. Monday of the week that would lead to Friday.

He whistled while he hauled the last loaf of frozen bread out of the freezer and made toast, in such a good mood he pretended he didn't complain that the radio wasn't playing his morning news but was tuned to the local music station the girls loved. He even found himself laughing when the girls jumped up from the table in unison, grabbed air mics and sang along with a Korean girl group.

The radio announcer voiced over the last bars of the song with some smarmy hype and he stopped listening, scanning the newspaper business section while he chomped his own toast.

A twin shriek had him dropping the paper to watch as the girls fell over each other lunging for their phones.

"I got through," Grace all but screamed.

"AAAH! Put it on speaker," Olivia yelled. "Let me listen!"

They were both jumping up and down like identical demented pogo sticks.

"What the...

"SHHH!" the pogo sticks hissed in unison.

"I can't stand it. Do you think we were the sixth caller?" Olivia asked.

"I don't know. We're on hold. But we got through."

"I can't stand it. My fingers aren't fast enough."

He watched the eager flush change to abject disappointment. Olivia pulled away and Grace said, "Okay. Thanks anyway."

"We were sooo close. Eighth. He said we were eighth."

"What is going on?"

"Shhh!" Olivia said again, and dashed to the radio to turn the volume up.

"Congratulations!" The DJ boomed across his kitchen. "You're the sixth caller."

Some girl, who could have been either of his daughters, screamed. "I can't believe it! You're kidding!"

"No, I'm not," the DJ promised her, and she screamed again.

"You and your three best friends will be going to see Pretty Girl in concert when the Pretty World tour hits Seattle next month."

"I can't believe we were so close," Grace wailed.

"And that's not all. Our very special prize package includes a backstage visit with the girls and an autographed CD and a prize pack."

More screaming from the radio. More groaning from the twins. Jeremy was getting a bad feeling in the pit of his stomach and his good mood was ebbing. "What was that all about?"

"The Pretty Girl concert. You can win tickets from the radio," Olivia informed him.

"I figured that part out. The bit I don't get is what you two would do with tickets." He kept his voice carefully neutral.

A desperately anxious, pleading expression suffused both faces. "Please, Daddy. Please, can we go? If we win the tickets, it won't cost a thing."

"You girls are ten. Do you seriously think I'd let you go to a concert at ten years old?"

"But, Daddy, it's the Pretty Girls."

"Maybe when they grow up to be the Pretty Women, you'll be old enough to go. Finish your breakfast or we'll be late."

"Macy's mom is letting her go."

Deliberately, he switched the radio back to his news station. Although he could have saved himself the effort. The world could have ended, and he wouldn't have heard a thing over the commotion in the kitchen. Cajoling turned to pleading, turned to shouting, until he finally snapped, "Not one more word. Go upstairs and brush your teeth."

"I bet mom would have let us go," Olivia sobbed as she slammed out of the kitchen.

SIXTEEN

"Japonica, I think," Libby mused aloud, sketching a low bush into her design.

"Apple tree," Mia murmured gravely, a beat behind her mother, her chubby fingers busy with a green crayon, a look of utter absorption on her face.

It had been a hell of a week. The twins were snarly and miserable because they couldn't see Pretty Girl in concert. Tyler was snarly and miserable because he was missing his weekend baseball clinic with Jeremy—even though Jeremy had come home from work early on Wednesday so he and Tyler could fit in their practice.

The weather all week had been as miserable as the kids. Rainy and dreary.

Only Mia remained sunny, but at three she hadn't got the hang of laying on a guilt trip yet. A couple of years and she'd be right up there.

Plus, this landscape design thing was starting to build. She'd been up until midnight almost every night this week working on designs for Brooke Mattson's oceanfront home and a client of Megan had asked for a quote and hired her on the spot.

All of which was good, since it took her mind off the big weekend. The sun had suddenly arrived, which seemed like a good omen, but now there were hours to go and she was as nervous as she'd ever been.

Jeremy was a nice man she'd known for months. It was a weekend away to relax.

She almost laughed aloud. Relax? Oh, yeah. That was going to happen.

Maybe she should call it off now before anyone got hurt.

Or rejected.

Or had to bare their sore ass in front of a stranger. She'd worked out every day and had the aching muscles to prove it, but she hadn't seen any change in her body yet.

She gave up and explained to Mia once again that nice Mrs. Lowenthal, whom the kids had already met and liked, was coming to stay with her. Mia hadn't been too sure about the arrangement until she'd found out that the twins were staying over too. This put the weekend in the category of major treat for her.

Libby was all packed. She was shaved, plucked, exfoliated and mani and pedi'd.

She was as ready as she'd ever be.

It was normal to be nervous taking on a new lover, she reassured herself. Once she got that first time out of the way, she'd be fine.

Mrs. Lowenthal arrived before the kids got home from school and they all shared a snack together and got to know each other. Then Jeremy arrived and gave everybody a hearty hello. He barely looked at Libby, but when he did, she felt breathless. The gleam in his eyes was unmistakable carnal.

No, she thought, relaxed would not describe how she felt.

"How come we can't come with you?" Tyler asked in his best whiny tone.

"Shut up, dork," Grace said.

Instead of chastising her, Jeremy ignored the interruption and spoke to Tyler. "Because it would be boring for you guys. We're looking at gardens to give your mom some ideas for her work." He flicked a glance at his watch. "And we should go now, so we can get some good hours in before dark."

Tyler stared at Jeremy as though he was completely letting down the guy team. "Gardens? A whole weekend of gardens?"

Mrs. Lowenthal rose with tactful timing. "Have a wonderful time. We're going to be fine. I've got games and books and movies and the older girls are going to help me take care of the little one, aren't you, girls?" They nodded. "And Tyler, as the man of the house, will have a great deal of responsibility."

Tyler still looked belligerent, but she could see his chest swell with the implied, if sexist, compliment. Yes, she thought, Mrs. Lowenthal was going to be fine.

Jeremy was wearing a fine wool shirt, open at the neck, and jeans she hadn't seen before. She wondered if they were new. After they'd kissed everybody, and got into his car, she said, "I can't believe you lied to those children. Gardens indeed."

He pulled smoothly out of the cul-de-sac and headed for I-5. "I did not lie. I have a surprise for you."

He wouldn't say any more and she decided to sit back and enjoy the spring sunshine in the Pacific Northwest—and the fact that she had Jeremy all to herself.

They headed north and she realized she didn't even know where they were going. Nor did she care. They had plenty to talk about with the kids and her business ideas. One thing about Jeremy, he was an excellent sounding board she'd found. He listened to her and his advice was always sensible. "You know," she said, turning her head to look at him, "You are my favorite banker."

He lifted her hand from the seat between them and pressed it to his lips. "And you are my favorite client."

"Delinquent payments and all?" She was making her

payments, now that the grace period was up, and managing to scrape by. But she still had middle-of-the-night terrors when she wondered if she was going to make it.

They left the highway and meandered through farmland. It wasn't until she saw the first sign that she figured out where they were going. She laughed. "The Skagit Valley Tulip Festival?"

"Gardens," he said smugly. "I promised you gardens."

Soon they saw them. Fields and fields of tulips. Rainbows of tulips in every color. "Do you know, I've never been here before?" How odd. It wasn't far from home and she, who loved flowers, had never made the trip.

"I'm glad," he said. "I want everything this weekend to be different."

Her stomach lurched. Everything?

He followed the signs and parked in a slightly muddy lot and they got out of the car.

Then he reached for her hand and the warmth that both soothed and excited her was in his gaze. He brushed her lips in a quick kiss and walked her into the rainbow.

She read all the signs, and wandered every path. She couldn't believe the colors. It was almost magical.

He wanted to buy her a bunch of tulips on their way out and she couldn't decide between the cheerful yellow, soft pink, brilliant purple or creamy white. So he bought her a bunch of each. And then they headed back toward Clamshell Bay.

"I thought we'd get settled in the cottage and then have dinner."

"Fine."

The light was fading as they pulled down the long drive that led to the secluded cottage. "Oh, my," she said when she saw it. When she'd heard "cottage" she'd expected something small and rustic, but this was anything but. Clearly architect-designed to fit its surroundings, the property perched on a rocky outcrop overlooking the lapping ocean. Beside it was a walk-on beach she'd never seen before and she lived in Clamshell Bay.

"A local Realtor rents it on behalf of the owner," he told her as he punched a code into the lock and then opened the door. She walked in, feeling as though she were walking into a dream. The cottage was built around the views, and every room seemed to have an ocean view.

"I never even knew this was here."

"Good. I wanted to surprise you."

She stepped into the main living area, drawn to the floor to ceiling windows and the restless sea beyond. "You did."

He came up beside her and gripped her hand over the colorful riot of tulips. "Fresh start."

She knew he was looking at her, but felt too shy to return his gaze. "Fresh start," she agreed.

"Why don't I bring in the bags while you look around?"

"Fine."

The main room was furnished in modern luxury with comfortable seating and tables that looked like they were made of driftwood and no doubt cost a fortune. A gas fireplace flared to life at the flick of a switch. The kitchen was high-end and seemed fully equipped, not that she planned to do a lot of cooking. She peeped into the master bedroom and noted the beautiful bed linens and more floor to ceiling views.

When Jeremy came in with the bags, he found her back in the kitchen, gazing at the wine fridge.

"Would you like a glass of wine?" Jeremy asked. "The Realtor said she'd stock the kitchen with a few things, but I made a dinner reservation in town for eight."

It was six thirty now. "Yes, please." At least it would give them something to do before dinner.

She found a vase for the tulips and fussed around, finding the perfect spot for them in the living room.

Jeremy came in with two glasses of wine and a plate of

cheese and crackers. She caught him glancing at her and took a big gulp of wine. "Are you as nervous as I am?" she finally asked.

"I don't think so," he said, with a shred of humor.

"I'm a wreck."

"Don't be."

She gazed at him. "It's been so long," she whispered.

"For me, too."

"There's been no one since...?"

A flicker of pain crossed his face. "No."

She reached for his hand, feeling stronger now she knew he was struggling too. "We don't have to do this if you don't want to."

He squeezed her fingers. "Funny, I thought that was going to be my line."

Putting her glass down, she reached for him, touching his face. Kissing him, realizing the sex thing was going to be a big issue until they dealt with it. "Maybe we should just go to bed and get it over with."

She felt his hands run up her back, tangle in her hair. He tumbled her to his lap and deepened the kiss. "No," he said, when he finally lifted his head, his eyes dark with passion and his lips wet from her mouth. "I've wanted you from the first day I saw you." He kissed her again. "There will be no getting it over with. I plan to take my time with you."

Tremors of desire ran over her skin at his words. And suddenly the passion she'd locked away for so long burst its bounds. She moaned, deep in her throat and kissed him back.

"Libby," he whispered into her hair, his hands unsteady as he reached for her pale blue sweater, pulling it up and over her head with help from her own unsteady hands.

She'd imagined their first time together would be tonight, after dinner, that she'd change in the bathroom and emerge in her full-length nightgown with her hair and teeth brushed. Not that she'd find herself tangled in her sweater and jeans, feverish with need, that she'd be tugging him out of his clothes with abandon, as restlessly and urgently as he was stripping her.

She tasted wine on his tongue and the same need she felt racing through her veins. When she nearly toppled off the couch, she grabbed for the table just in time. He laughed. She'd never heard him sound so carefree. He scooped her up, jeans and all, and carried her to the bedroom.

He undressed her slowly, kissing random parts of her as they emerged. Her shoulder, the slope of her breast, her belly, her hip, her knee. She'd imagined making love with him would be searing and emotional. But it was fun. Maybe there was a strong current of searing emotion underneath what they were doing, but right now she felt like those tulips. Fresh and just coming into bloom.

When they were both naked, he said, "Hang on a second," and walked, unembarrassed and gorgeous, to his case. He returned with a box of condoms. Thank goodness. Her last anxiety fled. She'd bought a few herself, but she was glad he was taking care of it.

As he placed the box on the bedside table she couldn't help teasing him. "The jumbo box?"

He grinned down at her. "I bought two of them."

Then he kissed her slowly, his naked body coming against hers so she felt her entire body taking part in that kiss.

She wrapped herself around him, giving and taking comfort, intimacy, and pleasure. Oh, such pleasure. He found her secret places, learned her body as she learned his. When he entered her she had an awful moment when she caught a glimpse of raw pain in his eyes. As though he couldn't bear to let her see his hurt, he closed his eyes and kissed her fiercely.

She had seen, though, and she even understood. He was making love with another woman. He was pushing his wife a little further away. Even as the knowledge of his emotional pain hurt her, she gave him what comfort she could. She was here, and warm, and alive. After that first bad minute, she felt him come back to her from that dark place where he'd been. And then he made love to her like she'd never been loved before.

In the end, they canceled their dinner reservation and ate the cheese and crackers and fruit in bed.

SEVENTEEN

For a bewildered moment, Libby didn't know where she was. Soft light filtered through fancy blinds, displaying unfamiliar furniture in a room that wasn't her own. She heard the sound of the ocean as close as though she were on a boat, and then consciousness returned fully, and she reoriented herself in the cottage bedroom. And the memories of last night.

Last night...

A smug little smile pulled at her lips while she thought about last night. She snuggled backward a little closer into the warm weight of Jeremy sleeping beside her in the bed. She heard a little rustling movement and then felt his lips on the nape of her neck in a sleepy caress. "How are you feeling this morning?" he whispered.

"If I were a cat I'd be purring," she admitted. She turned her head to gaze at Jeremy, almost unable to believe she could experience so much uncomplicated pleasure in one night. She caught the tail end of a very self-satisfied grin as he tried to swallow it. "Bet I could make you purr louder," he challenged, trailing a hand to her breast.

"Ow," she said, as she felt his stubbled cheek scrape her tender skin. "You need a shave."

He kissed the place he'd scraped, making her sigh, then he said, "Don't move," and bounded out of bed and headed for the bathroom.

Without knowing she did it, she snuggled over onto his side of the bed, where it was still warm from his body and smelled faintly of his scent. Through the open bathroom door came the sounds of water swishing, then Jeremy's voice, distorted as though he were talking while shaving. "What do you want to do today?"

She wanted to stay in that bed and make love. She was all keyed up and waiting for him to finish shaving. Had he lost interest so quickly? In a voice that sounded like one of the twins after she'd been told no to the Pretty Girl concert for the 50th time, she answered, "I don't know."

"I thought maybe we'd walk into town for breakfast. A very late breakfast," he said, striding back out of the bathroom and back toward the bed with an expression on his face that told her he hadn't lost interest at all.

"Oh, *after*." She flipped back the white cotton duvet to let him back in the bed. "That would be good."

Then he kissed her and she forgot all about breakfast. All about everything but the sensations bubbling through her body. The clean soapy smell of shaving cream and the taste of toothpaste on his lips. With a sigh of utter pleasure, she closed her eyes and began drifting toward the stars.

Some time later, she awoke for the second time.

"They'll be serving dinner, not breakfast, if we don't get going soon," she mumbled against Jeremy's ear.

"Room service," he huffed into the pillow.

"Not again." She giggled. "Anyhow, I need a break," she groaned, shuffling to a stand. "I've found muscles I didn't know I had."

The bathroom seemed to have moved four miles further from when Jeremy had made the trip earlier. She felt his eyes on her naked back and wanted to cover her drooping posterior and bolt. But pride, and something else, a newfound sense of herself, held her to a slower pace. More a speed walk than a hundred-yard dash.

"Did anybody ever tell you that you have a great ass?" His voice stopped her at the bathroom doorway.

"Not in about a hundred years."

He chuckled. "Bet they were thinking it. I know I was."

Luckily she'd hit the bathroom and, since she couldn't think of a thing to say, she shut the door. Had nine days of HIIT workouts done that much for her figure? She twisted around to get a better look at her backside in the mirror, but it still looked about the same as it had a week ago. But if he didn't care, why should she?

She made a face at herself in the mirror. Then did a double take. Was that really her? That woman with the tousled hair, swollen lips, and bright, sparkling eyes? That was the face of a woman who'd spent the greatest night of her life making love to a considerate, inventive, and humorous lover.

She stepped into the fancy shower with at least eight showerheads and let the hot water pummel her naked body. She experienced a new awareness of the way the water felt against her skin, the way the soap slid across the slope of her breasts, the way her flesh glowed pink and healthy as she toweled herself after.

She emerged with the slightest twinge of shyness. It was, after all, full day now, and Jeremy had opened the blinds with the remote control. So fancy. No more darkness and closed-eyed caresses. They'd be looking each other in the eye all day. Talking. And all the time, this new sex thing would be between them.

But she hardly had time to be shy. Jeremy handed her a cup

of coffee, kissed her shoulder, and took her place in the bathroom. Soon she heard the shower and took the opportunity to dress in her black jeans and a soft pink sweater that was cut a little low in the front. The intimacy of dressing in front of him seemed too much like a marriage, somehow.

Taking her coffee out to the wraparound deck outside, she stared out at the view. She watched a couple of bald eagles soaring high above the trees that edged the bay, then, unable to stop herself, checked in with the babysitter. Everything was fine, she assured Libby, who said she'd keep her phone on and not to hesitate if anyone needed her.

"Of course," Mrs. Lowenthal said, as though she hadn't left her cell phone number and Jeremy's on the fridge in plain sight, even though everyone had her phone programmed into their phone. "I'll call this evening to say goodnight," she promised.

"All right."

Then Jeremy joined her. "Do I need to confiscate your phone?"

"I can't help it. I worry about them."

"They'll be fine. We'll call tonight, like we said we would."

"I know."

"Hungry?"

"Starving."

"We could go to the bakery? I haven't been since Kelly and I used to go, but I haven't forgotten those cinnamon buns." He smiled at her. "Do you need a coat or anything?"

She forced herself to smile back. "I've got one in the car." *Kelly.* He'd mentioned her name like you would an old and dear friend. Not with anger or pain. The memory wasn't going to spoil his day.

Maybe he'd been telling her the truth. Maybe he had moved on.

However, she wasn't ready to waltz into the bakery on a Saturday morning with a new man. Cleo already knew about

Jeremy, but the chances were pretty good one of them would bump into someone they knew.

"Why don't we take a drive. There's a nice little restaurant a few miles from here that does an excellent brunch."

"Sounds good," he said, and she wondered if he was happy to avoid people he knew in town as well.

He reached for his car keys and she felt her eyes widen. "Your ring. Your wedding ring. It's..."

"Gone." He regarded the naked ring finger self-consciously. "I didn't think it would be right to wear it. With you, I mean. I wanted us to have a fresh start."

"Oh, Jeremy." At that moment, an eagle swooped past as a teary-eyed Libby threw herself into Jeremy's arms and said the words she'd never thought she'd say to another man. "I love you."

His sad, sexy eyes glowed. "I love you, too." And then he kissed her.

I love you. Such easy words to say. They might have been oiled, they'd slid so easily out of her lips before she could stop them. She could have kicked herself. Now the casual no-strings weekend was spoiled.

For once in her life she threw caution to the wind and dashed off for a wild weekend. And what happened? She awoke to find herself in love. A scary kind of love that felt as deep as her bone marrow. And as permanent.

As they headed out, hand in hand, she could picture them twenty years from now. Like one of those retirement ads on TV, she imagined herself and Jeremy, gray-haired and lined, in a tasteful, air-brushed way, heading off into their golden years.

She wanted to scream.

This was supposed to be a wild, glorious, sinful, no-holds-barred, maybe-I'll-call you-again-sometime kind of weekend. If she could take back those three little words she'd grab them and stuff them carefully away. And the most humiliating part was that she'd said them first. Oh, he'd parroted them readily enough. What was the poor guy supposed to do?

"Penny for them," Jeremy said when they were sitting over brunch and a silence fell.

"Hmmm?"

"That's what my English grandmother used to say. 'A penny for your thoughts.'"

"They're not worth a penny." She sighed. "You know, if your grandmother had put her penny in the stock market when it first opened, it'd be worth millions of dollars today. Millions. I read that in a budgeting book I borrowed from the library." A bitter laugh shook her. "I couldn't afford to buy the book."

He reached for her hand across the table. "It hasn't been easy for you and the kids. I know that. But it will all change when we get married."

She nearly choked on her Denver omelet. "I thought we weren't getting married."

He looked at her, puzzled, and she heard her own stupid words echo around them both. "I assumed you'd changed your mind."

But she didn't want to jump at his offer of marriage because it was an easy way out of her financial troubles. She wanted to be absolutely sure before she married again. "I wish I could go back in time and deposit that penny. That would change everything."

"It wouldn't change this," he said, almost angrily. "It wouldn't change the way we are together. This is right, Libby. We're right."

She tried to separate her head from her heart, but the foolish thing was banging away inside her rib cage making her lightheaded. How could she possibly think straight? "If I had more money there wouldn't be any hidden agendas between us."

"You mean you're marrying me for my money? I should warn you, my grandmother spent that penny." He was teasing, but only half. She saw the serious expression in his eyes. "There's no big inheritance or windfall in my future. I'm in pretty good financial shape." He made a comical expression, "As you'd expect from your banker. But all I have is what I've saved and invested from my earnings over the years. We'll be comfortable, but not jetsetters."

"I don't care about that. All I want is a good life for my kids. But money always comes between us. What happens if we get married and we fight? Will you think, she only married me to get out of debt?"

"No. That's like you thinking I only married you to make our babysitting arrangement permanent."

"Exactly."

A growl of frustration came from across the table. "Sometimes I wish I could meet that ex of yours to pound his head in."

The idea made her so gleeful she knew she should be ashamed of herself. "You do?"

"You picked the wrong guy first time out. It happens. He was a bad man. What can I say? Some men are. But not all of us. Don't let him spoil what we have."

"I don't want us to marry out of desperation. Either of us."

He looked at her with grim lines around his mouth. "I know desperation. I've been there. I could draw you a road map of the place." His fingers tightened on hers. "You must know you helped pull me out. I'd been there so long I'd forgotten I could leave."

"Oh, Jeremy."

"I love you because you brought me back to life. But that's only part of it. I love you because you're a wonderful mother and you're great with my girls. I love you because you're a terrific woman. Gorgeous, and sexy, and brave. I love you because I'm better with you than I can ever be without you."

She had never felt so flattered and yet she knew he believed those things to be true. "Jeremy, I'm scared."

"Trust me. Trust us. We can do this."

While they finished their food, he began talking about the future. From the way Jeremy was talking, it seemed they were engaged.

Every time the little voice in her head sounded its fearful alarm, she'd put a determined smile on her face and remind herself of Jeremy's words. She did trust him. And she did love him.

He must love her. He'd told her so, hadn't he? Not only with words, but with little thoughtful gestures and the expression in his eyes when he glanced her way. He'd loved her with his body deep into the night. So, she quelled the voice that said it was too soon. He wasn't ready.

Jeremy was the answer to all her hopes and prayers. She was delighted. Really, she was.

Maybe she was having so much fun being single and enjoying an attractive man simply for sex that she wasn't quite ready to be a wife.

"Eat up. You'll need your strength for tonight," he taunted as she pushed the last bit of food around her plate.

She felt absurdly shy at his words, and the images they immediately conjured in her mind. She might have blushed, except that the blood all seemed to have rushed to the intimate parts of her body. "Didn't you get your fill last night?"

"Darling, with you, I don't think I could ever get my fill. Just to help you get in the mood, I've booked you a full massage and I don't know what all else. Some kind of spa package."

"You did? For when?"

"This afternoon. I promised you a decadent weekend, didn't I?"

She gave a low chuckle. "I'm really starting to like being your weekend mistress."

"Well, it's a short-term assignment."

She blinked.

"Until we get married."

Abandoning the last of her breakfast, she sipped the fresh coffee their waitress had poured. "I don't know. We shouldn't rush into anything. This is a big step for both of us. We're not impulsive people." She glanced up with a wry grin. "Look how long it took us before we made love."

He reached for her free hand and ran a thumb over her knuckles. It was his left hand. The mark where his wedding ring had rested for so long was a shade paler. He'd only taken off one woman's ring a day ago. Was he really ready to replace it? "How do you see this playing out then?"

When she raised her brows, he continued. "Do I kiss you in front of the kids? Do we have complicated sleepover arrangements every time we want sex? Are you going to be okay with Tyler and Mia seeing me come out of your bedroom some mornings but not others?"

Slowly, as the impact of his words sank in, she shook her head.

"I know it's a little soon for us. I get that, but I can't see another way for us to be together than to get married. We're not impulsive people, you and I. And I don't think either of us are going to be comfortable carrying on in front of the kids unless we're married. Please say yes."

She did want to marry him, and she knew she'd be good for him. Instead of arguing, as part of her knew she should, she gave in. "Yes."

He looked thrilled at her answer. But she held up a finger of warning. "I may become your wife, but promise me you'll always treat me like your mistress when we're alone."

He chuckled, deep and dirty. "I don't have a lot of personal experience with mistresses."

She cocked a severe eyebrow at him.

"Okay. I don't have any. But I think a man's mistress has to do anything he tells her to—of a sexual nature, I mean."

"Really?" Little shivers of excitement raced up and down her spine. "Like what?"

He gave her a few ideas, and suddenly she couldn't wait to get back to the cottage and follow his instructions explicitly.

EIGHTEEN

He felt as excited as a kid at Christmas. After escorting Libby to the door of the day spa, where they seemed to do a lot of very expensive things with mud and seaweed, he'd dashed to his car and headed to a nice little jewelry store he knew.

He'd seen the trepidation in Libby's eyes and knew she was scared silly to get married again. To him, getting a ring on her finger was like a signature on a contract.

Marriage was the answer for both of them. Now that he'd made his decision, he wanted to get the thing done. He'd push for an early wedding, too. Once they were married, she could get rid of that too-big house of hers and her financial burdens. He had plenty of room.

"May I help you, sir?" A buxom, middle-aged woman with twinkly blue eyes behind some heavy-duty glasses asked him.

"Yes, I..." Now that he was here, he was getting the feeling his collar was too tight. He raised a hand to loosen his tie, only to discover he wasn't wearing a tie. Or collar. How could an open-necked polo shirt be choking him? "I'm looking for an engagement ring."

The woman slid the heavy glasses off her nose and let

them dangle from a silver chain around her neck. Her eyes were on major twinkle now, and something about the motherly way she regarded him made him breathe a little easier. "I see."

He got the uncomfortable feeling she did see. More than he wanted her to. "And the bride to be? Will she be joining you?" The woman squinted toward the door behind him.

"No. I want to surprise her."

"All right then. Of course, you can return the ring if she wishes a different style, or..."

"She throws it back in my face?"

The woman's laugh was musical and young. He found himself grinning. "I hope it won't come to that. But yes, we'll take it back for any reason. Now, what did you have in mind?" She led him to a staggering display of glistening, glittering gems. All neatly paired with wedding bands. The imaginary collar tightened another notch. Absently, he rubbed his ring finger, only recently naked.

Was he ready for this? He remembered picking out Kelly's ring. God, he could almost hear her giggle beside him, ghostly and far away. They'd gone together and chosen the set of rings that currently resided in a safety deposit box for when the twins grew up.

After a long silence, the woman said, "This isn't your first marriage, is it?"

He dropped his hands. Pondered getting huffy with her, and glanced up to see such a motherly expression on her face that he felt a momentary urge to bury his head in her ample bosom and tell her all his problems. "No. I'm a widower."

"I'm sorry," she said quietly. "And the lady?"

"Divorced."

"I see." She glanced down to unlock a display case containing rows of black velvet trays, each one loaded with diamond twin sets.

"Whew. I don't know where to start," he said, swallowing against the constriction in his throat.

The woman eyed him with professional interest. "Why don't you tell me a bit about her."

"Well, I love her, of course. That's why we're getting married." He said it in his bottom-line voice. So there'd be no mistake.

Two thin-penciled eyebrows rose. "Naturally. I was thinking more of her interests. That can have a bearing on jewelry. If she's a plumber or competitive swimmer you'd want one kind of setting. If she's a model or stockbroker you'd want quite another."

"Oh, I see. Well, between us we have four active kids. She loves to cook. And she's building a business as a landscape designer."

"She'll be getting her hands dirty then." The woman's own perfectly manicured hands, sporting quite a glitter of their own, fluttered over the trays and, selecting one, removed it and placed it on the glass display case.

"No," he said. "Too showy."

"What are her hands like?"

"Huh?"

"Are her fingers short and thick or long and slender?"

"She has beautiful hands." He flashed back to the way they'd looked trailing over his body last night, and almost groaned. "Ah, long and slender for sure."

"Take a look through these and see if anything strikes your fancy. The prices are all marked on the bottom."

He realized all at once that this was a more delicate operation than he'd foreseen. He had no idea what Libby had worn when she was married the first time. He was determined to get something completely different. He reviewed what little he knew of Mr. Victor Brown and immediately figured the guy would buy something huge and flashy, and probably full of flaws. He wouldn't care so long as it was shiny and big.

"I want a perfect diamond," Jeremy said. "Something elegant, but understated."

From the smile the woman beamed his way, he felt like he'd passed some kind of test. She opened a small drawer and pulled out a jeweler's loupe and a square black velvet tray. She plucked two diamond engagement rings out of the lot and replaced the rest of the rings. She scanned the rest of the offerings and plucked a third ring from another tray.

With only three brightly winking rings in front of him, Jeremy felt better. She picked the first one up and squinted at it through her scope. "One very slight occlusion," she informed him. Really, as close to perfect as you can get in this size. It's just under a carat. The setting is very simple, no claws or curlicues to get in the way of gardening or child-rearing.

He knew the moment he saw it was the one. He pictured it on Libby's finger and it felt right. It wasn't a showy ring, but it was both simple and elegant. And, like Libby, nearly flawless.

He studied the other two because he felt he ought to have a reasonable comparison, but he came back to the original.

"I'll take it," he said. "Wish me luck."

"Oh, I do, sir. Both of you. I hope you'll be very happy. We can alter the ring to fit, obviously, so bring her in anytime to size the shank properly. And, if she wants to change it," the woman shrugged, obviously thinking if Libby wanted a different ring than the one she and Jeremy had picked out, she must be insane.

He gave himself a pep talk all the way back to the cottage. Libby was good for him, good for the girls. He was crazy about her and about Tyler and Mia. He was doing the right thing.

He was.

He picked up champagne. Back in the cottage, he couldn't

sit still and wait for her, so he tucked the ring into his toiletry case, and went out for a walk on the beach.

After a while, he sat outside on a log feeling the crisp breeze on his skin, staring at the ocean. So long as he stayed here, nothing changed. The minute he put that ring on Libby's finger, he entered a new phase.

He blew out a breath. That was good, he reminded himself. Good.

He'd gone for the afternoon pampering package which included hair and makeup and when he picked her up all his apprehension vanished. The woman standing in front of him was stunning. Gorgeous and sexy, and he was crazy about her.

"You look fantastic," he said, "for somebody who spent an afternoon covered in mud and seaweed. How do you feel?"

"Like a new woman. Thank you, Jeremy," she whispered, her red lips curving deliciously. "I feel...pampered."

"You look amazing." She did, too. She looked blissed out. Her hair and makeup were different than he was used to, more obvious and very, very sexy.

"What was the best part?"

"Mmm. The massage. Definitely, the massage. Did you find something to do while I was being pummeled and painted?"

"Yep. I did some shopping, then went for a walk." Now that the time had come he felt his collar starting to choke him again.

Her professionally made-up eyes widened, then crinkled when she giggled. "Shopping. Right. Every man I know can't wait to go shopping."

When they got back to the cottage, he said, "I need to shower and change. Can you find something to do for a bit?"

"I'm going to do something I rarely do at home. Absolutely nothing," she said, and sank into the comfy couch and put her feet up on the table.

He'd been torn between presenting the ring in the restaurant, which they'd rebooked for tonight, and doing it privately.

But as soon as he was showered and dressed, he knew he had to do it here and now and get the whole thing over with. When he was with her he had no doubts. Why would he? Any man would be lucky to find a woman like Libby.

He dug the jewelry box out of his toiletry case where he'd stashed it, opened it and studied the ring for a long moment. He'd never imagined doing this a second time in his life. Closing the lid carefully, he dropped the box back into his pocket and emerged into the room to find Libby exactly as he'd left her, reading one of the magazines from the basket beside the couch.

"I should get dressed," she said, looking at him.

Clearing his throat, he felt as foolish as a boy asking a girl for his first date. He didn't have a clue how to act or what to say.

"I bought you a present."

"But, Jeremy, you've already given me so much. This weekend, the spa. I saw the prices in there."

"You've given me much more, Libby." His collar was so tight it seemed to choke him, making his words come out hoarse. "You gave me hope. And a future." It was now or never. He slipped the jeweler's box out of his pocket and held it out. "Please marry me."

For a moment she stared at him. Then slowly she extended those beautiful hands he'd come to love, red-tipped at the ends from a fresh manicure.

They trembled as she took the velvet box. She didn't open it right away. He could have sworn she was praying or making a wish. Then she opened the lid.

"Jeremy. It's beautiful." She stared at the ring, and he knew he'd guessed right. "It's perfect. But...are you sure?"

He took a couple of jerky steps toward her. "Yes. Trust me." And as he slipped the ring onto her shaking finger, he said, "I love you."

"I'm going to ruin this very expensive professional makeup

application," she cried. Sniffing and blinking rapidly. She held out her hand. "It fits perfectly."

"If we don't get out of this room, I'm going to ruin it even more." He kissed her lips swiftly. "Come on. Let's get a bottle of champagne and the best dinner in the house."

She admired her ring in the light, and he told her how good it looked on her finger. Which it did. She could be a hand model.

She slipped into the bedroom and emerged a few minutes later in a black dress that took his breath away. She was beautiful.

They made their way to the restaurant, which was decorated in cedar and glass, with vast windows overlooking the restless ocean.

When they were seated at a quiet table for two overlooking the water, he ordered champagne and waited until it was bubbling in two glasses to toast her. "To us," he said simply.

She sipped, watching him over her glass.

"You haven't answered my question, you know."

Her eyes dropped to the ring sparkling on her finger.

"Will you?" he asked softly.

"Are you sure you want me to? Really sure?"

He stifled every qualm. "Absolutely."

"And you're positively sure you love me? I won't ever marry another man who doesn't."

It must be love, this feeling he had for her. This combination of raging sexual desire, gratitude for all she was doing for him and the girls, and this indefinable sense of need. "I love you, Libby."

She took a deep breath and closed her eyes for a moment. When she opened them, they were bright with excitement and a tinge of fear. "Yes. I'll marry you. And I promise to love you forever."

Forever.

Til death do us part.

The unaccustomed sparkle on her left hand snagged his attention and gave him a safe way to back off from the intensity of this conversation. "We can exchange the ring if you want to pick out something else."

She beamed at him, totally eclipsing the diamond's sparkle. "This is exactly what I would have chosen myself. Well, I would have selected a smaller diamond. Are you sure we can afford this?"

He lifted her hand and kissed it. "I hope I have absolutely nothing in common with your ex. One thing I sure as hell don't have in common is financial recklessness."

"You have better taste in jewelry, too. I should have realized he was all wrong for me when he gave me the ring. It was so obvious. Like him, showy on the outside, not worth much when you got deep." She sighed. "I didn't get nearly as much as I'd hoped when I sold it."

He'd guessed right. Oh, he had the unlamented Victor's measure.

"Well, one problem we are never going to have is ex-spouses interfering with our marriage or causing trouble with the kids."

A tiny frown marred her smooth forehead. "I hope not." He didn't know whether she was referring to her ex or Kelly. He didn't press for details.

"Another good thing is how smoothly we mesh. My daughters will have the mother they need, Tyler will have somebody around the house who likes guy stuff, and you won't have to worry about money the way you have been."

"Hey, don't knock my hard times. I've learned a lot about making do with less. It's got to be such a habit, I kind of like the challenge. I'm proud of my new frugal skills. This dress for instance that you admired earlier?" She twinkled mischievously. "Twelve bucks at the thrift store."

He threw back his head and laughed. He had to. There she

sat, the most elegant and beautiful woman in the room, looking easily like a million bucks. In a thrift store dress.

"It's not funny. I figured out the difference between buying this dress and a brand new one, invested for my children's college education, would be a better use of my money."

"Sweetheart, you were meant to be a banker's wife."

"I've learned a lot in the last year. I'm through pretending to be something I'm not."

While she ate her fresh halibut surrounded by crisp vegetables, and he plowed into his rack of lamb done with an amazing sauce made from local berries, they talked, for once not about their kids, but about them.

"What are you going to do about your landscape design business?"

Those pretty hazel eyes that had been regarding him, widened and he saw a flash of panic. "I love what I do. I'm not giving that up."

"No. Of course not. I don't want you to. What I was thinking was, that if you want to start expanding, adding some extra services or hiring staff, you'd be in a better position to do it. That's all."

Her expression showed her relief. "Oh. For a second there I thought you were going to tell me you wanted a stay-at-home wife."

"Libby, I want you to be happy. And whatever makes you happy is fine by me."

She leaned closer. "I think I just fell a little deeper in love with you."

He snorted. "I haven't started getting on your nerves yet. It'll happen"

"I know. I'm kind of looking forward to it. There's so much intimacy in somebody's annoying little habits." She laughed softly. "Victor used to do this thing..." Then she clapped her newly-engaged hand over her mouth. "Oh, God. I'm sorry. What a tactless thing to say."

He finished chewing and swallowed. "Not really. He was part of your life for a long time. What did he do? I'll make a note never to make the same mistake."

She leaned forward and spoke softly. "He threw his dirty clothes at the laundry hamper. About sixty percent of the time they went in. The rest of the time they'd be draped over the edge, or socks would lay where they landed around that hamper. I'd end up picking the stuff up. It drove me nuts."

"I don't do that."

She grinned at him. "Good. What about Kelly?"

Suddenly, this wasn't such a great idea anymore, this conversation, but he was the one who wanted to go on when she'd tried to stop it, he reminded himself. What could he do but share something of Kelly the way she'd so easily told him of her ex?

"She, uh..." What? He tried to think of Kelly as the woman he'd married, the woman he'd lived with day in and out for nine years. The woman she'd been before she got sick.

And there it was. A memory as clear as the food in front of them. He sipped wine and then said, "She wasn't the neatest person in the world. And she liked to sew."

Suddenly, he was grinning at the memory of her surrounded by scraps of fabric. Orange and black as she worked feverishly at two identical pumpkin costumes for Halloween. "She made great stuff for the kids. Costumes and clothes. She was really careful about pins and needles and things because of the girls. But she wasn't too neat about everything else. There would be slivers of fabric and pieces of thread everywhere. For weeks after. And that sewing machine would sit in the middle of the dining table until we had somebody coming for dinner or I couldn't stand it anymore and put it away."

Libby touched his hand bringing him suddenly back to the

present. "I'm so glad you told me that. I was getting scared that she was perfect."

He shook his head. "No. She wasn't perfect. But she was a good woman. The best."

"And you'll always love her."

"Yes, but that doesn't mean I don't love you."

"I know. I don't want to take your memories of Kelly away from you. Not ever. What we have is our own."

The moment was so intense he felt that he needed to escape from all that emotion for a bit. "Anyhow, what I was saying earlier is that if you want to branch out and expand your business, I'm behind you all the way."

"Thank you for believing in me. But no. I'm not ready yet, and when I am, I think I'll go to the bank and get a loan. This is something I need to do myself."

"Good for you. Dessert?"

She shook her head. "Uh-uh. I'm stuffed."

"Coffee?"

"I couldn't."

"Sex?"

She giggled. "Oh, yeah."

NINETEEN

Libby opened her eyes, conscious of a feeling of wellbeing. Today, she knew exactly where she was. Already the snuggled warmth of Jeremy's naked body wrapped around hers was familiar.

With a pang of regret, she decided they'd have to wait until they were married to spend any more nights together. Today was the last day they could simply devote to each other for a while.

Married. A wedding. In her mind she'd skipped over that part and simply pictured her life going on pretty much as always, only without the money worries and with Jeremy in her bed every night when she went to sleep. And every morning when she woke up. She sighed. She'd have to get that lock on the bedroom door fixed. And turn the guest room into a bedroom for the twins. She'd get them to help her decorate. That would be fun.

"Penny for them," Jeremy mumbled in her ear, his voice sleep-groggy.

"I was wondering how quickly we could get married."

"I thought you liked being a mistress." He nibbled her ear lobe. "You're certainly good at it."

He traced a finger lazily round one nipple and her body started turning to liquid, just like that. She felt him hardening behind her and wiggled her hips against him. "I do like it, but I won't get any more practice until we're married."

The nibble turned into a bite that made her cry out and the hand on her breast went rigid. "What?" he demanded in a tone so peevish she smiled into the pillow.

Turning to see his outraged face, she said, "How do you suggest we conduct an affair with four kids?"

"We're engaged. They'll know we're getting married."

"I can't do it, Jeremy."

He flopped onto his back with a grunt, crossed his arms under his head, and stared moodily at the ceiling. "Tell you what," he said at last. "I'll meet you at city hall tomorrow at lunch. No, wait a second, I've got a meeting at one. Tuesday, then. We'll get married Tuesday."

"What about the kids?"

"They'll be at school."

"No. I mean, they'll want to be there. I want them there."

"Well. We could go after school, get married, and take them out for pizza afterwards."

She chuckled helplessly. "That is, without doubt, the most pathetic idea I've ever heard."

"Who cares about the marriage part? I want to get to the wedding night."

"I care. The kids'll care. This is forever, Jeremy. I want it to feel like forever."

He groaned again, sending her a pleading look. "This isn't working up to one of those magazine-type weddings with three hundred guests, is it?"

"Oh. No. I had that kind of wedding once. I don't want it

again." She hesitated a moment. "What kind of wedding did you have? The first time?"

"Same. Crowds of relatives I didn't remember ever meeting. Speeches. Bridesmaids. God knows, I love you, Libby, but I'm begging you, don't put me through that again."

She chuckled.

"There were plastic bells on every table. Swear to God. Plastic bells."

"Paper roses. My mother sat at home night after night and made one hundred and seventy-five paper roses." She sighed. "No. I don't want to go through that again, either. But I wouldn't want to hurt people's feelings. Tracy would want to come. So would my neighbor Paula and the women from my bread baking class. I couldn't get married without them there." Her heart sank. "And my dad."

"My parents will fly in from Florida."

"It's already getting complicated."

"I've got a great idea. Let's take the kids away somewhere. Hawaii maybe and get married. They can be part of it and we don't have to invite anybody else to the wedding. Then, when we get back, sometime we'll have a party to celebrate."

"Can we really go to Hawaii? I've always wanted to."

"Nothing easier. I'll book the tickets tomorrow. Let's say, a week from now?"

"Spring break is in two weeks."

"Right. Perfect. Then they won't have to miss any school."

This was feeling so much like a fairy tale, it was scary. She could picture them, the six of them, posed against a tropical sunset like a postcard. But it was good scary.

"I love this idea. We'd be legally married, so that would take care of the sleeping arrangements, and then we could have a garden party to celebrate when we got home. It's perfect, don't you think? Gardens are my thing." She glanced at him from under her lashes. "I might even get some business out of it from all your stuffy friends."

"How do you know my friends are stuffy? You've never met any of them."

"That's right. I haven't." They'd probably all known Kelly, though. They'd compare her, of course, to her predecessor. How would she stack up?

"You'll meet them soon enough."

"What have you told people about me?" she asked, feeling deliciously girlish.

"I haven't told them anything."

"Oh." It was crazy to feel disappointed. She hadn't told anyone about Jeremy, either, apart from Cleo, Megan, and Brooke. And Paula. In fact, she'd discussed her feelings for him at length with her closest friends. Falling in love with a new man was the most significant and exciting part of her life at the moment. He was definitely top of mind.

Oh, well, she reminded herself. Men are different. They don't love to communicate the way women do.

"Two weeks to wait," he complained. Before she knew what had happened, he'd flipped her on her back and rolled his full length on top of her, a very wicked expression in his eyes. "Better get our fill in now."

Then he kissed her, and she thought what a long time fourteen days was. And then she couldn't think at all.

They went for a long beach walk and then the weekend was coming to a close. It was time to go home.

"Hawaii!" the three older kids all screamed at once. Little Mia's voice echoed right behind them. "Hawaii!" then she whispered to Grace, "What's Hawaii?"

The kids had seemed pretty enthusiastic that their parents

were getting married. But their reaction to the trip to Hawaii practically had the windowpanes rattling.

Tyler, who'd been practicing surfing on the couch cushions, crouched and leapt into the air, riding an imaginary wave. It dumped him soundly on the ground where he rolled and bounced up again. "When do we go?"

"In two weeks."

"Woo-hoo. Wait'll I tell Ryan Doran. He thinks he's so cool cause he went to Disneyland for Christmas. I'm going to Hawaii, *and* getting a new Dad."

Something funny squeezed in Jeremy's chest. It was pretty obvious he placed a distant second to two weeks in Hawaii, but Tyler seemed totally willing to accept him as a surrogate father. He and Libby hadn't got as far as figuring what the kids would think about them becoming a blended family. He'd mentally budgeted a few thousand for counseling fees, and here everybody seemed delighted.

Everybody, that is, except Olivia, who'd suddenly gone pale. "Two weeks?" She asked in a hollow voice. "Will we be in Hawaii on the nineteenth?"

"The nineteenth?" He glanced at Libby but she looked as puzzled as he felt. "No. We leave on the twenty-first. Why?"

"The Pretty Girl concert is on the nineteenth."

He felt his jaw clench. "And on the nineteenth, you'll be sitting here at home. Because there's no way on earth I would let you two go to a rock concert."

Grace opened her mouth and Jeremy gritted his teeth even harder, but he was saved by Olivia, who took one look at his face and dragged her sister out of the room. He heard them whispering and muttering all the way up the stairs.

"What?" He challenged Libby who was grinning helplessly.

"I was wondering if we could postpone the wedding a little. Say, until they've finished being teenagers."

"At least with two of them, and two of us, the odds are a

little more favorable." He flopped down on his favorite chair, and wondered fleetingly whether Libby would make him move it when she brought her own stuff over. He had to admit, that what she hadn't sold was in a lot better shape than his own stuff.

He glanced around the living room, noting the dingy, finger-marked paint, and how shabby the furniture was. Mostly because he let the kids have free run of the house when they were home. He couldn't ask Libby to move in with the place looking like this. They could have a decorator come in and put a new touch on the place. She'd like that.

He watched her bend over and replace the couch cushions Tyler had upended before roaring off somewhere with Mia in tow. He opened his mouth to tell her not to bother, then closed it again and decided to enjoy the view. If it weren't for four very good reasons all over his house, he'd be sneaking up behind his new fiancée right now and messing up those sofa cushions again.

"I want you," he said low in his throat.

Her hands, busy smoothing the cushions into precise geometrical lines, stilled. He saw the diamond wink on her finger, heard her sharp intake of breath. Then she turned to face him, and he knew without words that she wanted him, too.

He stood, and in two strides had her in his arms.

"We can't," she murmured into his ear.

"Lunch tomorrow. Can you get a babysitter for Mia?"

She chuckled. "You have a meeting tomorrow, remember?"

Puzzlement turned to self-conscious laughter as he recalled his crazy idea to get married on their lunch hour. "Right. I remember."

"But Mia has playschool on Tuesday, if you could take an early lunch."

"I'm hungry now. Okay. Tuesday, then. I'll run home for a nooner."

She chuckled again, a deep sexy sound that made him kiss the side of her neck and try and get a hand up her shirt.

A slap took care of the hand. "Are you going to make a habit of nooners when we're married?"

"Damn right. Morning, noon, and night. You and I have a lot of celibate years to make up for."

"Mmm." She didn't seem to dislike the idea, so he tried sneaking his hand back up her shirt and got another whack for his trouble.

Regretfully, he gave up and pulled away. "Tuesday."

She smiled and nodded. "Tuesday."

"Oh, well. If we can't have sex, let's eat. I'll order some pizzas for dinner and we can celebrate with the kids."

"Well, all right. But we'll have to leave early. I want to bathe Tyler and Mia tonight."

"You're such a good mother."

She pinkened with pleasure at the compliment. "I'll try to be a good mother to Grace and Olivia as well."

"Don't worry. We're going to make this thing work." He wondered who he was reassuring.

TWENTY

A nooner? Sex in broad daylight? Libby felt both excited and foolish. She wasn't even sure if he'd been serious when he suggested it. And really, she shouldn't waste her time when she had the house to herself. She should catch up on work.

But then, she reminded herself piously, even she was entitled to a lunch break.

Should she make him lunch? The etiquette of a nooner completely baffled her.

Not to mention the correct apparel. Should she wear a negligee and stand at the bottom of the stairs holding a martini, a trail of rose petals leading to her bedroom? Or wear jeans and a T-shirt and give him a chicken sandwich, and let events proceed as they would?

She was peeling apples for the after-school snack. She sighed, following the paring knife, which went round and round the apple, spiraling like her thoughts. Her phone ringing interrupted her reverie.

"Hello?"

The voice on the other end of the phone made her gasp and

muff the unbroken circle of peel. "Jeremy. I was thinking about you."

"Me, too. What are you doing?"

"Making applesauce cake. I'm peeling the apples."

"Peeling the apples." He sounded like he was laughing at her. "Haven't you ever heard of canned applesauce?"

She shook her head, even though she knew he couldn't see her. It was a good thing she was marrying him. He needed her. "It's not the same." Suddenly inspired, she continued with forced casualness. "Maybe I'll let you try a piece tomorrow." She let her voice drift at the end, in a question. Hopefully, his response would let her know if it was a negligee or jeans date.

"Sweetheart, I can't make it tomorrow. I'm sorry."

"Why not?" It suddenly didn't matter what she was supposed to wear. She really wanted a nooner. Disappointment seeped over her.

He sighed deeply on the other end of the phone. "Our bank financed a combination residential and commercial development in California that's got a bad feel to it. I'm going to fly down and check it out, meet with the developers, before we advance any more funds. I leave tomorrow, and I'm swamped getting things cleaned up before I go."

"How long will you be away?"

"I don't know. A few days."

The apple was wobbling in her hand and she realized her hands were shaking. It bumped into the sink and she put the paring knife down with a snap. *He's not like Victor. He's not.* But the term business trip to her was synonymous with extramarital affair. And they weren't even married yet.

"Are you okay?"

"Yes. I'm fine. Just disappointed." *I trust him. I trust him.*

"Me, too."

"Can you come for dinner tonight?"

"No. I'm scrambling here to get everything ready."

"Oh. Of course."

"I have to ask you a favor."

She picked up the paring knife and started idly pressing it into the peeled apple in the sink. "What is it?"

"Can I leave the girls with you until I get back?"

"Oh. Sure, of course."

"You've still got a key to my house?"

"Yes." He'd given it to her a couple of months ago when one of the twins had forgotten her homework. He'd told her to keep it.

"Sweetheart, I don't even have time to pack the girls some clothes. Do you think you can manage?"

"Of course. Sure."

"You sound funny. You're not mad about tomorrow?" He lowered his voice and she imagined him sitting at his desk, with that awful Linda trying to listen from her desk outside. "If there was any way I could see you, you know I would."

"Yeah." The pressure in her chest was increasing. She needed to be honest with him. "I have some trust issues around business trips. It's not your fault."

"Oh, Libby, I'm sorry. You know I'd never do anything to hurt you. You can trust me."

There was a pause. "I know," she finally whispered.

"Look, I'll—" She heard an urgent voice in the background.

"Be right there," he snapped. She heard the sigh of frustration. "I have to go." He lowered his voice and murmured, "I love you."

"I love you, too," she said, but he'd already gone.

"Do you think Anne's going to marry Gilbert?" Grace wanted to know.

"Blech." Tyler made gagging sounds and accompanying retching gestures.

"You are such a child," Olivia said. It wasn't clear if she was referring to Tyler or her sister, younger by a few minutes. "Anne has to marry Gilbert. He's her soulmate."

Libby smiled. "I'm not going to tell. I've already read all the Anne of Green Gables books." She wasn't sure how the routine had started, but since the first fateful day she'd tried to interest the twins in something other than Pretty Girl and she'd handed Olivia Anne of Green Gables, the series of books about the turn of the century orphan girl from Prince Edward Island had become part of their lives.

At first, Olivia had asked so many questions, and read so many passages aloud that Grace had wanted to read the book, too. Libby ended up reading the book aloud, chapter by chapter, on afternoons when the kids were all together. She wasn't sure that Mia understood a lot of what was read, but she curled up in her mother's lap and copied the intent listening pose of Olivia.

Tyler pretended utter disgust, but even he'd laughed aloud when Anne, horrified by her red hair, had tried to dye it and it had turned green.

"What did she use to get it green?" he'd asked with interest.

"Don't even think about it," Libby had warned.

"But all the teenagers do it."

"You can't have a ring in your eyebrow, either."

"Aw, Mom."

He'd given up trying to get green hair, but he'd started listening in on the chapters anyway. Now, with Jeremy away and the girls staying over, they'd taken to reading at night before bed. They'd moved on to Anne of Avonlea, the second book in the series. After Jeremy's harried phone call earlier in the day, Libby thought gloomily they might get the whole series finished before he got back.

She stilled the flutter of panic that occurred every time she thought of him so far away. He wasn't anything like Victor. He wasn't off having an affair. She knew that. She trusted him completely but she'd sure be glad when he got home and she could stop reminding herself a hundred times a day about how much she trusted him.

"Gilbert loves Anne," Olivia continued. "Like my dad loves you, right, Libby?" It was reassuring that even his ten-year-old daughter could tell he was in love with her. Of course, he wasn't off on a spree.

"Right." She smiled.

"When's he coming home, anyway?"

"He's hoping to be home by the weekend. His meetings are taking longer than he thought. But think what a surprise he'll get when he sees we've got your room all ready." With the girls' help, she'd removed the wallpaper in the guest bedroom. They'd chosen a bright apple green color for the walls, and, unable to talk them out of their choice, Libby had managed to convince them that it would look nice striped. And it did. A little bright, but nice. She'd painted white and green stripes on the walls, helped the girls brighten up an old wooden dresser by gluing on pictures out of magazines. She'd imagined something tasteful, like the Victorian decoupage she'd showed the girls from one of her decorating books. Instead, they'd covered every square inch of the dresser in little glued-down pictures of their favorite music stars, mainly Pretty Girl.

They'd learn a good lesson about the fickleness of fashion trends when they had to scrape off their decoration a couple of years from now. In the meantime, they were happy, and Libby felt it was important to make them feel at home in their new room.

She'd rummaged through the remnant pile at the local fabric store and raided her own stash of "someday" sewing projects for enough scraps to make each of the girls a new quilt for their beds. It was her idea of a housewarming gift for them.

It was comforting to know that Jeremy would be leaving the painful memories in his house behind when they became a family. She wondered if they should redecorate her bedroom as a kind of symbolic gesture. She'd have to ask him when he got back.

Once she had all four kids asleep, Libby donned her pajamas and crawled into her own bed with her latest design project. Brooke was so delighted with her garden that she'd given Libby's brand-new business cards out to everyone she knew who had a garden. Megan was also handing out her cards and showing off the couple of designs Libby had done for her clients so things were shaping up.

Now she'd been asked to work on the display home for a new subdivision. The homes there were gorgeous and, unlike a lot of new subdivisions, the developers hadn't gone in and leveled every tree, they were working them in as eco-friendly a way as possible. Her designs were a whole lot more interesting because she had some natural features to work with. This yard had some huge boulders in the backyard with a couple of big cedars brooding over top. She imagined a pond with a small fountain to keep the water moving. A stone bench and a lot of shade-loving plants. Ferns, hostas. Some Rhododendrons over here. She started scribbling, then stopped. Sure, the rhodos would love it, but weren't they a little obvious? Who was going to pay for a design you could get from your local garden store clerk?

With a sigh, she settled back among the pillows and let the unease she felt rise up and make its point.

Jeremy had delayed his trip home by a couple of days. Big deal. He'd told her to trust him and she did. He'd told her he loved her and she believed him.

And maybe if she kept reminding herself of how much she believed him, one day she actually would.

Knowing that sleep wasn't going to happen anytime soon,

she got out of bed and wandered the house. After checking that everybody was asleep and tucked in, she padded to the computer in Victor's old home office. She'd found some excellent resources for plants and design ideas on the web.

Having asked Google for help, she visited a lot of garden sites, bookmarked a few, made some notes.

Then she sat back, brooding. Maybe it was being here in Victor's old office, but she couldn't stop thinking about him tonight. Comparing him and Jeremy wasn't fair. And perhaps she wasn't comparing them. Maybe, in the same way Jeremy had needed to accept his wife's death before he could move on, she needed to accept that Victor had really gone too. And yet he wasn't dead—or was he? The idea sent a strange shiver down her spine. It was late at night and she was getting maudlin. Of course, he wasn't dead. She'd have heard something. Wouldn't she?

Her fingers started typing. Good old Google. She entered his name, certain it couldn't be this easy to track down the man who'd yanked up the roots she'd so carefully planted and disappeared.

It took her less than an hour to find him. The arrogance of the man. He had a blog all about himself and his new business, exporting antiques and artworks with his beautiful young partner, Irina. The blog led to a website for their export business.

She waited for her blood to boil, but strangely, it didn't. The feeling was more like a simmer.

Naturally, a person wouldn't have a website and a blog promoting their business without having an email address. She wrote to him.

Libby emailed her AWOL husband and imagined the message traveling from Clamshell Bay, Washington, to Somewhere Unspecified in the Czech Republic. What would he think when he read it? Would he reply?

"Daffodils are the happiest flowers, aren't they?" Libby said to Mia.

Mia regarded the bright blooms thoughtfully. "They're yellow."

"Yes, they are. I think yellow is a happy color." Or maybe it was her mood that made everything seem right. Jeremy was coming home tonight. And Victor had replied to her email as she'd somehow known he would. Oh, he was full of apology that he hadn't been in touch, work had been busy, he was having a bit of a cash crunch, but of course he'd be sending her money soon, *blah, blah, blah*. Libby had phoned around. She'd put her problem out there in the network of women and she'd been referred to a lawyer who specialized in family law. A woman.

She felt, even if she never got another penny out of her ex, that a burden had been lifted off her shoulders.

Maybe it was the smarmy, lying email that had made her see so clearly the difference between him and Jeremy. Maybe she was simply over him. But that morning she'd gone and bought herself a pretty dress to wear on her wedding day.

"Why? Why is yellow a happy color?" Mia wanted to know.

"Well, it's the color of sunshine and butter, and what else?"

"Bananas?"

"Good one. What else?"

"Eggs in the middle?"

While they played an impromptu color game, she sliced the oatmeal squares that the kids all loved. Dinner was in the oven. They hadn't discussed it in the rushed phone call, but she assumed Jeremy would stay for dinner when he came home tonight.

In a little more than a week's time, they'd be married and then he'd be coming home for dinner every night. Excitement and a little skitter of nerves filled her at the thought. *Please let this work out.*

They had tickets booked, a hotel on the beach, and today she'd found a dress. A simple long, sleeveless dress in primrose. Such a happy color.

She was pulled out of her reverie by the doorbell.

She wiped her hands and walked down the hall and opened the front door. There was a woman on her doorstep and a boat-sized silver Cadillac in her driveway. The woman wore absurdly high heels, for some reason that was the first thing that Libby noticed. She wore a stylish pale gray suit, bleached blond hair in a backcombed, upswept style and jewelry glinting off her hands and wrists as she beamed a toothy smile at Libby and handed her a business card.

"Mrs. Brown? I hope I'm not too early. I'm Candace Schwartz." The woman had a southern accent with a touch of eastern European.

Libby stared at her blankly.

"The Realtor? Jeremy set up the appointment. I don't see his car so I guess I'm early." The woman extended a thin hand with cinnamon-colored nails and Libby was so stunned she took it. She felt like she was going to have her home sold out from under her by Zsa Zsa Gabor.

"Jeremy made an appointment with a Realtor? Jeremy O'Toole?"

"Sure he did. Did he forget to tell you about it? Honestly. Men." She smiled, big preternaturally white teeth. The woman could be a walking ad for Crest White Strips. "Congratulations, by the way. I can tell you that there will be a lot of very disappointed women when they find out he's getting married."

"Thank you. But why are you here?" A headache was starting behind her eyes.

"To put your house on the market, honey. Jeremy says it's in excellent shape. In this area and this market?" She flapped one hand back and forth like a middle-aged blond rapper. "It'll sell in no time."

"I think there's been a mistake, Ms. Schwartz," she said as firmly as she could.

"Why, you can call me Candace. Or Candy, I like to say that's 'cause I have a sweet tooth for real estate." She tittered as though she'd never said those words before. "And you have a real nice home here."

"Thank you. I plan to keep it. I mean, we plan to keep it. It's Jeremy's home that will be going on the market."

A sigh, so sincere sounding it could have been genuine, wafted from between thin cinnamon-colored lips that matched the nails. "I'm getting the feeling you two never discussed this."

"Well of course we..." She stopped in mid-sentence, then slowly shook her head. "I assumed we'd live here."

"I'm guessing he did the same thing."

A curtain fluttered in the Carmody home across the street.

"Would you like to come in?" She couldn't stand there explaining this hideous mix-up in front of every nosy neighbor on the block.

"I'd love to. I've always wanted to see inside this house. Real estate's not only my job. It's my addiction."

She stepped into the hall and Libby shut the door behind her. "Oh," she said, putting a hand to her heart. "You baked. You do that every time we have a prospective buyer and the house will sell like that." She snapped her fingers.

"Make yourself comfortable in the living room. If you'll excuse me, I'm going to call Jeremy."

"Sure, honey. Don't worry about me. I'll just poke around."

That's what Libby was afraid of. She bolted into the kitchen and grabbed her phone. She called Jeremy's cell but it was turned off. Called his private line at the bank and got his recorded voice. However, she could press 1 to speak to his assistant, so she did.

"Linda Hornby, how may I help you?"

"Oh, hi Linda, this is Libby Brown. I'm trying to reach Jeremy."

"Mr. O'Toole is out of the office. May I take a message?" the frigid voice informed her.

"I know he's out of the office. His cell phone's turned off. I need to reach him."

"If you'd like to book an appointment, he has space Thursday."

"An appointment? No, let me speak to..." Who? Who did Jeremy talk about at work? Who might actually treat his fiancée like a human being? "Melanie Kwan. Is she in?"

"I'll transfer you," the arctic voice said.

"If it's not too much trouble," Libby said sweetly, but her sarcasm was lost since she'd already been transferred. Fortunately, Melanie answered her phone.

"Hello. I'm sorry to bother you, but this is Libby Brown. I'm trying to reach Jeremy."

"I'm sorry, Ms. Brown, Jeremy's not in the office until tomorrow."

Her brows drew together. "I know he's not. I'm trying to reach him on a personal matter."

"Personal?" Curiosity zapped like an electric current across the line.

"Yes. I'm his...girlfriend." Stupid term. Why hadn't she said fiancée? What was the matter with everybody today? What was the matter with her?

Melanie squealed. "What? Jeremy has a girlfriend?" Then she gasped. "Oh, I'm so sorry. That was tactless. I'm...ah, kind of surprised, that's all."

"I-uh, I didn't realize no one knew."

"Yeah. Um. Did you try his cell?"

"Yes. It's off."

"He checked in earlier, right before he got on the plane. He should be back sometime this afternoon."

"Okay. If you hear from him, can you tell him I'm looking for him?"

"Sure will. Uh, it was nice talking to you. I hope I get to meet you soon."

"Yes. So do I." When she hung up, she stared sightlessly out of the kitchen window. No one knew about her. No one. It wasn't only his friends, but the people he worked with every single day. He hadn't mentioned her or their upcoming wedding to anyone at all. Except the Realtor. What did that say about her importance in his life?

Maybe if she weren't already so wretchedly insecure she could tell herself he was only keeping his private affairs to himself, but after being dumped by one husband, she really didn't want to be hidden away like a guilty secret by a second.

She walked slowly back to the living room to find the Realtor in the dining room. "Lovely wainscoting," she said, then looked at Libby and her smile dimmed. A look of concern took its place. "Please don't look so worried. This will all work out. Misunderstandings happen all the time between couples. You know, communication is the toughest skill to master in a marriage."

"Yes. I know." And right now, the communication she was receiving from Jeremy was unnerving her.

"We'll sort this thing out. Ah, looks like we can sort it out, now," Candace said, and going to the front door, flung it open.

Sure enough, a maroon Volvo pulled up and a very tired Jeremy emerged.

He took a step, paused, squinted at the Realtor and then at Libby. He shook Candy with the sweet tooth's hand, gave Libby a peck on the cheek and said, "I think I forgot to tell you about Candace coming."

"That's not the only thing you forgot to tell me," she said as pleasantly as she could considering she wanted to smack him.

TWENTY-ONE

The crescent was experiencing its post-school rush hour. Kids shuffled, skateboarded and cycled past on their way home. Moms and nannies walked to the school to pick up younger children. With horror, she noticed that Candace used her boat-sized Cadillac as a rolling billboard for her services. Any minute now, she'd be hailed by some nosy parent or neighbor. She gestured into the house, "Why don't we talk about this?"

"Dadd-ee!" came a twin chorus and there were the girls, with Tyler hot on their heels, sprinting toward Jeremy.

She steeled herself for the inevitable inquisition about the realty sign on the Cadillac, but they were too wrapped up in greeting their father, in the twins' case, and his hero, in Tyler's.

"Guess what? We're putting on a play at school and I'm going to try out," Olivia panted.

"I'm going on the track team," Tyler reported.

"Did you see our new room?" Grace piped up. "Me and Olivia and Libby decorated it ourselves."

He'd been grinning and hugging the jumping, wriggling bodies, until Grace spoke. Then he glanced up with mixed horror and embarrassment.

"Come and see." The girls each took one of his hands and dragged him toward the open door where Mia stood, a big smile on her face and her arms upstretched.

She thought he paused, as though no longer sure of his place, then dragged Mia up high the way she liked. She squealed her approval.

That left Libby and the Realtor staring at each other. "Why don't I let you two talk about things. You can call me when you're ready. I do have the nicest family that would love to locate into this area."

"We'll call you," Libby said firmly. Then added a thank you. The woman was only trying to do her job, and she'd been pretty decent under the circumstances. "Thank you for understanding."

"Honey, I've been married for twenty-eight years." She paused, her car keys glittering in her hand. "Do you want some advice?"

No. But she nodded to be polite.

"Go in and let him have it. Have that fight I can see you working up to."

"Don't worry, I intend to."

"But don't let your pride and your hurt blind you to a good thing."

"I won't. Thanks."

She followed the gang up the stairs to the room she and the twins had been working on every night since he'd been away. She could hear their excitement from here.

"Isn't it great, Dad?"

"Do you like the color?"

"Libby let us put Pretty Girl on our dresser. She said we could bring our clothes over, too. After we come home from Hawaii, this'll be our new room."

"I...uh..." His hand crept to his belly, and he rubbed it absently. She could see he was in pain. Well, so was she. "I need to talk to Libby for a while."

"About Hawaii?"

"In private. Olivia, Grace, take the other kids downstairs and put on a movie."

"Libby always makes us do our homework first."

With a distracted air, he waved them away, and Libby thought she'd never seen him treat his daughters so dismissively before.

The twins gaped.

She finally found her voice. Or maybe it was somebody else's. It sure didn't sound like her, that flat, hopeless tone. "Grab a snack and watch a movie. It's okay."

"Cool." They thundered down the stairs whispering and giggling. Libby was pretty sure she knew what they'd be watching, but Pretty Girl seemed like saints compared to the man she was suddenly alone with in the bright apple green and white striped room.

He walked to the doorway, listened for a moment and then shut the door, closing them in together in the girlish room.

"I don't know what to say. I assumed you and Tyler and Mia would move in with me. I've got plenty of room."

"But I'm closer to the school. Everyone's used to being here." And she didn't even mention that the state of her house and garden were a lot more desirable than his.

It turned out she didn't need to mention it. "I know my place needs some updating. I thought we'd get a decorator in."

"But that's always going to be Kelly's house." She thought about the way he'd first taken her to the guest room. "I'd feel like an intruder."

His face darkened. "What do you think this place would feel like to me?"

"I never thought about it."

"Yeah. It was another one of those conversations we should

have had. Forget it." He flicked a glance at the bright walls. "Your place is fine."

But the vise around her heart didn't ease. "How come when I phoned the bank no one knew who I was?"

"What?" His surprise seemed genuine.

"Your secretary offered me an appointment for next week when I introduced myself, and then I got transferred to Melanie Kwan. You talk about her a lot so I figured she'd know who I was. She pretty much fell off her chair when I identified myself as your girlfriend."

His eyelids jerked as though she'd come at him with a pitchfork. "I don't talk about my private affairs at work."

"You were planning to get married in a week and you didn't bother to tell your co-workers? Must have forgotten to pencil it in your calendar." As she finished speaking, she noticed she'd spoken of their marriage in the past tense. Her hands felt cold. She glanced down and noticed they were clenched into fists.

"I was going to tell them. I've been busy."

She was working up to her mad now. Maybe if she hadn't been married to Victor Brown she wouldn't be so angry about her fiancé making sure not to mention her to the people in his life. But she had been married to Victor, and no one was ever going to treat her so lightly again. "In the fifty hours or so a week you spend with these people, you never found a minute to say, 'by the way, I'm getting married in two weeks?'"

He shifted, looking uncomfortable and sad and confused. "I don't want to make a big deal out of it. Frankly, I want to get the whole thing over with."

The silence was so heavy she found it hard to breathe. "Getting married is a big deal. It's a big deal to me."

"I didn't mean that the way it came out. Damn it, Libby. You know I didn't."

"I only know one thing. I'll never, ever marry a man who doesn't love me. ME! Not the babysitter or the corporate wife or the cook and cleaner. Me, Libby. For who I am." Her throat was aching and her nose tickled, but she was determined not to cry. Not today.

"Don't dramatize a misunderstanding. You know I love you."

"Would you want to marry me if you didn't need a mother for your girls?"

His lips clamped together in his anger-darkened face. She could almost hear him mentally counting before he answered. "We wouldn't have got to know each other if it weren't for the girls."

"No. It was the twins who brought us together, wasn't it?"

"So what? Was I supposed to fall in love with you just because you were beautiful and gazed at me with big helpless eyes? I'm trying to do what's best here for everyone."

"What's convenient, you mean. I won't be anyone's convenience. Never, ever again. I can make it without your help, thank you very much."

"And what about the kids? Are you going to deny them a family because you don't feel special?" He sneered the last word. She knew he was hurting, but right now she needed reassurance big time. Sure he was scared too. But she'd been planning a wedding, telling anyone she felt like telling that she was getting married again. The only person Jeremy seemed to have told was the Realtor.

She sank to one of the single beds awaiting its new quilt. She felt so cold, she wished the quilt were there so she could wrap herself in its cheerful warmth. "I know this is hard for you. I do understand." She shook her head, cursing herself for a fool. "I even knew you weren't ready. Not for marriage." She swallowed. "It's too soon."

He sat down on the opposite bed. Finally, they were talking about the real issue. She knew the trouble between them wasn't about which house they were going to live in.

"I put Kelly's pictures away. All but one. I have moved on."

She smiled a little. She managed that. "I know you have. You've come a long way. But we rushed into marriage so we could sleep together without embarrassing our kids. That's not a good enough reason."

"It's not true, either. We love each other."

She gazed at him. "Do we?"

He shifted, and dropped his gaze.

"I found Victor."

Jeremy stood with a jerk, turned away and strode to the window. Stood, looking out. "Where is he?" His voice sounded like it came from a long way away.

"He's in Czechoslovakia."

"You were right then."

"Yes. I found him on the Internet. Can you believe the arrogance of the guy? He didn't even change his name. He's got a new business, a new life." She hesitated. "A new woman. I emailed him."

"Did he reply?"

"Yes."

Jeremy still wouldn't turn around. "Is he coming home?"

She stared at the line of his spine, so straight, painfully straight. "Could you possibly believe that I would want that man back?"

"Libby, I can't figure out what you want."

"I guess maybe I want closure. I want him to..." She petered out, the truth was she wasn't entirely certain what she wanted from Victor. Or what was best for the kids. "I want him to take his responsibilities seriously. To pay what he owes us and..." And what?

"What did his email say?" Jeremy turned back at least to look at her, but he still had that remote expression on his face. She knew him well enough to understand he'd locked away his emotions behind that façade.

"He said he was sorry, that he'd been meaning to get in touch and threw in a bunch of excuses. He's going to figure something out, he says. He promised he'd take care of us."

She glimpsed the swirl of anger and pain in Jeremy's eyes, and then he clamped his emotions down once more. "And that's what you want?"

"Yes. I want him to do what's right. What he promised."

"What's right is for us to get married and make a family. Put aside our own problems and give those kids stability."

She gazed at him, wishing this could be easier. She wanted them to be happy so badly, she was tempted to take second best. But something stopped her. Maybe it was selfish to marry for love rather than convenience. If so, she was selfish. "I can't, Jeremy."

She could make out the noise of the television. Oh, God. How were they going to tell the kids?

"I..." She glanced up, and the words died in her throat when she saw his face, so pale and grim she wanted to reach out and make everything all better. Even though his hands were jammed in the pockets of his slacks, she could see they were fisted. He stared out the window, but it was pretty obvious he wasn't admiring the landscape. The younger Libby, the naïve one, would have gone to him. But not this Libby. Not the woman who had finally learned her own worth.

She shut her mouth and silence ruled again.

Finally, he jerked round to face her. "Just don't say anything for a few days. Will you do that?"

"But what's the point?"

"Please. All I ask is a few days."

He appeared so desperately in earnest that she agreed. It wouldn't change anything, but maybe in the next few days she could find a way out of this mess. Get things straightened out with Victor so she could finally have the closure she needed.

Yeah, and maybe Jeremy would throw a meet-Libby cocktail party for his friends and co-workers.

Jeremy left soon after with his girls and Libby operated on autopilot, helping Tyler with his homework, getting dinner on the table, dishes done, and the kids to bed. She felt shell-shocked. As though some horrible explosion had robbed her of her normal senses. But beneath the numbness she was aware of the pain.

If she'd had any doubt before, she knew now, beyond the shadow of a doubt, that she loved Jeremy.

There was something else she'd learned in the last few months as well, and that was that she would survive. All by herself, with no support from anyone. She could give her kids a home and she could make a life for herself.

Her little garden business was growing like chickweed. She probably had enough work for at least the next year. And, by then, Mia would be in kindergarten. With luck and hard work, she could make a go of it on her own.

Losing the love she thought they'd had was cruel. But, if it was only one-sided, it was doomed anyway.

Libby stood outside the storefront realty office and took a deep breath. Megan's pep talk was fresh in her mind. "You've got this," Megan had said when she'd practiced her pitch. She could do this. She had nothing to lose.

There were planter pots outside that probably spilled over with geraniums and blue lobelia in the summer, but right now contained a couple of dry-looking weeds and a few cigarette butts. They should be full of spring bulbs, she thought, her mind flashing painfully back to the Tulip Festival such a short time ago, when she'd so foolishly given her heart away. Even in winter she could keep those pots looking inviting.

Somehow, those empty planters filled her with confidence and she put the same firm smile on her face that the Realtor had greeted her with when they first met.

"Hello," she told the young woman at the reception counter. "I'm here to see Candace. I have an appointment. I'm Libby Brown."

"Okay, I'll let her know."

"Libby. Great to see you," Candace said, emerging from an office with her big smile beaming and her hand extended. She glanced behind Libby. "No Jeremy today?"

"No," Libby said, keeping her smile intact and her voice firm. So she'd come under slightly false pretenses. She'd wanted to make sure of an early appointment.

"Well, come on in." If the woman noticed that Libby carted a portfolio case with her, she gave no sign of it.

Candace had a desk and computer in one corner of her office, but she motioned Libby to a round table with padded chairs around it and sat opposite. "Can I get you some coffee or tea or anything?"

"No. Thank you."

"Jeremy called me. He said you two had decided to slow things up a little. I'm sorry."

"It wasn't your fault," she said. "We went into the whole thing too fast. I think we need to make absolutely sure before we go any farther."

Candace gazed at her for a moment, then said, "I sold Jeremy his current house, you know. When he and Kelly were expecting the twins."

A shudder crossed her skin. Her mother used to say, "somebody walked across your grave" when she shivered, but in this case, it was Kelly's grave they were crossing.

She glanced at Candace, the question in her eyes. "She was nothing like you. She was one of those bright, bubbly people who talk a mile a minute. You could tell they were happy the way they looked at each other. I remember thinking, this is one house I'm never going to have to put on the market because of a divorce."

"You were right." She smiled sadly.

Candace sipped from a coffee mug, then grimaced. Probably the coffee was cold and she'd forgotten.

"Well, I guess you didn't come here to talk about old times."

Libby managed a chuckle. "No. I didn't come here to buy or sell a house, either."

"Too bad. That family I had in mind can't find anything they like. I drove them by your place and they loved it." She let an unspoken question hover in the air. "With a little work, they could even make Jeremy's house work for them."

"I honestly don't know what's going to happen. We're both taking a breather right now and trying to figure things out."

"Well, keep me posted."

"I will, thanks." She took a breath and said, "I'm here on different business."

"Aha."

With a flash of entrepreneurial zest she saw her opportunity to sell herself, and before she could talk herself out of it, said, "In fact, *you* could use my services."

The professional smile froze. "Really."

"Landscape design. That's what I do. You said yourself, it's easier to sell a house that looks good. I could shape up gardens on properties you're trying to sell."

"Did you do your own garden?" She had the woman's attention, now. And that patronizing, *I don't think so*, expression had been wiped off her face.

"Sure did. Front and back. I also did several other gardens in the neighborhood that you could look at. And they're finishing the planting this week on the display home near me." She placed her portfolio on the table. "Would you like to take a look at what I can do?"

Candace nodded and soon was poring over the portfolio. She nodded a couple of times. Murmured "nice" when she got to the display home's garden.

Cinnamon nails drummed the tabletop. Entrepreneurial zeal glowed on the Realtor's face. "Smart girl. I own the realty company, you know. Sometimes we mow lawns. I've been known to trim shrubbery myself to make a property more visible. Some people just have no idea how to make their homes look good." She was talking to herself now, Libby could tell.

"That's right. I could offer a consultation, draw up a plan and let them do the work themselves, that would be the cheapest. Or, I could do it all for them."

"Do you have brochures?"

She shook her head. "I've got business cards. That's all. I've been working strictly on referrals and word of mouth, but I need to expand my business." Especially if she was going to be on her own.

She didn't have to explain. Candace nodded. "I can't make any promises, you understand. I'd have to think about it and talk to some people. But I think you're on to something. Promise me you won't go to any other Realtors until I get back to you?"

Libby opened her mouth to agree, then remembered she was an entrepreneur. "I can wait until next week."

The hard mouth softened in a grin. "You'll do fine in business. I'll introduce you myself to the local business women's network. I know a great company, two local gals, that do the most darling brochures. They do all my stuff."

Business women's network. It had a nice ring to it. "Thanks, Candace. If I ever do sell..."

And in that moment, it hit her. In her way, she was hanging on to the ghosts of her past as badly as Jeremy was. Did she really want to start a new life with Jeremy or anyone in the house where so many memories of Victor remained?

But that was the house where Tyler and Mia had lived their

whole lives. What about those memories? And the love and time she'd put into her garden and the house.

And yet, she'd asked Jeremy to do exactly that. And his memories were a lot more poignant. Maybe she had to stop feeling threatened by the woman who'd loved Jeremy first and who'd brought the twins into the world. They weren't rivals. They ought to be a team.

She packed up her portfolio, then said quickly, before she could change her mind. "I'm making no promises, but if your family would like to come through the house. I might consider an offer."

Candace's eyes lit up. "Can I bring my people by tomorrow?" At Libby's nod, she hauled a cell phone out of her purse and in minutes a house tour was arranged for ten the next morning.

Jeremy picked the girls up that afternoon, as he did every day after he was done work, and he and Libby chatted briefly about the back and forth of the children's lives. They tried to sound normal in front of the kids, but it wasn't easy. When she looked into his eyes, she saw the same confusion and hurt she imagined he was seeing in her own.

She didn't know how long she could keep doing this, seeing him every day when it hurt so much.

Mia decided to have a full-blown temper tantrum that night, and Tyler was stuck on the nine times table and Libby—who'd never been strong at math—was having to stop and think as she tried to test him. Some role model she was.

"Nine times nine," she yelled over Mia's howls of outrage because it was time for bed and she'd decided she wasn't going until Tyler went. Libby knew her little girl was overtired, but it didn't make it any easier to listen to her scream.

"You keep asking me that one. Eighty-one," Tyler yelled back, a lot less bothered by the noise than his mother.

"That's because I'm sure of the answer. Look, keep memorizing the sheet and I'll test you after Mia is asleep." Which better be soon. She was worn out. Exhausted. She wanted that trip to Hawaii so badly she could taste the salt-tinged air and feel the warm breeze on her skin. And right now, she wanted to go alone.

She'd barely got the kids asleep and she was sitting in the kitchen thinking she might never get up, when the phone rang.

"Hello?"

"Hi. It's me."

"Jeremy." Her insides went liquid with wanting and sadness that it was all such a mess and they were both so scared.

There was a tiny silence rife with all the things they couldn't or wouldn't or didn't know how to say. Finally, he said, "I miss you."

"Me, too."

"You sound tired," he said. Oh, if she'd ever needed a shoulder to lean on, it was tonight.

"I had a rotten evening. Mia threw a temper tantrum and Tyler had trouble with his math."

"He should have called me. I'm a whiz at math. It's my thing."

She traced a pattern on the tabletop with her fingertip. "I don't think it's fair on Tyler to let him start relying on you. If..."

"I don't want to keep doing this. It's crazy. We can't go back to the way things were before, when we were practically strangers. I stand there in the doorway dropping off and collecting the girls and all I want to do is hold you. I can't pretend nothing happened with us."

"No. We can't. It's too hard."

"Look. I've been thinking. It's a house. Who cares? I can't believe we're putting our futures in jeopardy over a house."

She closed her eyes. She found she was clutching at the phone with both hands, hanging on for dear life. "It's not the house. Is it?"

A heavy sigh. "No."

"I think we rushed into things. We need some time to cool down and think it all through."

"I've had lots of time to think. We've known each other for months. We had a great time on our weekend. Our kids even like each other. How can we let this go?"

She sucked in a breath. "I've got a family coming tomorrow who might be interested in buying my house."

"You have?" He sounded shocked. "I thought we decided your place made more sense."

"I haven't even decided if I'm going to sell it yet. But I'm exploring the possibility of maybe being open to the idea," she said, trying for a light tone.

"It's tougher than you think to let go of the memories, isn't it?" he said after another silence.

"Yes."

"So, what are we going to do about Hawaii? The kids are already dragging out their summer clothes and arguing about what to pack."

She closed her eyes. "Why don't you take the girls and have a holiday?"

"Because I want us all to go. We could all have a holiday and put the wedding on hold."

"That doesn't make any sense. If we're not going to make it as a couple..."

"Don't you give up on us," he practically yelled. "I'm sorry I screwed up with the Realtor. I'm sorry about a lot of things. But don't give up. Not yet."

"I don't want to give up." She loved him so much it hurt, but she wasn't sure enough that he loved her. She had a feeling he wasn't sure either.

"You won't come to Hawaii?"

"No. But you and the girls should go."

"If you're not going, none of us are going."

"I'm sorry." She glanced around her quiet kitchen, at the cabinet door he'd fixed, and the tile he'd replaced. Already he was part of her life and her home. How could she bear to lose him? "I think I'd better go. I've got some work to finish up."

"One last thing."

"What?"

"Are you still wearing your engagement ring?"

She glanced at the diamond winking from her left hand. "Yes."

"Good."

TWENTY-TWO

The doorbell rang at precisely ten o'clock the next morning. The family that stood on her doorstep, along with Candace, were perfect, Libby had to admit, as she shook hands with both mother and father and the children. After greeting the Realtor and her clients, she'd pretended she and Mia had to go out, unable to watch strangers going through her house wondering if it would suit them.

She took Mia to Clamshell Bakery and Café where she poured her troubles into Cleo Duvall's ear. The cheerful baker had long, red hair threaded with gray and a gym-hard body from all the years of carting heavy sacks of flour around. She'd taught Libby to bake artisanal bread but she was also a good friend and, while she drank coffee and Mia sipped juice and nibbled a peanut butter cookie, she listened.

"I don't know what to do," Libby wailed, sounding as mature as her three-year-old.

Cleo left the serving to her assistant, Pepper, and grabbing herself a coffee, joined Libby and Mia. "I married the wrong man, too," she admitted. "About as no-good as yours. We didn't have children, at least. But he scarred me for years." She sipped more coffee. "I never did marry again." She shot Libby a mischievous grin. "Doesn't mean I couldn't love again, though."

She'd fallen for a once famous TV actor who'd found himself in Clamshell Bay looking for a coffee and ended up falling for the baker. Ethan Crisp had wanted Cleo to go away with him and travel the world, but she was too much of a homebody. So, they traveled when she could get away and felt like it. He came and stayed in Clamshell Bay for weeks at a time. "Is it working out with you and Ethan?"

Cleo nodded. "He's spending more and more time here. I think we're rubbing off on him."

"Or he can't stand to be away from you."

"I am pretty special." They both laughed, but even in her own misery Libby was happy that her friend seemed to have made her unconventional relationship work.

"Maybe if we didn't have four kids between us, we could take our relationship one day at a time."

"But you do have four kids between you and you're not the casual type."

Libby didn't bother to argue. "I don't know what to do. There's a family touring my house right now. They seem really nice." She glanced at her phone. Candace had promised to text her when the family left. No text had appeared. "They've been in there a long time. They must be interested."

"Who wouldn't be?" Cleo said. "Your house is gorgeous. Your garden, too. Which reminds, me, Jennifer Weaver—do you know her? She's got two boys at the school. She took one of my baking classes."

"Is she the one who's always organizing those fund-raising political dinners?"

"Used to. Now she's a Buddhist."

Libby put her coffee mug down. "A Buddhist?"

"She found a truer path to enlightenment, I guess. Anyway,

she wants to turn her garden into a meditation center. I gave her your phone number."

"Gee, thanks."

"Hey, it's work. Anyway, she's probably kept a lot of her old contacts. You never know."

But Libby had stopped listening. "There's a text. Candace said she'd wait for me at the house. Her people have left." She felt her stomach jump. "What if they want to make an offer? I feel sick."

"You don't have to do anything you don't want to."

Libby felt foolish. "Yeah. I know. It's just so hard to say goodbye to that part of my life."

"You've already moved on in so many ways. When you came to my class you were such a pleaser you could hardly bear to pound dough. Now I see an assertive woman who's building her own business and raising a family on her own. You're going to be fine, with or without Jeremy O'Toole."

She began to gather her things and helped Mia put on her coat. "You're right. I feel so much stronger and surer of myself than I did when I first met you. Even if I don't sell my house, I might get some work from the Realtor. I think I have more entrepreneurial spirit than I ever knew." Briefly, she relayed her conversation with Candace, when she'd pitched her services to the Realtor.

Cleo laughed. "Not that you need it, but good luck."

"I'd better go. She's obviously waiting."

"I've got good news," Candace the Realtor sang from her front door as she approached.

"They want to offer. I told them you're reluctant to sell so they've given me the top price they can afford." She named a price that made Libby's eyes bug out. She knew prices had risen in her neighborhood, but not that high. She could pay off all her debts and have money to live on for a couple of years while she built her business.

"When? When would they want it?"

"They want to be all moved in before school starts in September. Lots of time."

"Can I have a few days to think about it?"

"Obviously, they're anxious to get things settled. They have to go back to California and sell their house. He's been transferred up here."

"I understand. Give me a few days?"

"Sure. Now. About that other matter. I talked with some of my Realtors and everybody likes the idea of being able to offer your services to our clients. Exclusively, you understand."

Libby's head was whirling. The woman in front of her was a deal-making machine. From one project to the next with lightning speed. She realized she'd better learn the technique if she was going to make a success of her own business. She managed a noncommittal "Uh-huh," and tried to turn her thoughts from the fear of finding herself imminently homeless, to business wheeling and dealing.

"I'll put up the money to get a brochure done that will describe your services and include our logo and a short blurb. I want to get right on this. We'll—"

"I'll want creative control of the brochure," she interrupted.

A beat went by. "Naturally."

All right. Score one for me, she thought gleefully. By the time they'd hammered out a deal, Libby was feeling all the euphoria of her newfound skills. And there was a lightness in her chest, like a weight had been lifted.

It wasn't till later, when Candace had left and she wandered the quiet house once more, that she realized it was the weight of the house itself that had been lifted. The worry, and hopeless aim of keeping a house she couldn't afford, and that didn't fit her anymore, was over. In that moment, she realized she'd made up her mind. She was moving on.

That night, she was the one who called Jeremy.

"Hey," she said. "How's it going?"

"All right. You?"

She took a deep breath. "We need to tell the kids that we're not going to Hawaii."

Jeremy said, "I have a better idea. We go. We get married. We can make this work."

"I can't marry you if I don't believe you love me," she said, feeling as though her heart really was breaking. There was a pain in her chest.

"I do love you. What the hell am I supposed to do to prove it?"

"I don't know," she whispered.

There was another of those awful pauses that had punctuated their conversations ever since Candace had shown up in her driveway. Finally, he said in a low, expressionless tone. "All right. We'll do it tomorrow."

"Libby, you have to marry Dad. We have to go to Hawaii."

Her heart went out to the little girl scowling at her. Olivia's eyes were puffy and dark-circled. Too much crying and not enough sleep, Libby diagnosed the problem without a second's hesitation, knowing she suffered the same ailment. "I'm sorry, honey." She held out her arms, but the older twin took a step backward and scowled even more fiercely.

"You promised! You said we'd be a family. We painted our room."

"It hurts me, too." And it had hurt to see Jeremy's face this morning when he'd dropped the girls off. Where the twins' stormy expressions gave away all their feelings, his face gave nothing away. He'd locked all his emotions away somewhere.

If she'd expected that he might try to win her back at seven forty-five in the morning, in her driveway, she was wrong.

He was in the car, backing down the drive, the kids all in the house, when she ran to the car and motioned for him to roll down the window. "Did you tell them Hawaii's off?"

He nodded. For a second, she thought the blank expression cracked and she had a glimpse of a man in pain. Then the mask was intact again.

There was half an hour until she had to walk the kids to school. It was going to be a very long thirty minutes.

Maybe another cup of coffee would help.

"You're a bum-head and I don't want you for my sister anyway," Tyler shouted. So much for that quiet cup of coffee. She ran into the hallway and saw him halfway up the stairs, his face beet-red and his arms waving wildly.

Mia was crying noisily.

Grace sat slumped and quiet on the hall stairs, and Olivia, equally red in the face, was about to answer Tyler in kind.

"Stop," Libby commanded. Her own heartbreak had to be put on hold for now, while she dealt with the very real pain in the young faces all around her.

She picked up Mia and crooned softly.

"But she called me—" Tyler blustered.

"He said—" Olivia shouted.

"Stop," she ordered again, in the voice that brooked no arguments. When she was certain the imminent battle was over, she shepherded all four kids into the kitchen.

The three older ones sat stiffly on chairs around the table, while Mia clung to Libby's leg in a way she hadn't for a long time. It took some soothing words that almost choked in her throat, a few animal crackers and some juice before Mia would sit at the table, sniffing quietly.

Libby prepared three cups of hot chocolate and then poured herself that much-needed cup of coffee. Then she broke one of her rules and put a plate of chocolate chip cookies in the middle of the table. So they ate cookies at eight o'clock in the morning for once. What the hell.

Although she felt a ripple of shock flow round the table, it was a measure of their distress that not one of the kids reached for a cookie. Glancing at each face in turn, she read shock, anger, fear, disbelief...and from Olivia, glaring back at her, blame. Keeping her gaze on the elder twin's face she said simply, "I'm so sorry about Hawaii. I know how much everyone was looking forward to going." Her voice wavered piteously, and she swallowed hard.

For an instant she glimpsed the naked hurt in the child's eyes, then it was gone. "That's crap."

"Olivia."

"My dad still wants to marry you. He said so, and *he* never lies. It's you. You don't want us."

"I do. I do want you. This has nothing to do with you and Grace. But sometimes adults make mistakes." She stopped to take a sip of coffee and regain control of her voice. "Your dad and I..." What? What could she tell them? She was terrified she couldn't compare to their dead mother? Horribly afraid he was marrying her for convenience? "We need to take more time. It's too soon."

"You pretended you loved him."

"I do love him."

Olivia still glared, Grace had yet to say a word and Tyler hadn't lost the belligerent, perplexed expression he'd worn ever since she explained to him that they weren't going to Hawaii after all.

"If you love him so much, why don't you get married?" Olivia challenged.

"It's not that easy."

"I'm never getting married. It sucks." She glared into her hot chocolate. "No Hawaii, no Pretty Girl concert. The whole thing blows."

Ignoring Olivia, Tyler glared at his mother, his color blazing once again. "We have to go to Hawaii. The kids at school'll call me a liar."

"We'll go."

"When?"

She sniffed miserably. "I don't know, honey. Maybe next year?"

"Next year?" He stormed to his feet, a study in impotent fury. "You're all a bunch of boogers." Then he stomped out of the kitchen.

"I wanna go Hawaii," Mia wailed, snuggling deeper.

"Well, that went well. Call us next time you want another one of these little talks." And Olivia, with a jerk of her chin, left the table, followed meekly by the still-silent Grace.

With a sigh, Libby reached for a chocolate chip cookie.

"I don't believe it," Paula said in a voice of amazement.

"Don't believe what?"

"You have a butter mold. And it's been used."

Libby pulled a foil sack of coffee beans from the freezer. "Of course, it's used. It makes a really elegant star-shaped butter pat. I've also got a fleur-de-lys mold somewhere in that drawer. I don't entertain anymore. Why don't you take them?"

"No. Really. A tub of margarine in the middle of the table is as elegant as I get." She replaced the butter mold and got the coffee spoons out of the drawer. Then she reached for the mugs. They'd done this so often, they had an unspoken ritual.

"I don't know what I'd do without you, Paula."

"Are things any better with the kids?"

Libby made a face. "Armed neutrality. The twins barely speak to me, Tyler's rude and uncooperative, and Mia pretty much whines every second she's not sleeping."

"It'd be nice to ship them off to camp."

"Huh. Camp David maybe. Someplace we could figure out how to declare a truce. Maybe I'm not going to be their stepmother, but I love those girls."

She poured the beans into the grinder. After the machine had finished roaring, she measured the freshly ground coffee into the coffee maker and added cold water.

"And the hot banker?"

"He barely glances at me when he brings the girls and picks them up. He treats me like some evil homewrecker."

"Are you?"

"What?" Libby slopped the milk she was pouring into a jug onto the counter.

"I wonder if maybe you panicked. That's all."

The milk puddle blurred before her eyes. "Maybe. It's like we're locked into this pattern and neither of us know how to get to the next stage, you know?"

"Yeah. I appreciate your scruples, but I'm not sure it would have ruined those kids forever if you'd gone ahead to Hawaii and tried a family vacation. Maybe you'd find out he really does love you."

"I don't know. I already lost one husband to another woman. I'm not going to marry a man who's in love with a ghost." She poured two aromatic cups of coffee, passed one and then drank from her own.

"He offered to move in here," her neighbor reminded her.

"And then I could feel guilty forevermore for taking them away from all their good memories. I'm not that awful a person. I'm not."

"Life." Paula shook her head.

She stared out at the rain drizzling down the kitchen

windowpane. "We would have been on our way to Hawaii in a few days. With the family."

"I can understand you throwing over a handsome, successful man, but giving up two weeks in Hawaii?" Paula shook her head in mock despair.

Libby gave the expected chuckle. "Think of the money I saved on sunscreen."

Before the kids were expected home, Libby brushed her hair and freshened her makeup. It was a silly ritual, but once begun, it had become a habit.

As she looked at herself in the mirror, she noticed how tired her face appeared. A couple of lines she'd never noticed before had taken up permanent residence between her eyebrows. And she was tired. Not only was she trying to police a war zone, she was already the proud owner of her own business. Complete with business cards, brochures, and letterhead from the ultra-efficient Candace. Megan had put her in touch with a designer for her new website.

And when she had little time for business, the calls had started to increase. Financially, she needed the work and somewhere deep down in her entrepreneurial soul, she was thrilled by each call. But the toll of trudging out to job sites, dredging up enthusiasm and enough creativity to wow clients and design fabulous gardens was leaving her seriously depleted.

The irony was that her favorite current project had turned out to be the meditation garden. The part of her that craved quiet and peace and contemplative solitude yearned for such a place to escape to. And so, it was easy to imagine the little trickling fountain, exactly there. The small stone bench here, under the shade of this maple. The lavender there, where its scent would soothe the soul.

And, in between times, she pretended she didn't notice Olivia's sarcasm, Grace's painful silence, Tyler's boisterous rudeness or Mia's whining. The children were working out their feelings. She tried to respect that.

It was more difficult to respect Jeremy's brooding anger, which she knew was directed at himself as much as her.

As for her own feelings, she'd tried to push them into a mental cupboard. And most of the time, she was so busy they stayed locked up. But every once in a while, like now, she'd feel the overwhelming sadness.

She picked up Mia and her little friend Sarah from playschool and drove home in a daze. What had she done? Was she really considering selling her home? She walked in and prepared lunch, and then the girls went downstairs to the playroom.

She was tidying the hall closet when the phone rang. Maybe it was Candace canceling. But no, the woman's voice said, "Is this Libby Brown?"

"Yes."

"This is Tracy, Jeremy's sister? We met on your birthday."

"Yes, of course. How are you?"

"I'm fine. Listen, I get off early today. I'd love to buy you a coffee somewhere and talk."

Jeremy's sister wanted to talk to her? "Can I ask what it's about?"

A low laugh came through the phone. "It's about my dumbass of a brother."

"I can't leave the house. I've got my daughter and her friend home. Would you like to come here for coffee?"

"Sure. That would be fine." She told Libby she'd be there in fifteen minutes.

Libby ran into the kitchen and put coffee on. There were muffins left from breakfast, so she threw a few in a basket and got out napkins and cups. She felt like she'd had a lot of emotional conversations lately over coffee. Now she was entertaining Jeremy's sister? What if the woman was coming to yell at her?

Well, she thought, she might just yell back.

But when Tracy arrived ten minutes later, she didn't look as though she was going to yell. She was dressed in black wool trousers and a blue blazer and she held a box of chocolates in her hand, which she pushed toward Libby with a wry grimace. "I had no idea what to bring you, but chocolate always seems appropriate."

Libby laughed, sensing that a chocolate offering meant she wasn't going to be yelled at. "Thanks, come on in."

"I hope you don't mind me coming. Jeremy would kill me if he knew I was interfering." The flicker of hope that Jeremy had sent his sister to mediate on his behalf died.

"I've got coffee on in the kitchen."

"Wonderful. Wow, your house is beautiful."

"Thanks."

She fussed around with coffee and muffins and Tracy waited until she was sitting. Then she said, "I know this is pushy of me, and you can throw me out any time, but I wanted to beg you to give my brother another chance."

A feeling like an electric shock zapped through her. "He told you what happened?"

Tracy leaned forward looking anxious. "Please don't think he was being disloyal. The thing is we've always been so close and I could see he was upset, so he told me you guys were having trouble."

"Trouble? Tracy, you're the only person in his life who knew we were a couple. I feel like some dirty secret." She blew out a breath. "You've known him a lot longer, but I was there, when we cleaned out Kelly's room. I knew then. I should have known. He was still in denial about her death."

Tracy squeezed her hands together. They were plump and freckled, the kind of hands that could soothe a crying child or write for hours on a chalkboard. A teacher's hands. "He's come a long way since he met you."

"I can never be Kelly," she cried. "I'm jealous of a dead woman. I'm not even like her."

The other woman reached forward suddenly and touched her hand. "No. You're nothing like her." She studied Libby. "You're obviously a more reserved person. Maybe a little more serious. And you're right. He loved Kelly with all his heart." She swallowed and her voice grew choked. "We all loved Kelly. She was the sister I never had. And when they looked at each other you felt their love. But you know what's funny? When you and Jeremy look at each other, I get the same feeling from you two. I thought to myself, after I met you, I can't believe he got that lucky twice. And when we worked together that day cleaning out her room, I thought, maybe I'm going to get another sister." She sniffed and Libby passed her a box of tissues, then pulled out one for herself.

"I never had a sister, either."

"I know he's hopeless, but please don't give up on him yet. He loves you. I know he does."

"He didn't tell anybody he works with. None of his friends. He didn't tell anybody about me. How can he love me and hide me away like that?"

"He's never been a man to wear his heart on his sleeve. He's more like you, reserved." Tracy plucked another tissue out of the box. "When Kelly was dying, those terrible last months, he still went to the office every day. He did his job and I doubt any of the customers even noticed anything was wrong. That's the kind of man he is. It doesn't mean he doesn't have deep feelings because he doesn't show them."

"I don't know, Tracy. I'm so terrified of making another mistake."

"I think that's what's really bothering you. More than the house or Jeremy not telling people. You're scared."

Libby blinked at her.

"Hey, I'm not criticizing. I'd be scared too. It's not easy trusting someone to love you forever. But what if it's possible?"

"What if?"

"By the way, our parents are dying to meet you. They wanted to book Hawaii as well, to be there for the wedding."

She felt her eyes widen. "They did?"

"Sure. Jeremy told them it's immediate family only. But they can come to the garden party to celebrate your marriage."

"He actually phoned his parents and told them about me? You're not telling me that to make me feel better, are you?"

Tracy pulled out a cell phone and even as Libby waved her hands and protested, she hit a button and the next thing Libby knew, Jeremy's sister was saying, "Hi, Mom, it's Tracy. I'm here with Libby Brown. She wants to talk to you." And she passed over the phone.

"Ah, hello," she said.

"Hello, Libby. I'm so happy to make your acquaintance. I've written you a letter to let you know how pleased we are that you'll be joining the family. But a phone call is much better. Why didn't we think of that."

She sounded a lot like Tracy, so Libby imagined Tracy, only older. "It's nice to talk to you."

"I'll get my husband on the extension." Then she yelled, "Van? Van! It's Libby on the phone. Jeremy's fiancée."

In five minutes, Libby knew that Tracy took after her mother and Jeremy was more like his dad. One was all chatter and plans, the other quiet, but sensible. They'd heard so much about her, they said. They couldn't wait to meet her.

They didn't care when the garden party was, they were coming up soon after the Hawaii trip for a visit.

"I'll look forward to it," said Libby, realizing that Jeremy had told her the wedding was on, and not that it had been postponed. She hadn't mentioned the delay, either.

When she disconnected, she glanced at Tracy. "I think I need one of those chocolates."

After Tracy left, Libby picked up the phone to call Jeremy. But she put it down again. She needed some time to think about this. Maybe she'd suggest they set a wedding date for six months away. Give them both time to get used to the idea.

She cleaned up the coffee things and set out cookies, juice, and fruit for the kids' snack.

Maybe this can still work, she thought as she heard the front door slam. The kids were late but she wasn't going to start an argument. "Hi." She called out.

"Hi, Mom."

There was a rule that the older kids all had to walk home together. Puzzled, she moved toward the front door where Tyler was kicking his shoes off into the hall closet. He knew she hated him to do that. "Where are the girls?"

"I dunno. They never showed."

She counted to ten. "You know I don't like you walking home alone. You should have waited for them. Maybe they were kept in after school."

"Nope. I went to their class and checked. They left before me."

Unease fluttered in her belly. "If they left before you, why aren't they here yet?"

"I don't know. Those girls in their class are all nuts. All the girls were yapping on about the big concert tonight."

Her legs were suddenly boneless. She slumped to a sitting position on the stairs. "Oh, no. Not Pretty Girl."

"Oh, yes. Pretty Giiiirl," he mimicked the girl group. Any other time Libby would have laughed at the impression. But not today.

A surge of panic wiped her mind blank. What to do? Where to begin? Then reason reasserted itself. There was no cause to believe the girls had gone to the concert. Where would they have gotten the tickets? How were they planning to get to the King Dome? How would they have pulled something like this off without raising her suspicions?

Then she remembered the hostility. They'd been acting strange ever since they found out the wedding was off. And she hadn't exactly been her usual perceptive self, either. "Tyler, did the twins say anything to you?"

"'Bout what?"

"About coming home late today? Or...uh...anything?"

"No. But they gave me a note. At lunchtime."

"Well, why didn't you tell me?" She took a breath. Shouting at Tyler wouldn't help anything. "Can I see it?"

He dug through his backpack and hauled out a crumpled piece of foolscap with a smear of butter at the top. It was addressed to Libby.

Hey, Libby,

Don't worry. Me and Grace are going to the Pretty Girl concert tonight. We know how to get there and everything. Tell Dad we will get home late. We are writing this note so you won't worry or get too mad at us.

Yours truly,

Grace and Olivia O'Toole

"Oh, my God," she said, leaping off the steps and running to the phone.

TWENTY-THREE

"Jeremy!"

"Hmm?" The way Melanie's voice had sharpened, he had a feeling it wasn't the first time she'd called his name.

"I've got the layouts for the new brochure. Do you have a minute?"

"Sure. In fact, you're exactly the person I wanted to see."

"That's unusual," she muttered, placing the mock-up on his desk.

He glanced at the thing. "That looks great, Melanie."

"Are you feeling all right? You always hate everything I do."

"No, I don't. We have differing opinions from time to time. You do a fine job." He smiled warmly. He'd been smiling warmly at everyone today. And the reactions had shocked him. From puzzled looks to nervous grins to Melanie here, with her mouth hanging open. It gave him an uncomfortable feeling that he might have been less than pleasant the last few days.

"You go out a lot. What's the most romantic restaurant you know?"

"La Pergola." A dimple appeared. "So that's why you've been so weird lately."

"Sorry about that."

"You had a fight and you want to make up?"

"Yeah."

"That's so romantic. No wonder you've been such a bear lately." Her face brightened in a smile. "As soon as you initial approval on this brochure you like so much, I'll give you directions. It was written up in Best Places to Kiss in the Pacific Northwest."

He ignored the blackmail and signed. Best Places to Kiss... that sounded good. "How's the food?" Like he cared.

"Mouthwatering. You'll kiss and make up before dessert. At least I hope so, for all our sakes."

"I'm sorry I've been kind of...uh...grumpy. It's been a tough time."

The phone shrilled insistently on his desk. He glanced at it and frowned. Linda always held his calls when there was someone with him. Unless it was important. "Excuse me." He muttered to Melanie. "Jeremy O'Toole here."

"Jeremy. It's Libby."

Pleasure coursed through him at the sound of her voice. "Libby, I was just thinking about you."

"I'm so sorry, Jeremy." She sounded near tears. He made bye-bye motions to Melanie, who was eagerly listening in.

"I'm sorry, too, honey." Melanie gave him a thumbs up and waltzed out with her signed layout.

"Did they leave you a note?"

"Who? What note?" He reached for the extra strength antacid pills his doctor had recently prescribed.

"Oh, God, Jeremy. It's the girls. They've gone to the Pretty Girl concert."

"They what?" he shouted, jerking to his feet.

"They sent home a note with Tyler. I'm going to drive down to the stadium and try to find them." She had that super calm voice he remembered from the first day he met her when the twins had the baking disaster. But now he knew her better. He heard a quaver underneath the calm.

"Don't move. I'll be there in ten minutes."

He sprinted out of his office. "Linda, if the twins call, find out where they are, tell them to stay put, and call me immediately on my cell."

"Trouble?" the startled woman asked.

But he was already through the stairwell door and he didn't pause. Oh, yeah, there was trouble.

When he pulled up at Libby's house, Tyler and Mia were waiting outside with their coats on. "He's here, Mom," the boy shouted through the open door.

Seconds later, Libby appeared with her coat and purse, and locked the door behind her. He couldn't believe it. She wasn't planning on bringing a couple of little kids on a manhunt, was she?

Her eyes were wide and anxious as she opened the rear door of the Volvo.

"Wait. Libby, they'll slow us down." He motioned to Mia, already half in the back seat.

Her tragic eyes widened. "All right. I'll take my car. We'll meet you there."

But he couldn't do it. He'd only be worried about her and her kids as well as his own two gone AWOL. "No. Get in."

She hesitated.

"Please." He got out and opened the other rear door for Tyler.

She nodded briefly and within a minute they were on their way. "I called the school, but no one there knew anything, except they were at school all day, so they don't have too much of a head start." She was calm. Businesslike. Whatever fear she was feeling, she had it under control. "I also called the bus line while I was waiting for you. I have the probable route they took. If we can overtake the bus, that's our best chance."

She didn't explain, and she didn't have to. If that concert wasn't sold out, it was damned close. Tens of thousands of concert goers would be milling around. He pictured drinking, drugs, even a riot. Anything could happen. If they could nab the girls before they got off the bus...He pressed down on the accelerator.

He could practically hear Libby's teeth grinding in the seat next to him. Momentarily, he'd forgotten Mia and Tyler in the back seat. Ashamed of taking foolish risks with those he loved, he slowed the car.

She gave him directions to help him track the bus route, and he followed them.

"I think that's it," Libby said beside him.

And sure enough, ahead of them was a bus. He pulled in behind and followed it. The tension in the car was palpable as they followed the lumbering vehicle. Several blocks went by before the bus signaled.

"It's stopping," Libby said.

He nodded. "If there's a place to park, I'll find out if they're on the bus."

Already she was grasping the handle. "Pull in behind. I'll go."

So, he did. And she did. After several tense minutes of waiting she returned. Alone. Her head shake was pretty unnecessary under the circumstances.

He watched the bus pull away as she slipped back into the seat beside him. "Given the timing, the driver thinks they've probably already reached the stadium. He's going to try and get hold of the other drivers and if anyone remembers the girls, they'll call your cell."

He nodded. Grim. Knowing she was as worried as he. And that he could trust her completely. She couldn't love them more if she were their biological mother. The thought didn't even surprise him, the way it would have a few months ago. He pulled away from the curb. "Should we call the police?"

"Won't there be police outside the concert? For crowd control?" There was an awkward pause before she resumed, with false brightness. "Not that they'll be hard to spot. Being twins."

"Are Olivia and Grace getting arrested?" Tyler asked hopefully from the back.

"I'm thinking about it."

"Cool. Can I visit them in jail?"

He shot a glance at Libby and they exchanged a look—the kind of look that parents everywhere swap when a kid says something outrageous. There was a world of unspoken communication in that glance. Understanding, and the kind of intimacy of parents who work long and hard raising children together. He pulled his gaze back to the road, but not before he'd seen her small, reassuring smile. "It'll be okay," that smile said. He had to believe her.

Apart from Mia getting all excited every time they passed a bus, since she'd picked up that this was somehow a very special event, the rest of the drive passed in virtual silence. As they drew closer to the stadium, the traffic got heavier, the sidewalks and crosswalks were thronged with people, scruffy-looking deadbeats, most of them, as far as Jeremy was concerned. And bus after bus came from all directions. "What the hell were they thinking?" He finally roared in mingled frustration and terror.

She didn't murmur any safe platitudes, merely reached over to squeeze his hand in sympathy and support. He felt the trembling in her palm and knew she was as anxious as he.

The traffic was hardly crawling, and somewhere out there with all the riff-raff, druggies, drunks, and perverts were his precious daughters. He couldn't sit here. "Take the wheel, Libby. I'm going to flag down a cop and get some help."

"Yes. All right."

"Everybody got their doors locked back there?" He craned his neck around and checked to be certain.

"I hate to leave you like this," he said to the outwardly calm woman at his side.

"No. You're right. We can search different areas. Let's make a time and place to meet."

"No. Honey, take the kids home. I'll call you."

"We're not leaving, Jeremy."

His cell phone rang. With a quick glance at Libby, he answered, "Jeremy O'Toole."

"Daddy," a small, scared voice said, bringing an immediate lump to his throat.

"Olivia. You okay?"

"Yes. We're so sorry, Dad. Please don't be mad at us."

"It's okay, baby. Where are you?"

"At McDonald's." She sniffled.

He glanced up, and hallelujah, there it was a few blocks ahead. He'd never been so glad to see those golden arches in his life. "Is it the one near the stadium?"

"Uh-huh."

"Is Grace with you?"

"Yeah."

"We're on our way. Stay put."

Through the aggressive use of his horn, and shouting the word "emergency" out the window until he was hoarse, he managed to cut his way through the jammed cars. Of course, the restaurant parking lot was full when he finally got there.

"Go on in. I'll park. We'll join you in a few minutes," Libby's calm voice said.

"I can see them in the window," Tyler said. "Look." And there they were. Two identical dark-haired heads, in identical dejected poses, slumped at a table near the window.

All the relief he felt was mirrored in Libby's eyes. He didn't have time to say everything he wanted. He leaned over and kissed her lips swiftly. "See you inside."

She was flustered and blushing. He grinned as she pulled away. Then stowed the grin as he marched toward the restaurant.

"Hey there, kiddos," he said softly as he approached.

Both girls threw themselves at him. "We're sorry, Dad."

"Please don't be mad."

He hugged them both tight, not sure which of the three of them was trembling hardest. "I'm glad you're safe. We've been worried sick."

"We?" Olivia searched behind him.

"Libby and the kids are with me. She's parking the car. We started tracking you the minute she got your note."

"I'm sure glad we left that note," Grace said.

"We weren't going to," Olivia admitted.

"Let's all sit down again and you can tell me about it." He sat on the hard plastic chair and listened.

The confession was halting at first. They'd won four tickets from the radio contest. "We wanted to surprise you and Libby and take you to the concert," Olivia said. He'd told them to their face about fifty times that they were too young for a rock concert, but he refrained from reminding them of that now.

"Then, when we were going to Hawaii, we figured we wouldn't be able to go. I mean, I guess you guys getting married and us going to Hawaii is more important than one Pretty Girl concert." He had to hide a smile. She sounded pretty unsure of the equality of the tradeoff.

Olivia seemed to have stalled, so Grace took up the tale. "Then you weren't getting married anymore, and it was so awful. Everybody was mad at everybody and we figured you'd say no if we asked anymore." She shrugged. Guilt written all over her face. "So, we didn't ask."

"What made you change your mind about going through with it?"

They both blushed. Olivia finally spoke. "On the bus it was fun, but when we got here, it was awfully crowded. There were lots of kids, but they all had grownups with them." She glanced at her sister, as if wondering how to proceed.

"Then this guy came up to us," Grace continued. "He was weird. And he smelled funny. You know how Uncle Charlie used to smell before he started going to AA?"

The familiar burning started deep in his gut. He nodded, dreading what might be coming.

"He hung around and kept trying to talk to us. He said stuff about 'little twinnies.' We were totally grossed out. Then Olivia yelled, 'Hi, Dad.' I was scared because I knew you'd be mad at us, but she grabbed my hand and started running. It wasn't you. It was somebody else's dad, but we tagged along behind them and pretended we were with them. They came in here, then we hid in the bathroom. We didn't come out for a long time, but the weirdo wasn't here."

"But we were too scared to go back on the street. So we called you."

There was a pause, while he searched for the right words to say. "You were wrong, girls. You know that, don't you?"

Mute nods.

"But, I guess you've learned firsthand why Libby and I refused to let you come."

"But lots of families are together. It would have been okay if you guys had come with us."

"But not alone," he reminded her sternly. "I guess you've learned your lesson, though. It wasn't very pleasant what happened tonight, was it?"

Mute headshakes this time.

"I'm also proud of you." The heads jerked up, identical questioning looks on their faces. "You handled a difficult situation very well. That was smart of you, Olivia, to attach yourself to a family. And even smarter to call me and stay here until I arrived."

"I love you, Daddy," Olivia said.

"Me, too," Grace said.

A great wave of tenderness engulfed him. "Me, too," he replied a little huskily.

TWENTY-FOUR

"Hold my hand tightly, Tyler. We don't want to lose you, too." Libby let the crowd sweep them along. She had Mia in one arm and Tyler hanging on to the other hand. The golden arches were like a mirage shimmering in the distance. She'd finally found a private lot in somebody's yard for twenty bucks.

She consoled herself, and her aching shoulders, with the thought that Jeremy would have more time alone with his daughters before she and her kids intruded. After all, it wasn't like she was anything more in their lives than the temporary babysitter.

Except for that odd kiss, a little voice reminded her.

That was relief, she explained it away.

And he called you honey, the voice continued.

It was a moment of stress, she countered.

But she couldn't explain away the fact that she and Jeremy had acted like an experienced mom and dad team all through the crisis. And they made a good team, too.

"Can we go to McDonald's house?" Mia chirped when she saw the familiar yellow M.

"Can I have a Big Mac?" Tyler added.

She couldn't remember the last time they'd eaten at a place like this. "We'll see," she said. A lot depended on how Jeremy and the girls were doing.

When they finally reached the door, it opened magically, and there was Jeremy, suddenly precious and familiar standing there with an expression on his face that made her heart do a funny kind of lurch. He eased Mia out of her arms.

"I asked for a Big Mac, but Mom said 'we'll see,'" Tyler informed him. He caught sight of the girls. "Hey, did you guys get arrested?" he yelled across the crowded restaurant.

Jeremy laughed, looking years younger than he had an hour earlier, and way too sexy for her peace of mind. "Do you mind if we eat here?"

"No. The kids'll love it."

"I had somewhere more intimate in mind for tonight, but..." He shrugged.

More intimate? Who with? The way he was gazing at her, her first guess had to be it was herself he'd hoped to spend an intimate evening with. But then, why had he given no indication of the fact that morning when he'd barely glanced her way as he let the children off?

It was a puzzle. As was his good mood after the atrocious stunt the twins had pulled. "Where are you parked?"

"Somewhere in Canada, I think."

He laughed again, shepherding her to where the twins had Tyler enthralled with their tale of adventure. Mia insisted on sitting with the other kids and, since the table only sat four, Libby and Jeremy sat at the next table munching burgers and fries and Cokes while Jeremy filled her in.

"I was so scared in the car when I saw all the drug pushers and derelicts heading this way."

"The band's not exactly Mega Death, Jeremy. I saw lots of families and young children on our way here."

He licked a dab of ketchup from the corner of his mouth,

looking thoughtful. "The girls have four tickets already. I wonder, now that we're here..."

She nodded. "I think they were punished enough just experiencing such a fright. They'd be so thrilled to see the concert."

"And you?" He grinned.

"I wish I'd brought my earplugs."

"Will Mia be all right?"

"She had a long nap this afternoon. And she knows those Pretty Girl songs about by heart."

"Right. Don't say anything yet. I'll run across and see if I can get two extra tickets."

"You know you'll be paying scalper prices?"

"Don't remind me."

She watched him stride out, tall and confident, and a pang of sadness pierced her. He was exactly the man she would choose. If only she could be certain he was free to be hers.

With a hopeless sigh, she drank the last of her cola and cleaned away the remains of their meals. After that, she insisted all the kids take a bathroom break and wash up. By the time they'd finished doing that, Jeremy had returned and gave her a thumbs up.

He held the two tickets out in his hand and waited. Olivia clued in first and gave a shriek that stilled conversation in the restaurant. "You mean we can go?"

"Libby and I decided you've learned your lesson. And, since we're all here now, anyway..." The girls, then Tyler, threw themselves at Jeremy. Mia, who hated to be left out, followed suit. He swung her up in his arms and the six of them headed out.

"We won't be able to sit together," Libby warned Jeremy in an undervoice. "We should decide now who sits where."

He stopped her with a kiss. "Have faith."

She hadn't been big on that lately. Maybe she'd give faith a try.

And sure enough, when they got to the crowded arena and found their way to the four seats the twins had won, Jeremy went ahead and she saw him chatting to a couple of teenagers who obviously had the adjoining seats. By the time Libby and the kids reached him, he had six seats together.

"How on earth did you get those kids to change seats with you?"

"I told them we need to be together because we're a family," he said, looking at her in a way that made her heart flip. "And then I gave them a hundred bucks."

Libby hadn't been to a concert in years, and, despite herself, got caught up in the enthusiasm. Pretty Girl was fun, especially as she knew most of the songs. The kids' enthusiasm was infectious, and when "Who's a Pretty Girl?" finally came on, they all joined in. Jeremy caught her eye and mimicked the movements of the lead singer, making her stop singing as a giggle choked her.

He grinned, and behind the backs of their own singing and dancing quartet, pulled her close. Surprise widened her eyes. "Thanks for being a good sport," he said, and kissed her.

Her heart started banging in time to the band's frantic percussion, and the kiss, which had started out friendly, deepened suddenly. They were grasping each other, gripping and hugging wordlessly while the music blared around them. The cacophony created a sort of intimacy, since it was impossible to be heard. "I missed you," he yelled into her ear.

"Me, too," she shouted back.

They left when Mia began to droop. The concert wasn't over, and yet there wasn't a peep of protest from the three older kids. They really had learned a lesson tonight.

The walk back to the car didn't seem so long with Jeremy carrying the sleepy Mia and soon they were all buckled in and driving home. For the first little while it was almost as noisy inside the car as it had been at the concert.

"That firework thing was so cool."

"She saw me, I know she did. I did that special wave and she did it right back at me."

"I bet they got paid a million bucks. At least."

"Who cares, Tyler. You are so lame."

"Not as lame as gushing over girls with dyed hair and miniskirts," her stung son retorted.

And so it went on as they drove through Seattle and headed for Clamshell Bay. Slowly the energy level depleted, and long before they reached home the back of the car was silent but for snuffling sounds of children sleeping.

She and Jeremy didn't talk much. She felt jumpy and uncertain, scared to break the mood and yet determined not to fall back into the old bad patterns. She was a strong woman, she'd discovered that. She loved Jeremy. She doubted she'd ever love another man as deeply, but if his heart wasn't hers then she couldn't continue. It was as painful, and as simple, as that.

But it had been nice tonight. She lay her head back and stared out the window as the streets grew more familiar. It had stopped raining hours ago, but the heavy sky threatened more drizzle.

"You took a wrong turn, Jeremy. You must be getting sleepy, too."

"Can I take you on a little detour? There's something I want to show you." She noted the intense tone under the casual words as she automatically agreed.

She was almost certain they were headed for his house. What was he planning to show her? His etchings? She kept quiet and waited, her tension mounting as they neared his house. When they turned into his crescent, she glanced sharply at him, but he refused to return the glance.

He didn't drive into his driveway but angled the car and left the engine running.

"What are you doing?"

She gasped as she saw, illuminated in his headlights, a familiar real estate sign. Candace's, the same one that was featured on her brochure. A red Sold sticker slapped across the front.

"I love you, Libby. I couldn't think of a better way to tell you."

"But where..."

"I accepted an offer this morning. I didn't want to tell you about it until the house was sold. It's as close as I can come to proving what I feel." He took her hand and his eyes shone in the dim light of the car. "Please marry me."

"And if I don't?"

He flicked the lights off. Darkness filled the car. "Then the girls and I will find a place on our own. You told me to move on. You were right. It was time. With you or without you, I'm moving on, physically and emotionally." She heard the catch in his voice, and knew how tough it was for him to talk about this. "I loved Kelly. I'd have stayed with her forever if she hadn't died. But she did. It wasn't until you cleared out her stuff that I realized I hadn't let her go." He stopped and she felt a lump form in her throat. "Now, I have."

"But it was her home, your memories are there."

"I'll always have my memories. They move with me. Kelly will always be a part of me and of the girls, but you showed me that I can respect her memory and still live a good life." He touched her face. "Acceptance. I finally got there."

"I hope you'll share those memories with me. I owe her so much. I wish I could have known her."

She felt him nod. Then, after a moment of silence, he said, "Oh, one other thing."

"What?"

"I'm taking you for lunch one day soon and giving you a tour of my office. You can meet everyone."

"Really?"

"Melanie's going to kill me if she doesn't get to meet you soon. She's the one who recommended the restaurant I was planning to take you to tonight."

"And on the way we'd drive by your sold house?"

"I'm such a man of mystery."

"God, I love you."

He really did love her. But there was one thing she had to set him straight on. "We haven't talked a lot, lately. I think you should know that I'm taking on a lot of work with my garden design business." She tried to keep the pride out of her voice as she said those last four words, but it was tough. "I won't be there every day when the kids come home from school. Sometimes there will be a sitter."

The lights flashed on again and he turned to face her, an amazed grin on his face. "Do you by any chance think I want to marry you to save myself your daycare fees? Because let me tell you, that was highway robbery."

"It was not. Where else would they get such nutritious food, a trained medical—" He shut her up by the simple method of kissing her senseless. And she was kissing him back.

Her hand was around his neck, the lights were out again, and they were going at it like a couple of teenagers. "I'm going to have to write these down," he mused when they stopped for breath.

"Pardon?"

"I'm writing my own chapter on Best Places to Kiss in the Pacific Northwest. So far tonight, I've got the McDonald's parking lot, the stadium during a K-pop concert, and the car out front of my house. What do you think?" He asked, pulling her close once more.

"I think you'd better re-book those tickets for Hawaii right now."

"I never canceled them," he said with smug satisfaction.

"And while we're gone, the movers can take our stuff over to your place."

She rested her head on his shoulder. Heard a tiny snore from the direction of the back seat and smiled. "That was a broken home."

"Hey, I did a lot of work patching up that place."

"I know. Tyler said it wasn't our home that was broken, it was our family."

"I'm a handyman, remember?"

"The thing is that Candace's got this nice family wanting to buy my house. Maybe it's time for all of us to move on and find our own home. For a fresh start."

"Do you have any idea how tough it is to find a home in this neighborhood?"

"Follow my directions," she said, excitement filling her as she realized she had the perfect solution.

———

"I've already done the garden," she said, as they drew up in front of the display home for the new subdivision. "All the lots are sold now, so they'll be selling the display home." She turned in her seat. "I've been inside and it's gorgeous. Four bedrooms and a den that could be a fifth bedroom if the twins ever want their own rooms. The main floor has a big kitchen and family room, and downstairs there's room for a playroom, even a home theater if we want one."

"A fresh start, for all of us."

"What do you think?"

"Candace's going to get three commissions is what I think."

She laughed, and leaned over to give him a quick kiss. "Let's wake the kids and tell them the good news."

A LETTER FROM THE AUTHOR

Dear Reader,

Thanks for reading *The Cottage at Clamshell Bay*. While the Clamshell Bay stories are fiction, they are inspired by my experiences and those of my friends. As women, we bond and support each other by sharing our stories with laughter and sometimes a few tears. I wouldn't have made it through some of the tough times without my friends, my Cleo and Libby and Megan and Brooke. I really love hearing from readers like you. You're welcome to drop me a line at Sara@SaraJaneBailey.com.

If you'd like to join other readers in keeping in touch, here are two options. Stay in the loop with my new releases by clicking on the link below. Or sign up to my personal email newsletter on the link at the bottom of this note. I'd be delighted if you choose to sign up to either – or both!

www.stormpublishing.co/sara-jane-bailey

If you enjoyed reading *The Cottage at Clamshell Bay* and could spare a few moments to leave a review that would be hugely appreciated. Even a short review can make all the difference in encouraging a reader to discover my books for the first time. Thank you so much!

Join other readers in hearing about my writing (and life) experiences, and other bonus content.

www.sarajanebailey.com/newsletter

I hope to see you in Clamshell Bay again soon,

Sara Jane